UnStuck

Would You Trade Your Job to Be a Pop Star?

Natalia Hooker

Cover illustration by Aleksandra Kolesniak.

Cover design by Hanna Mykytuk.

Interior formatting by Alaya Books.

ISBNs

Paperback: 978-0-6486447-7-4

Hardcover: 978-1-7642504-0-5

Ebook: 978-0-6486447-9-8

www.nataliahooker.com

www.alayabooks.com

Author's Note & Disclaimer

This is a work of creative nonfiction based on personal life experiences. While the events depicted are inspired by true stories, all characters have been fictionalized for the purposes of storytelling.

To protect the privacy of individuals, the names, identifying details, nationalities, appearances, and life circumstances of people portrayed have been changed. In some instances, characters are composites, or certain scenes have been altered, reordered, or dramatized to enhance the narrative.

Any resemblance to actual persons, living or deceased, is purely coincidental, unless explicitly stated otherwise.

This book is a reflection of personal perspective, memories, and interpretations at the time of writing. It is not intended to be a factual account of others' experiences or points of view. The intention is to entertain, reflect, and inspire, never to harm or expose.

Thank you for reading with an open heart.

Natalia Hooker

Alaya books

The world needs your story.

www.alayabooks.com

NATALIA HOOKER

About the Author

Natalia Hooker is a writer, publisher, and creative adventurer. Born in Australia to a Polish mother, she has lived and worked in Sydney, Warsaw, London, New York, Paris, Milan, and Barcelona. Her career has taken her from banking to singing to publishing, and her greatest passion is storytelling, especially stories of transformation and reinvention.

Natalia also writes and publishes illustrated children's books that help young readers explore the world with wonder and curiosity.

Also by Natalia Hooker

Coming soon: *UnBlock*

LJ Hooker The Man: The Untold Story of an Australian Icon

Messages from Angels: Notebook

For Young Readers

Kitten Tails: Life is Better Shared

Flower Book

Are You?

Wish Upon

Misha the Travelling Puppy: ABC

Misha the Travelling Puppy: Spain

Misha the Travelling Puppy: Australia

Misha the Travelling Puppy: England

Misha the Travelling Puppy: America

Misha the Travelling Puppy: Italy

Misha the Travelling Puppy: Mexico

Misha the Travelling Puppy: India

Misha the Travelling Puppy: Christmas

Misha the Travelling Puppy: Colouring Countries ABC

NATALIA HOOKER

In memory of Bill.

CHAPTER 1

Slow down and enjoy life. It's not only the scenery you miss by going too fast – you also miss the sense of where you are going and why.

- Eddie Cantor

October 1997

A sunset-orange leaf lands at my feet – my first New York autumn. I take it as a sign. A new season, a new home, and a new life.

As I walk down 16th Street, I admire the tree-lined road and brown-stone buildings. Cafés and restaurants toward Union Square are already buzzing with life. I love this area – and I'm hopeful today's viewing will end my seemingly endless apartment hunt.

Striding along at my usual fast pace, flicking back my shoulder-length hair, I scan the buildings for number thirty-seven. The house where I grew up in Australia was number thirty-seven. My first office job in Sydney? Thirty-seventh floor. That number has always been a good omen for me.

When I reach the building, I clamber up the murky-blue-carpeted stairway, wobbling in my heels on the steep, uneven stairs. The door to apartment 2B is open, so I walk in. Two dim spotlights light the far corners. A balding man sits in the middle of a large black leather sofa.

1

"Sit there," he booms, pointing to a lonely desk chair in the middle of the room.

With my short, tailored beige suit, I perch carefully, feeling like Sharon Stone being interrogated in *Basic Instinct*. I gently swivel on the seat, eyeing the parquet floor, exposed brick walls, tall windows facing an internal courtyard, and an original marble fireplace.

I do some quick redecorating in my head to brighten it up. After weeks of trudging through cockroach-infested hovels in my price range, this place feels like a dream.

Getting a decent deal on a place in Manhattan is no small feat. I sell myself hard. I'm SO clean. I'll always pay early. I'll stay for years – if that's what you want, of course. But he's noncommittal. A slew of applicants, he tells me.

So I call the guy every day without fail until he crosses off all the other candidates one by one and I successfully convince him the apartment is meant to be mine. He later recalls what a pain in the butt I was. "You were *very* persistent," he admits.

The first night in my new apartment, I celebrate by pouring a glass of Australian cabernet sauvignon bought from the handy liquor store on the corner. Sitting on the black leather sofa, I look up at the high ceiling. *This is my space. My studio!*

I jump up and do a pirouette, followed by a few pliés using the mantelpiece above the fireplace as my ballet barre. I go back to the sofa, inspired to write on a notepad:

PRIORITIES
1. Lifestyle – check.
Yay, I'm living in a cool apartment on 16th Street in Manhattan.

2. Career – check.
Having completed a successful summer internship with a boutique investment bank, they offered me a full-time job. The decision for me

as a single, twenty-six-year-old Aussie to stay in New York City was a no-brainer; the last three months have been the most fun of my life, not to mention the great work experience. I can't help but get excited as to what this stint in the finance capital of the world will do for my curriculum vitae.

3. *Relationship – no check.*
Work in progress. Come on, there are millions of men in this city!

Over three years later

In New York, I'm all in. I go to every show, every dance company performance, every ballet and opera that hits the stage at the Met. I have subscriptions, seat preferences, favorite bouncers. The velvet ropes? They part for me. I don't know if it's the way I speak or just pure confidence, but somehow, I can always get a group in – best table, hottest spot, no problem. The city hums with energy, and I move in time with it. Work hard, play hard. Everything moves at a dizzying pace and I'm keeping up, heels clicking down Fifth, coffee in hand, life flashing by like a montage.

My friends call me Velcro – I have a knack for picking people up wherever I go. Strangers don't stay strangers for long. Whether it be someone waiting for a drink at the bar or someone at the next table at Cipriani, I end up talking, connecting, adding another number to the contacts in my phone. New York is mine. I absolutely love it, but I am constantly sleep deprived, and the question would always niggle inside, is my life here sustainable?

I lean back on the green leather desk chair in my office. Papers are piled high on the long bench behind me. There are stacks of investment committee memos, abandoned deal proposals and folders of nothing important. They are collecting dust, and I don't need them, but I never get around to sorting through the mounds.

The phone rings. I recognize the country code: +48 – Poland.

"Hi, Ma."

"Hi, my baby," she beams. "So nice to catch you!"

Mum is always upbeat. Sometimes nicknamed Zsa Zsa Gabor, she's a bubbly, petite blonde with a thick Polish accent. She met my dad in Poland during the Communist period, followed him to Australia, became an actress, and earned her seaplane pilot's license.

I look at the clock on the wall. Already three p.m. *Where has the day gone?* "I'm swamped," I say. "Can we chat on the weekend?"

"Oh, just a minute, *darlink*. It's nice to hear your voice," Mum insists. "What about the guy you were seeing, anything interesting?"

What guy? I can't even think who might have been of interest enough to tell my mum.

"Nothing new on the man front," I say. "This deal I'm working on is huge – I haven't had time to focus on a relationship."

"Just tell me quickly," Mum continues. "How is it going at work?"

"Same as always. Surrounded by a mob of young, balding men in matching yellow ties with egos the size of the Empire State Building." Not to mention their pink shirts (yikes) and Brooks Brothers cufflinks – colorful, knotted material ones. I look down at my own attire. I am wearing a tailored black pantsuit with a fitted ruby-red lace shirt. The young guys in the office tell me I have a "downtown look."

"It's a good company, baby, and just remember that Bob adores you. He'll look after you."

Bob Davis, our Chairman and CEO, is a class act. White hair, understated manner, a legendary dealmaker. He's been my mentor, and like family. He, too, wears pink shirts and yellow ties – somehow charming for a man of his stature. Within twenty years, he built his company from nothing into a multibillion-dollar enterprise. Over the past years in New

York, he's nurtured my career, trusted me with secrets, and given me much-needed confidence.

"He's handed me over to a pack of tormented souls," I mutter.

"Don't be so dramatic. He'll be there when you need him."

I wish I could share her optimism. For the past year, I have been reporting directly to a young boss who is consumed by his own career path. Like all the other senior executives, he's busy vying for Bob's attention and demanding back-patting for his own achievements.

"All I know is after this deal is closed, I'm going on holiday."

As I leave the office that evening, I reach for my coat, and that's when I see it – like noticing something for the very first time.

The printout had been on my wall for years. Crooked, curling at the edges, pinned beside an unused yoga pass and a photo from last summer's team building trip.

Desiderata.

I'd read it once or twice when I first put it up – probably during a rough week. But this time, the words tug at me. Especially one line: *"Go placidly amid the noise and haste, and remember what peace there may be in silence."*

I stand there for a long moment, the city glowing through the glass behind me, headlights threading their way through the streets below.

For once, standing still feels like progress.

That evening, I enter my building, stopping to open the mailbox. There is a wad of papers bursting out of the rather angry-looking mouth above the 2B plaque. The sign on the door that says NO JUNK MAIL is completely ignored. I sigh and grab the papers and envelopes, clambering up the familiar stairs to my apartment. My 375 square-foot Chelsea apartment (that's small by most standards) still feels awesome and it suits my intensely New York lifestyle.

I place the lump of mail on a table and head in the direction of my tiny kitchen. *Maybe there's something left over from last night's takeaway?* The refrigerator's meager contents total some leftover soy sauce packets from ordered-in sushi and a half-empty can of Coke. I close the fridge door, disappointed.

This is the home that I have come to refer to as my "Parking Spot." A place where I change from office attire to going out gear, a refuge to nurse a hangover while watching MTV's *Behind the Music* and reruns of *Friends*, and where I store my steadily increasing collection of business suits and cocktail dresses. Even my cactus has died because I haven't watered it.

I look at my watch: it's already 8.30 p.m. I need to be at LOT 61 for an event at nine ... I quickly change and fluke getting a taxi up 6th Avenue.

At the bar, I spot a suited-up, handsome thirty-something. Tall. Clean-cut. He catches me looking. He smiles, runs a hand through his hair, and approaches.

"Seems I caught your eye?" he asks. "I'm Carter. What's your name?" He bites his lower lip rather sexily with his straight white teeth.

"Luna," I answer. My head bows slightly as I sip through the straw of my gin and tonic, fixing my green eyes on him.

"Luna, pleasure to meet you." He puts out his hand for me to shake.

"Pleasure to meet you too," I say giving him a big smile. I take his outstretched hand.

"Hey, you have an accent. Are you from England?"

"No, I'm Australian."

"Awesome, 'put a shrimp on the barbie!'" he says, feigning his best Australian twang, and lets out a robust laugh. I've gotten used to this line, so don't fault him for it, but then he asks, "And what do you do in the city?" This is the formidable New York question.

I know the rest of the banter ahead. This is part of the usual questions: "What do you do in the city?" followed by, "Where do you live?" then, "What is your job title?" And sometimes even, "How much do you earn?"

"I work in an investment bank," I answer him, and then the conversation starts to drift from "awesome!" to not-quite-so-interesting. As I answer his next questions one by one, he finds out I'm a Second Vice President, which sounds very senior and important, but it's really no big deal. My newfound friend's eyes glaze over. A banker? I can almost see the word "disappointment" engraved on his forehead. He's a banker too, weren't we supposed to bond?

The reality is, though, I don't want to talk about my work. I want to talk about anything but. In New York, it seems you are defined by what you do. I used to be a passionate dancer, loved to go clubbing, was really into music, and have always been a big traveler open to learning languages. However, we never get to the interesting aspects of possible conversation. I really would like people to see the creative side of me, but that somehow gets lost in corporate New York.

I start to wonder if I've done myself a disservice by working in what is still considered by many to be a man's world. Cute men in New York want to be with actresses or models. Something easy, glossy, light. They don't know what to do with an ambitious, downtown-suited finance girl. They, like me, want to have breezy conversations about a different slice of life. My job is certainly not exciting to talk about. While I give a big yes to the money, *who have I become?*

Flings come and go – rich, broke, shy, Dutch, Belgian, banker, non-banker, male model (that was nice). I even kissed a Bosnian refugee on a plane coming back from Amsterdam one time. That was really nice, until they put me in the refugee line when we arrived at JFK because they thought we were married.

None of it sticks. Life in New York skips along at double speed, and lately, it's started to feel hollow.

I worked so hard to get here. I have the degrees, the job, the lifestyle. But somewhere along the way, I lost touch with the part of me that used to dance, write, and dream.

CHAPTER 2

Go confidently in the direction of your dreams! Live the life you've imagined.

- Henry David Thoreau

"What's all this?" Dani says, looking disapprovingly at my table piled high with mail.

Dani, also from Sydney, started her corporate stint in Manhattan at the same time as me. During our first weeks in the city, we ran into each other downtown. It was a sheer coincidence, and we quickly became close friends.

"Dans, I look at paper all day in the office. I can't handle it when I get home. I'll get to it."

"What's all this under the desk?" My skinny, freckled friend looks at me with her intense eyes. "If you just deal with it every day, you won't have this problem."

"I do go through the essential stuff."

About a year back, I decided there was no way I was going to let the incessant flood of mail infiltrate the remnants I had left of a personal life. I let it pile up, and when the pile got too high, I put it into a huge brown paper bag and shoved it underneath the table, pretending it didn't exist. I'm now up to the sixth bag stacked full of mail like a cow's udder ready to burst.

Dani takes a recent addition from the top of the pile. "From BAM Properties. Important?"

"Yeah, haven't got to that yet. That's the building owner."

"May I?" she asks, opening the envelope. I nod and disappear into the bathroom to touch up my lip liner and gloss.

Dani reads out, "Apartment 2B – To whom it may concern: For reason of a complete building renovation, we hereby give all tenants six months' notice to vacate the building and make alternative living arrangements. Yours sincerely, The Bastards from Hell."

"Damn!" My lip gloss drops to the floor.

Dani and I are settled in a booth at one of our favorite places on my street, The Coffee Shop. I've never actually had a coffee there though – it's an American diner-come-late-night cocktail lounge with dark lighting. "I can find a new apartment," I continue, "but I just don't know if I'm into my life in this city anymore."

"Chin-chin," says Dani, chinking her rather huge margarita with mine. "I'm completely over being a lawyer. I'm going to move to the Caribbean and become a deckhand."

"Well, considering you're an admiralty lawyer, that's kind of related." I smile at Dani. I picture her in white shorts with a T-shirt tucked in, a red bucket next to her, on her knees scrubbing. "You'd really get into that?"

"I just want to be in the open air with the sea spray on my face, and I desperately need sun. I'm like a ghost in this city. Look at me!" She brings my attention under the table and exposes a leg. A little color remains from last summer, but yes, it's almost as white as her napkin. "And I'm developing a serious aversion to offices, computers, files ..."

"I really want to do something creative," I say. "I'm thinking about a stint in Paris. I want to finally speak French fluently."

"What would you do? Just study French?"

"No, I'd do loads of dance classes and get really fit again, then find a job with a modern dance company or something. I dunno, those creative types must need someone on the business side."

"Sure they'd need you, but they could never pay you."

"Cirque de Soleil made 400 million dollars last year."

"Run away and join the circus?" We laugh.

"The money's not what I'm after anyway," I explain. "I want to feel I'm doing something, you know, artistic and exciting. Dans, I'm turning thirty in May."

"Been there, done that." Dani takes my wrist, feigning a doctor checking for a pulse. "The prognosis is: you will survive." Dani lifts her cocktail for another toast.

"Here's to turning thirty and your am-a-zing creative career."

I'm aware of her sarcasm. Dani doesn't really believe people leave their corporate jobs. She just likes to fantasize about it.

"To nothing less!" I say, triumphantly holding up my glass again.

"Thing about you, Luni, you might just go and do it," says Dani. "And I'll still be here pushing files in my Zimmer frame."

"So," the hairdresser says, taking my thick brown hair in his hands, "what we do today?" He separates sections with his fingers and holds my hair in his palms as if weighing gold. I'm at Dani's new favorite hair stylist — an Italian named Mario.

"I was thinking just a trim and blow dry?"

He studies me in the mirror. He pulls my hair back and leans to view me from the left and then right. Then he declares with his strong Italian accent, "Bella, it's clear to me you should be blonde."

I am surprised by his comment but something about it rings true. My mother and I look very similar, and since her early twenties she has dyed her hair blonde. "I used to be blonde," I say, "when I was a teenager."

"You like it?" Mario asks.

"Yes, I liked it a lot. But it's a pain to maintain and I want healthy, natural hair."

"We all want healthy hair, but in the end you should accentuate your features. You are fair with green eyes – blonde will suit you." He must sense my reservations. "You trust me?"

"I trust you," I say, "but I don't want you to go crazy here. Just a few highlights."

"Okay. Let me put the color. I will be gentle, I promise."

In the mirror, my reflection is like a medusa with foil snakes weaved on my head. But a few hours later a new, golden me emerges. Mario has taken "just a few highlights" to mean an entirely blonde head. At first I'm taken aback, but then I think, why not?

Feeling great with my new look – hair blonde and bouncing – I step out of the salon feeling like a totally different girl. What's next for this new me?

CHAPTER 3

Chance is always powerful. Let your hook be always cast, in the pool where you least expect it, there will be a fish.

- Ovid

Kate is an Australian friend from university. Being sporty and somewhat tomboyish, she's always a lot of fun.

```
Date: January 15, 2001
To: luna@bank.com
From: kate@aspen.biz
Subject: skiing
Luni. I've arrived in Aspen. All good and sorted. Come
and stay whenever you want. Shared housing but spare
mattress on the floor with your name on it. I'll have
nights free. Loving being a lifty, so far has been
hilarious. Can't wait for you to get here. No phone.
Email me with dates.
```

I arrive a few weeks later and we have a blast. I've never been to Aspen before, and it's spectacular. I land a free bed, free lift tickets (bonus), and a great catch-up with an old uni friend.

Kate has her beanie askew and ski goggles permanently hanging around her neck. She talks fast but her walk is a saunter, radiating the kind of carefree energy that makes you forget your worries. She's working on the ski lifts and manages to take a few days off so I can ski with her.

Saturday night, we're invited over to Kate's friend's place for a party. We arrive at the chalet to find a tall blond guy standing outside the front door. He looks 6'4" and completely hot. *Oh my goodness, I am so happy I came to Aspen.*

I slip a bit in the slush when he smiles at me. Amazing thick, shoulder-length, sun-bleached hair; sculpted face with cheekbones higher than Ajax Mountain; tan as gold as the lid of my J'adore perfume bottle. He's got this cool skier dude look going on. I've always had a thing for guys with long blond hair since I fell in love with a gorgeous surfer in Australia when I was seventeen. *He is so my type.*

"Hi, I'm Luna," I say.

"Hal-lo," he manages, still smiling, while juggling three bottles of liquor in order to shake our outstretched hands. His hand is large and masculine, but soft in touch. I feel my cheeks are capable of melting snow. But one catch in the situation has already become apparent: I think his English might be non-existent. I keep an open mind, telling myself that no talk is perhaps better than the corporate drivel I've been subjected to for the past years.

The front door opens, and we enter the large chalet. The mute god scuttles off to join two friends. I meet our host, make small talk, and ever so casually saunter over in the direction of the blond and his handsome mates. They're in conversation, and their vocabulary consists of one repeated phrase. "How you doing?" they say time and time again using different kinds of intonations, some rapper-style hand gestures, and then burst out laughing.

Soon the guys stop their how-you-doings and break into a language that sounds similar to Polish. I can't catch every word, but I get the gist – enough to try my own Polish on them.

"Czesc," I offer, "Jak sie masz?" A look of understanding and surprise dawns on their faces. They understand me! They're from Slovakia and he's called Marek. His friends are both called Mirek. They're in their early twenties, studying at university in Bratislava, but taking a break to work in America and learn English.

So far their English is fairly tragic, but it does exist. Somewhere midst my rough Polish, their broken English, and Slovak (Polengsvak?), it seems we've found communication.

The guys hit the Jacuzzi and are doing vodka shots, and I have a salt-rimmed margarita shoved in my hand by a hospitable stranger. The guys call over for us to join them in the tub, but I don't want my handsome Slavic find to have the unnecessary shock of my white overgrown office butt bursting out of a swimsuit. I safely keep my body covered in my black pants and turtleneck, with hair neatly brushed and makeup on. My lips feel dry from the sun and wind (and likely something to do with the salt!), so I lather on oodles of luscious lip gloss.

Later, Kate, the Slovakian guys, and I go into town to an Italian restaurant for dinner. Marek has a raw quality about him, like a yeti being introduced to civilization for the first time. At twenty-two, he's seven years younger than me, and I find his manner totally boyish but totally appealing.

He sits next to me and eyes me intently as I put my napkin on my lap. He follows suit. He asks me how to use a knife and fork (I *think* he is joking ...), and how can I be so sure which one is meant to be the water glass? He needs help with the menu. I suggest grilled fish, but he quickly scrunches his nose. Okay, I get it, no seafood. When I say "spaghetti," he nods.

"How you doing?" says one of the Mireks from the other side of our round table.

"How you doing?" echoes the other.

I see Marek go to open his mouth. "Nooo. Pleeease say something else," I say. "No more how-you-doings for tonight, okay?"

The guys look at each other. Marek grins and says, "So." Pause. "How YOU doin'?"

We crack up laughing.

Kate is completely lost between language switching, while my stomach muscles start to ache from giggling so much.

After the meal, I reapply my lip gloss.

Marek leans in and says, "You mouth very shiny. Like ... disco ball." He adds. "Sexy disco ball."

My tube of pamplemousse-flavored Juicy is passed around the table and Kate and the guys put it on. There's a lull in conversation while we all sit there, grinning at each other while smacking our lustrous lips and waiting for our coffee. As we stand up to leave, I impulsively reach up to hug Marek around his broad shoulders. His lanky figure is stiff, and he doesn't reciprocate. *Have I been misreading signals?*

We go on to the diviest bar we can find in Aspen to have a dance. The guys have no money left, so I buy them a round of horridly overpriced Coronas. They explain that's why they drink spirits from the supermarket; it's the only way they can afford to get a buzz in Aspen. They pay the equivalent of thirty cents for a beer in their hometown.

We dance to Guns n' Roses "Welcome to the Jungle." It's so much fun thrashing around, we all really let loose. I so rarely dance in New York, I feel this is exactly what I need to let my hair down, literally.

"You come stay with me?" asks Marek, tilting his head and looking intently with his honey eyes.

"Maybe," I say, playing it cool but inside my heart is leaping with excitement that he does like me, yay! "I'll talk to Kate."

"Katey, do you mind if I stay with Marek tonight?"

"You'd be crazy not to," she says in her usual no nonsense way. "He's absolutely gorgeous, and he seems to be really into you. Enjoy!"

We soon leave the bar. Marek and I walk Kate home and then return to the Jacuzzi house where he is staying. We have no bed, so we pull cushions off the couch and he places his rather damp and heavy wool jacket on top of us like a blanket. We have an incredible view of a huge mountain outside the full-length window, with the moon reflecting off the snow.

We settle into our "bed." As we lie there, an excited tingly feeling is building in my stomach as I wonder when he's going to kiss me.

"The snow looks so beautiful," I say, breaking the silence. "The mountain looks almost blue, doesn't it?"

"Will be good ski tomorrow."

More silence.

I can't wait any longer. I precariously lean over to peck his cheek. It feels smooth and warm on my lips. I close my eyes, wondering if I just made a mistake. *He's the one that invited me here to stay with him, surely not just as friends?*

He turns to face me, and we simultaneously kiss each other. It's slow and natural, like we've been kissing for years.

I love his hairlessness, his small nose and ears, and almond-shaped eyes. His face and hair smell fresh and youthful. We kiss and kiss, and refreshingly, he doesn't try anything more.

We wake to a rich royal blue sky, and we hit the slopes. Marek's forecast was correct, it couldn't be a more perfect day for skiing. Marek carries my skis and does all the right things. Like Kate and the Mireks, he should be going to work, but after a week of clearing tables in a fast-food joint, he's fed up and says he'd prefer to take the day off to ski with me.

Marek is an absolutely top-notch skier. I swoon as he elegantly bounces between the moguls, his blond ponytail flying. We sneak kisses on the chair lifts and laugh our way down the runs with my rather disorganized skiing versus his stylish carving.

"You crazy!" he keeps yelling at me when I don't hesitate to hit the double black diamond runs with him, though I should be on the blue. Despite the fact that I do a few major face-plants, we get down rapidly enough and we're both back for more.

"No Fear Keti," he starts calling me, grinning all the time. "That's you name – Keti," he says beaming. I presume it's Slovak for kitten because then he says, "And I will be your puppy. I will just do whadever you say."

CHAPTER 4

Live and work but do not forget to play, to have fun in life and really enjoy it.

- Eileen Caddy

Thanks to loads of frequent-flier miles, we take our off-piste adventures to a new level. Marek's first trip to New York is a blast.

"This amazing! I never see such tall buildings and so many light. The cab really yellow, like a movie," he says.

I love showing him *my* city.

"There always so much peoples on the street?" he asks.

"Yeah, this is New York," I say.

"This best city in the world."

In the evenings we order some pad thai, which we chow down with bottles of Aussie red, then sit in my big, old marble bathtub for hours talking about life in broken conversation.

Strawberry-scented bubbles surround us while he massages my feet. He explains to me concepts from his studies, books he's read on philosophies of life, his mushrooming and wood meditation adventures in the depths of forests, and his crazy life experiences. He's a natural storyteller and I have endless patience to work out what he is trying to convey. His English improves rapidly, and the Polish soon diminishes from our conversations.

"Keti, I fink I know you much better than any girlfriend in Slovakia. It's like I know you for all my live." I oddly feel that I have known this guy for a long time as well, even though he's only been in my bathtub for five nights.

Something about the way he ticks draws me in. His outlook is optimistic and unaffected. He seems to have an innate connection with nature that makes him diametrically opposed to the business world I live in.

"My father, he make a wood house in the mountains. I want take you there. I fink it the best place on Earth," he says.

"Your dad built a cottage?"

"Yes, every year he do works. Now we have water, even toilet. It beautiful. We ski down the hill, but then have to walk up. I know you lazy New York Keti. You not like walk too much."

"I walk loads in New York!" I exclaim. I like the way he teases me, but even more, I like stories of his life in the Slovak Republic. After so many years in the corporate world, I want to feel closer to his world – plant my feet on the ground again.

Marek stirs something inside me. I feel like a new Luna is emerging, or perhaps it's the old Luna coming back. Suddenly, the walk to the subway in the morning feels lighter, and I catch myself smiling at strangers for no reason.

Old Luna's work day: 7.30 a.m. press snooze on alarm clock (at least three times), long shower to wake up, walk to F train – clomp, clomp, clomp, takeaway Starbucks coffee under Rockefeller Plaza, drink coffee at desk while checking emails, feel tired, but by 1 p.m. possibly feel more alert, work, meetings, arrange a night out with friends, go home 8 p.m., lay on sofa for ten-minute power nap, shower to refresh, wonder why I am going out because I am knackered, get dressed, makeup on, have nice time out but still tired, after wine and gin and tonic feel great, then time to go home (*one in the morning already, shit, will be tired again tomorrow*). Don't take off mascara, climb up to loft bed, sleep as close

19

to wall as possible so as not to roll off bed, press snooze on alarm clock (at least three times) ...

New Luna's work day: wake up to an orgasm, shower with Marek, skip toward F train, look up to enjoy the clear blue sky, decide to take a taxi to work (just because I can), check emails, and laugh to myself over the fun we had the previous night, by midday Marek calls to make lunch plans, butterflies in my belly when I see him, at 6 p.m. he's back at the office to pick me up, get some wine, go home, order in, listen to music, chat, and enjoy each other until about 4 a.m., 7.30 a.m. alarm, roll over and kiss Marek ...

Finally he leaves for Aspen after twelve days of sheer bliss. As we say goodbye, I clutch my large black leather handbag, placing it over my front as if it would protect my heart from pain. I haven't felt this strongly about someone since my high school boyfriend. *Will I ever see him again?*

"You must make promise," he says, wiping a small tear off my cheek. "You 'No Tears Keti.' We have to make each other happy, not sad."

I get back into a work routine that seems closer to reality. Marek calls me regularly and emails most days. His messages always make me giggle. I know he's in my life, and I like the feeling.

We repeat our rendezvous, in Florida, and then again in New York. Dani can't take my relationship with Marek seriously, and I know she might be right, but I can't help fantasizing that he might be the one. "He makes me feel so beautiful. He gives me everything I ever wanted. He *loves* my body, even my big bum from years of sitting perched at my desk. I feel so light and carefree and I want that feeling to last forever."

During his next visit, Marek and I are sitting in my lounge room. We have the music playing, and we're listening to my favorite Madonna album, *Ray of Light.*

When Madonna's song, *Frozen*, comes on, I sing along with the words. It says how if she lost him her heart would be broken.

I know this album back to front, but I had never focused on the intensity of the lyrics before. I feel like the words were written for me.

"You sing like Madonna," Marek says.

"I wish! She's amazing." Madonna has been my number-one idol since I was about thirteen. "Madonna is such an incredible business-woman, the way she is constantly reinventing herself and taking risks." By comparing me to Madonna, Marek could not have given me a better compliment if he tried.

"Sing again. It sound good."

"*Mmmmmm*," I hum along with the tune,

"Why you not sing more?" he asks me.

"Singing doesn't quite fit with a job in finance. I'm at work a lot and I don't even listen to music very often. Apart from when I am here with you, I'm never really home."

"You want listen this?" He brings out a selection of his CDs that are in a black plastic case. All the CDs are silver TDK brand with unknown names handwritten on them. "This really good."

"Sure, put it on."

Pumping trance music blares through my speakers and within a moment it infiltrates me.

"I absolutely love this!" I say. "This is the kind of music I listened to all the time in London."

When I studied law in London. I had a really intensive university schedule so couldn't have a busy social life, but I would religiously go out on Saturday nights to Strawberry Sundae in Vauxhall, a club in the arches under the train lines. I was in my element, and being so high on the dancing, other clubbers would often say to me, "I want what you are on." I would reply, "I'm on water," and show them my pint-size water bottle with a grin. I didn't need anything to make me feel like I was on Ecstasy. Suddenly, Marek brings that feeling back to me. *Where has the music from Strawberry Sundae been all this time?* I'm so thrilled he brought it here to New York.

"Why you have go to work?" asks Marek the following morning. We're in my loft bed, which has become our nest. We have even taken to eating sandwiches in bed rather than ordering in dinner.

"I go to work to make money, of course. Also, it happens to be interesting." I say this, not sure I'm being very convincing.

"Take the day free – play with me."

"I can't. I've got commitments – a presentation and meetings."

"Don't seem you like it much. You don't look so happy when you talk about it."

"I have been there almost four years," I say. "But most likely next year I'll move to Europe to do something else."

"So why you not leave now? You be happy in Europe."

"It's not that easy. I have a great income, friends, and a lifestyle here. I'm not sure if I'm ready to leave it all behind."

"What you scare of?"

"I'm not scared. I just don't want to rush things. I have a good job. I just want to be sensible."

"Keti, you born in heaven and will always be in heaven. You can do whadever you want. You cannot be always sensbul."

That day in the office, I don't get anything done. I am going through the motions but my thoughts are everywhere else. The spreadsheet in front of me is a blur. It's not just that I can't focus ... I don't want to. I realize how boring my job is.

Marek had asked something that stuck with me: *"When's the last time you took a day off?"*

I couldn't remember. I spent my days in heels, in elevators, in meetings. Even my weekends were scheduled.

Now, something in me ached – not for escape, but for grounding. For connection. Something slower, more honest.

My mind transports me back to when I arrived in London in 1994. The rain tapped against the windows as I sat cross-legged on the carpet, surrounded by university brochures. They were spread out like tarot cards. One was for a postgraduate law program at a top-tier university. The other for a language course that promised full immersion in French, Italian, and Spanish: Romance languages I'd long been fascinated by.

The idea of studying languages felt like a delicious daydream. I had imagined myself in Parisian cafés, in Roman piazzas, and in Spanish courtyards, speaking fluently and understanding the world through different voices. It was romantic and beautiful.

And then there was law. Structured, respected, reliable. A passport to a secure future. It had prestige and predictability.

I stared at the two brochures. My heart pulled one way, my mind pulled the other way.

In the end, I filled out the application for the law program. I told myself I could always learn languages later. That this was the sensible decision. The smart one. The right one.

But as I put the language brochure back into its envelope and slid it into a drawer, something inside me folded up too.

Lately, a question had begun to rise: *What's true to me?*

Not what looks good on paper. Not what makes sense. But what makes me feel alive.

What do I really want?

I want to live in Europe, speak different languages, and take up dance classes. And the key is, I actually have the savings to do it. *Is Marek right? Is it time I make the change?*

Corporate Luna: You gave up your dance classes at age sixteen to follow this path. You spent over a decade studying and working toward the high-powered job you wanted. You can't give that up on a whim. I won't let you! Don't let this guy get to you so much. What does he know? Calm down, get your thirtieth birthday over with, and I'm sure you'll return to normal.

Creative Luna: Normal? That's what you are. You're a boring, conservative banker who sits on her butt all day looking at a computer screen. That's not Luna! You just wanted to beef up your CV and get some money together – staying in a corporate job was never part of your grand life plan.

Corporate Luna: If you leave, you'll regret it, big time. Stick it out, at least for a few more years.

Will Corporate Luna always have the last word?

CHAPTER 5

Confucius says: "Beware of good-looking long-haired young men who are good in bed." Or maybe that's what my father told me when I moved overseas.

A few weeks into his third visit to New York, Marek comes to my office to check his emails. "I got massage from a girl in Aspen." I know by "massage" he means a message.

"Okay ..." Where is this leading?

"She say she want me come back there."

"Why are you telling me?" I am *so* not into games. *Is he trying to make me jealous?*

"She pretty, twenty years old that I meet at party last time. I know she like me."

"And, do you want to be with her or me?"

"With you of course, silly."

"So, why do you even care if she sent you a message or not? Why did you give her your email address anyway?"

He sits there with a smug look on his face. He loves female attention. He glances at himself in the mirror near my desk, as if double-checking the obvious: yes, still gorgeous. I have always been aware that he spends more time in front of the mirror than I do. I've been so smitten with his hotness and thought, *Who can blame him for being into himself?* But now a vain guy who is playing jealousy games? It was all so childish, and it hurt. I thought the idea was that we make each other happy, not sad. They were Marek's own words just a short time ago.

Though what did I expect from a twenty-two-year-old? Logic made total sense, except when I was in Marek's arms. I was addicted to him, and to the freedom I felt with him.

"You know, Keti," Marek continues. "I don't to see a future between us. We said we will always to be honest wid each other. I love be with you, but you can to find somebody better than me."

"If I want to be with you, it's my decision. For now, I'm perfectly happy."

"Yes, but what would happen in five years. I return to Slovakia soon. I can't promise I be with you. You want to marry and have children, no?"

"Yes, most definitely."

"Then I am not for you. I not want ruin you live."

I put my pride aside, tucking away the sting of his words like a letter I wasn't ready to read. I tell myself not to overanalyze, and just enjoy what we have.

We fall back into our rhythm – laughing, kissing, sharing stories late into the night. We continue to have a blast. Deep down, I know this isn't forever, but for now, I choose joy over expectation. I let myself be in the moment, even if it's fleeting.

Marek takes me out of the boardroom and into the bedroom. But it's more. He reminds me of who I really am, and who I want to be. Everything I do with Marek is exciting. I don't feel I belong in the office anymore. I arrive back to work as usual, looking well-groomed and conservative, continuing to play my part in a suit. Inside, though, my head is filled with fun adventures and ideas. I sit in meetings with Bob and other old-school men over sixty, and think to myself, "Gosh, if they only knew what I got up to this weekend."

"I've been thinking more and more about moving to Europe," I say to Marek one night, buzzed after an evening dancing at a large, Ibiza-style club. "I feel music in my life again, and I don't want it to leave." He doesn't hug me, or look happy. He actually looks a bit concerned. "Don't worry," I add, "if I move to Europe, it isn't for you."

And really it isn't. For as long as I can remember, I have wanted to speak French fluently, go to dance class each day, and live on the European continent. I'd lived in the UK, and Poland, but the western part of Europe was calling me. I start to fantasize: what better place to start than Paris ...

Of course, Corporate Luna tries to make me stay put in NYC.

Corporate Luna: You've got it made here. Great job, great income. Amazing city. Why throw it all away?

Creative Luna: Ignore that bossy boardroom babe. Follow your heart, not your wallet. Be confident that you'll land on your feet. C'mon, let's go live in Europe!

Recently it seems that Corporate Luna has less and less to say.

I request a lunch with Bob, the company CEO. His secretary calls to say we'll be going to the 21 Club just across the road at Rockefeller Plaza.

"What's on your mind?" says Bob, blue eyes piercing under his white bushy brows.

I swallow hard. I'm on the edge of being teary. Bob has always been so kind to me over the years. We have always connected on a personal level, and I consider his extended relatives my American family. Under his wing, I turned from an insecure university graduate into a confident businesswoman.

"I want to let you know that I'm leaving New York," I say.

"Really?" He moves in his seat, but his gaze is intent on me. "We'll miss you. What's your plan?"

"Various things have come up that have made me think it's the right time for me to make a change." I pause. He's waiting for me to continue.

"My thirtieth birthday is soon and it's made me reconsider my life a lot. I have to change apartments, so I thought, well, maybe it's a good time to move altogether. I feel it's time I pursue something more creative."

"Are you sure you know what you're doing?" He sounds completely unconvinced by my idea. "Another apartment can easily be sorted out. You're just going places in the company."

I feel myself wavering. Bob has been my mentor. How can I not heed his always solid advice?

"You really think so?" I shrug to show my disbelief. "For some reason I feel stagnant."

Corporate Luna comes back on the scene. What are you thinking? Your reasons for leaving are so weak. You don't even know exactly what you will do in Europe. He's telling you he thinks you have a great future with the company.

"What were you doing when you were thirty?" I ask Bob.

"I had a six-month stint in Australia and made my first million. That's the kind of thing you should be doing. You're just reaching your prime."

As much as I admire Bob's financial achievements, making millions is not my driver. I want experiences. The past years have gone so quickly, and I don't want to wake up turning thirty-five, realizing I'm still in New York doing the same thing – banking! I want to live in Europe, feel fit and healthy again, connect with my creativity and a non-corporate life.

"Well, since you went to Australia when you were thirty, can you understand that for me it might be time for a new adventure?" I say.

"New York is the hub of the world. Where would you want to go?"

"Europe. I'll start in Paris. I've always wanted to speak French fluently," I reply, conviction coming back into my voice.

"We're looking for a Chief Administrative Officer," Bob says. "I thought you would be a great candidate for the job. You would be made a partner."

Why is he making this so hard? Why didn't he ever mention this before? I try to keep focused on my goal. I've decided to leave. I didn't have lunch with Bob so that he could talk me out of it.

Corporate Luna: This amazing man is offering you a promotion and you are going to say a flat no?

"Your studies are such a powerful combination – business and law," Bob says. "You can't let that go to waste. My foundation deals with many creative initiatives. You could continue working here and I'll support your interests on the side."

I know myself. If I stay in New York, my life will not change. How, in addition to everything else I do in the city, would I find time to start some yet undefined creative venture? And when I'm working in finance, the truth is I don't have the inspiration. If I really want a creative career, I need to throw myself into a new life.

"That's very kind and generous of you, Bob, but I really want to live in Europe." My voice sounds meek and I can't believe the words are escaping from my mouth like wild animals from a cage. I'm turning down this incredible offer from him. *Will I regret this?*

"Does this have something to do with the young man you're seeing?" Bob asks.

The tears well and I can taste them building in my throat. I'm an emotional bubble ready to burst. "He's really too young and there's no future between us," I say. "I'm doing this for myself."

"Well you will always be welcome to come back."

"Thank you. You run an amazing company. Who knows, I might find myself back here – anything's possible."

We sit in silence for a moment.

Then Bob says, "Perhaps you can continue doing some part-time work for us over there. I'll look into it."

Now that is an offer I will not refuse. That would be a dream come true, to have part-time work based in Europe. *Bob is an angel!*

"That would be brilliant! Thanks so much for considering it."

I touch his arm and feel a tear escape. I quickly brush it away, hoping he didn't see.

As I walk out of the office that afternoon, salty tears sting my cheeks, but inside, I am strangely light. Saying no to Bob is like leaping off a cliff without knowing if a parachute will open – but I also feel the quiet thrill of free fall. Paris is just a dream for now, but for the first time in years, I'm giving that dream a chance. Maybe I'm not just leaving a job. Maybe I'm finally choosing myself.

CHAPTER 6

One needs to be slow to form convictions, but once formed they must be defended against the heaviest odds.

- Mahatma Gandhi

The boxes are packed. My apartment is nearly bare, just a scattering of furniture and a few half-used candles waiting for their final burn. I'm days away from leaving New York. Paris is on the horizon.

And just when I'm trying to steel myself for the leap, my inbox pings with an email from Marek.

```
Date: July 20, 2001
To: luna@bank.com
From: marek@hotmail.cz
Subject: abcdefgh
So how YOU doing ??!@@!@#$%^&*
Lunio ,move your nice bottom and come to visit me ,I
really want to see you!!!!!!!!
i met some girls ,with who i tryed to spend some time
,just go clubbing or do some sports and it was HORIBLE!!!
comparet to time which i spent with you … i can't compare
it, stupid stupid stupid.
```

```
seriously.i have great plan for you,listen: you want
to go to Paris ? stupit french guys or gays?, apartment
stress ,rain? YACKY! you will be sick soon! trust me!
But you can do something completly diferent,you can come
and have fun time with puppy. we can do whatever we will
want to ,travel ,ski, party ,go to cinema, hors riding,
ice skating … i miss it ;-(
  i know you'll do what you think is the best for you ,but
think about it at least, please.we can have fun togethA,
  marek
```

I sit back, the email glowing on my screen. Of course he sends this now – just when I'm about to move to a new country, just when I've finally stopped crying over him. The message is messy, impulsive, laced with bad grammar, and Marek's signature charm. A confusing cocktail, like always. One message from him, and it's as if every logical bone in my body has picked its skeleton self up and left me. *Should I feel his warm touch again?*

Later that evening, I'm back at The Coffee Shop with Dani, my gin and tonic glowing like a magic potion under the neon lights.

"Right when I'm about to leave for Paris, he sends me this!" I moan to Dani. "He's definitely a player," I tell her. "But I felt so alive when I was with him. Maybe I should squeeze in another rendezvous?"

"Get a grip, Luni," Dani snaps crossly. "You've had multiple last rounds with this guy."

Of course, she is a voice of reason. Marek's last New York tryst had been extra-romantic, with us endlessly listening to our favorite trance albums and lying tangled in conversation, convincing ourselves that love could somehow overcome reality. But even then, he said it himself: "I can't to keep away from you, but I know it not work forever."

"I can't resist him," I choke out, the words catching in my throat. "I love him, Dans."

32

"He's a tall, blond twenty-two-year-old skier. I think you want to call that lust."

"Last call!" the bartender shouts. I reach out to signal another round.

"Time to move on," Dans counsels. "Time to 'move your nice bottom,' as Marek would say, to Paris. And live out *your* dreams. You don't need a European man. You need Europe!"

"Thank you, Dans." She's right. In the fog of leaving, I let doubt creep in and took comfort in the familiar distraction of Marek. But the path ahead is mine alone.

I'll always be grateful to him for helping me find the courage to leave New York, but now, Paris is calling. As I step forward, I'll carry him with me, tucked in a corner of my heart.

CHAPTER 7

One does not discover new lands without consenting to lose sight of the shore for a very long time.

- Andre Gide

I'm in a relationship that's good, but not perfect. That's my relationship with Paris.

I read out in French class, *"Je sais qu'il faut partir."* I translate the words in my head: *I know I have to leave.* My lessons here at an illustrious Parisian university are anything but interesting. *Perhaps it is time to leave?*

Briiiing-briiiing. Briiiing-briiiing. Oh damn, my cell phone rings, rather loudly.

I catch the teacher giving me a look of death as I scramble deep in my black leather handbag to turn it off. I raise my eyes at her apologetically. *It really was a mistake.* I plead, *"Je suis très désolée."* *Do not kill me, you scary woman.* As I feared, my attempt to calm her fails.

"Je NE supporte PAS le telephone cellulaire!" she exclaims in an over-articulated way. She has a grayish-blonde bun tied up tight on her head and gold-rimmed spectacles that sit on her nose. A potentially quaint Mrs. Claus-come-primary school teacher look is transformed into the Wicked Witch of Paris.

It's like I'm stuck in a time warp back to high school. Not only because of the way the teacher is barking at me, but also because I'm about a decade older than most of the students in my class. Many of them are bachelor-degree students completing a semester of French studies abroad. I am thirty and had a professional career in New York. *What am I doing here?*

To make matters worse, everywhere I go in Paris, they call me "Madame." *Oui, Madame. Bien sur, Madame*. Why Madame? It sounds like I am a mother or something. I still feel very much like a Mademoiselle and would really like to be reverted back to that status until at least such time as I am married. *Do the Parisians think I'm that old?* At what age does someone become a Madame? Not only did I have to actually turn thirty (lots of parties eased the pain), but being called "Madame" feels like an official decree that my youth is over.

I write in my diary to remind myself of my goals for Paris:

1. *Get to know this incredible city.*
2. *Speak French fluently.*
3. *Attend regular dance classes.*

It doesn't help that I'm staying in a very dingy apartment rented out to me by a man who has a spare key. A few times he has entered unannounced. It's really unnerving – I need to find my own place.

After my morning French classes, I busy myself with finding a new apartment. I manage to rent a small, colorful studio in Saint-Germain-des-Pres, the famous 6th arrondissement. A bustling area in central Paris bordering the River Seine, it is completely overrun by tourists and dog poop, but it's the ideal place to live for my Parisian adventure. The apartment has a loft bed, exactly like my apartment in New York had. It immediately feels like home.

After months of silence, I thought my relationship with Marek might really be over. But then he emails.

February 12, 2002
From: marek @hotmail.cz
Subject: love
whooof,brush,poo,pee,love?

So after all that time, this is what he sends? Nonsense words and childish sounds. It makes me smile – then ache.

I close my laptop slowly.

The pain is real. Not fresh anymore, but dull and lingering. I haven't met a guy in Paris who I'm even vaguely interested in. But I also know I deserve more.

I don't reply.

It's not easy, but it feels right. This isn't about pride. It's about looking after myself.

With perfect timing, Dani arrives for a weekend visit.

Straight off her morning plane, we launch into a rigorous drinking session involving copious amounts of beer and rosé to celebrate her arrival. Although it seems that conversation of Marek is out of bounds because I know too well how she never approved of him, her visit is exactly what I need. Tourism and bar therapy!! Highly recommended for a broken heart!

We go on a boat cruise down the Seine in awe of the distinct bridges, visit Chez Paul (an absolutely scrumptious patisserie), walk around Le Marais (a gay area, full of charm), and drink at my local bar, Bar du Marche (which is so quintessential Paris), then enjoy happy hours in various cafés before starting on the red wine ... *ouch!* We pass out at eleven p.m. We wake up at three p.m. the next afternoon feeling awful. *How did we sleep so much?* Dani is jetlagged and exhausted from her hectic New York lawyer life, but I have NO excuse.

Feeling really hungover, we hit the streets of Saint-Germain, go to Chez Paul again (more croissants!), then do a walking tour of Paris along

Le Louvre and Jardin Tuileries, taking the Ferris wheel that has a great view over the city. I get vertigo, so cling to the center pole for dear life.

The day is a blur. Dani and I buy liquids at every possible stop – even a bottle of dodgy water from a passing fellow selling water bottles in the middle of the footpath out of a scummy bucket. The water isn't even cold, and we aren't sure if the bottles have been refilled with tap water, but we drink it down more than happily. *Liquids. We need liquids!*

We soon move on from dodgy water and start on wine, and realize that was what we needed to feel better.

"It's a great city, Luna," Dani says as we amble along a broad tree-lined pavement down by the river. "You seem happy."

"I'm really glad to be here," I say, "but I don't feel settled at all. I'm just one of so many tourists living in Paris. The locals all think I am American. I don't feel the Parisians see me, they just look through me."

"What about your French?" she asks. "You seem to be getting really good."

"Yeah, I enjoy speaking French. It's such an incredibly beautiful language. I remembered a lot from high school. The Parisians, though, they hardly let me practice. They insist on speaking to me in English." I roll my eyes. "Dans, I'm thinking of leaving."

"Already?"

"Now it's like I'm still half stuck in New York. I live here in Paris, but I'm back in New York for work all the time, and most weekends that I'm here I go to other cities in Europe rather than making a social life for myself in Paris. It just doesn't seem to be the right place."

"Where would you go?"

"I have no idea. I considered Geneva and Brussels because they're French-speaking, but they are not for me. Amsterdam? That's where Cirque du Soleil's offices are, but it's just too wet, and I don't think I'm ready to learn Dutch. Next weekend I'm going to check out Rome."

"Rome sounds good!"

"Yes! Viva Italia! Gotta love Paris though. Europe is just so amazing."

"Couldn't agree more!"

Dani has to get up early for her flight. She has Xanax for the trip to sleep well, and then will have a romantic get-together with her new man when she gets home. Yes, it seems Dans is in love. So she is not so sad to leave me and Paris.

I am left somewhat deflated after the hype and excitement of her visit. Back to my thoughts and the dilemma of where to live and what to do with this next phase of my career and life.

The following weekend, I venture to Rome with high hopes that the city will beckon me to live there. I have a chaotic four days of five-course meals with friends and visit the Colosseo, Foro Romano, Vaticano, basilicas, fountains, Gucci, and Prada. An amazing place, but the idea of making it home doesn't appeal. Its like a rough diamond, while Paris is such a feminine city with its pristine fairytale-like architecture. I return to Paris with added incentive to stay.

As the weeks pass, I learn to succumb to my new life, and work out a rather ideal *Parisienne* routine. Instead of continuing the course at the university, which is more focused on grammar, I know it's the French speaking I really have to focus on. I have private French lessons in the mornings at my apartment on Rue de Buci with an older woman who is very strict with pronunciation. Although she speaks perfect English, our conversation is restricted to only French and she doesn't let me get away with any errors.

After a grueling but extremely satisfying hour with her, I then hit the bustling Saint-Germain streets, enjoying a *jamon et fromage crepe* or baguette for lunch. In the afternoons I go to a dance class in Le Marais, which from my place is a thirty-minute walk along the Seine. I pass the statue of St. Michel, cross the island where the Cathedral Notre-Dame sits, and venture past the incredible Hotel de Ville. My brisk steps become part of the tapestry for outdoor café patrons who are rugged-up, chugging on Gauloises cigarettes.

Back in my cozy Parisienne pad, nestled in front of my computer, I work for the office in New York until late evening or perhaps meet up with some friends.

"Hey Luni, you got plans next weekend?" asks Elena, bursting with vigor. She's a Dutch fashion MBA student living in Paris who has become a good friend. We were introduced through a mutual friend in New York.

"No, just hanging out," I reply, wondering what she has in mind.

"A group from my fashion course, we're going to Milan and you gotta come. It's gonna be great!"

The answer is simple. "Okay. I'm in!"

CHAPTER 8

Look and you will find it – what is unsought will go undetected.

- Sophocles

I step off the train in Milan into what looks like a concrete wasteland. Not exactly the glamorous Italian escape I had envisioned. I almost regret my decision to go. I've booked myself into the same hotel where Elena and her MBA student friends are staying. The aptly named hotel "Diablo" (Devil) has a concrete facade reminiscent of post-war Eastern Europe. It's outrageously expensive and my room doesn't even have a decent bathroom. The shower sits awkwardly beside the bed, hidden behind a flimsy screen. The toilet? Communal. Down the hall. Dismal.

"Where are we?" I ask Elena's Parisian colleagues that evening. They are holding a rather tattered map of Milan upside down.

"Haven't we passed this street before?" asks Elena. "I remember that office building."

"This doesn't seem to be the town center," I say. "All the squares are completely deserted."

"But the map says we are here," says her petite French friend, pointing to an intersection.

I look up to find some corresponding street names to no avail. It's cold and dark, and it's almost ten p.m. I'm hungry.

"Let's just get a taxi," I say. "It might be a few euros but at least we'll get there."

"Sure," says Elena, brushing her long blonde fringe behind her ear. "But have you seen one?"

"No."

After another hour of walking, we find our destination. We head toward a big box-shaped building with a name written in bold on the side: ROIALTO.

We stand at a crimson velvet rope as the doorman mumbles into a microphone pinned to his suit jacket. He motions us to enter. We weave our way through a wall of colorful hanging beads into an enormous warehouse space.

Elena and I grin at each other. "Okay, so now I know why people come to Milan," I say.

"This is gonna be great!" says Elena, grabbing my hand with excitement. "I'm so sorry about before. Next time, we call a cab at the hotel."

Roialto has modern decor with a slight Middle Eastern feel adorned with bright cushions and large terracotta pots. There are giant fans that look like windmills protruding from the super-high ceiling. The people are dressed in trendy attire, and the place is pumping with conversation and ambient music. We put our names down for the next available table in the restaurant.

"What do you want to drink?" Elena asks me as she edges her way toward the bar.

"Ask the bartender for the specialty."

We are handed elaborately adorned Vodka Sour con Maracuja cocktails that have the bitterness of passionfruit mixed with other exotic treats. We are ready to mingle.

We meet bankers and students, all eager to try out their English. "You're from Australia! What a beautiful place. The cousin of my father lives in Melbourne. Do you know Frederico Colombo?"

"I can't believe everyone is so easy to talk to here," I say. "Do you find the French closed or is it just me?" Elena is about 5'10" with long blonde hair, and while I don't look that different to her, bar a few inches, I somehow presume because she is European her time in Paris has been easier than mine.

"The Italians are much friendlier," she says. "There's no comparison."

After dinner we go to Gattopardo, a club down the street that's in a renovated church. Past more velvet ropes and security, we admire the white marble interior. At the former altar, the centerpiece is a enormous chandelier that comprises thousands of lights, like the queen of disco balls. A saxophonist is standing up on the long bar, playing along with the DJ's music. The staff also jump up on the bar from time to time, performing rehearsed moves to retro-songs like "YMCA." We dance non-stop for hours.

This is just the beginning of a sensational weekend of visiting the most attractive shops I've ever seen, marveling at architecture such as the Duomo and Galleria Vittorio Emanuele, and going to a myriad of fun restaurants, bars, and clubs. We meet with locals, end up being driven from place to place, and everywhere we go we are greeted by more smiling Italians. It seems every venue has a distinct atmosphere; from the sleek white leather couches of Chatoulle to the zebra-skinned walls of Cavalli Caffè.

Everywhere I turn, something clicks. Maybe this isn't just a visit – maybe Milan is the place I was meant to land all along.

"Ouch," says Elena at our last lunch together in Milan. She scrunches up her face and is obviously struggling to swallow her pizza.

"Not feeling well?" I say, having already devoured half my delicious prosciutto and fungi pizza. It's on a delightfully thin base with succulent toppings. OMG, the Italians really do know how to make perfect pizza.

"We've been out partying and drinking every night," she says, holding up her head with her hands. "I feel ill."

"I'm exhausted," I say, but the reality is I'm strangely elated. "You know, Elena, I think I have an idea."

"Really?" She looks at me with her eyebrows raised.

"The idea came to me last night as I was going to bed."

"What is it?" Her deep blue eyes are completely focused on me.

"I think Milan could be the city for me."

"Milan?" She takes a long pause and looks puzzled.

"Something about it feels like a mini-New York in Europe. Everyone is well-educated and friendly, with the added bonus of the fun Italian way. I think it could be great."

"What would you do here?"

"It's the hub of fashion. Maybe that's my creative calling?"

"And the men here are so nice," she says, winking. Seems she's mustered up some of her usual energy. "Why not give it a try? It's so close to Paris. You can always come back."

"Yes, I am moving to Milan." I repeat it, just to make sure it's real: "I am moving to Milan!"

A few days later, I'm back in New York – where skyscrapers loom, my inbox is full, and my feet suddenly feel heavier. But the Milan decision buzzes in my chest. I meet with Bob and tell him my idea. His reaction isn't quite as supportive as that of Elena.

"Milan will not be different to me being in Paris," I say. "It has two international airports and there are direct flights to New York."

"I'm sorry," he says kindly, "but we think it's time to wrap up our part-time working relationship. We can't keep this going on indefinitely. We want you back here in New York, and if you're moving even further away in Europe, we'll have to find someone else to take over your role."

I know I have absolutely no power to change his mind, and something tells me it might be a blessing in disguise. I need to move to Milan with a clean slate and not drag my corporate life with me.

Corporate Luna: But what are you going to do without the income?

Creative Luna: That's what savings are for! You worked for years and saved up for a time like this. Spread your wings. Feel truly free. You always land on your feet, and you will in Milan too.

Corporate Luna: You might regret this.

Creative Luna: Give it a go. Worst comes to worst, you can always go back ...

I let Creative Luna have her way. Its high time I release the corporate life that I had in New York. I love being back in New York, and seeing colleagues and friends, but it's always wonderful to return to Europe. Something inside me knows that Europe is the key to my future life, I just need to find it.

Marek is now back in the Slovak Republic and keeps emailing.

Date: May 11, 2002
From: marek@hotmail.cz
Subject: news
cus lalunius!!

OK i have some news … i have new flat-mate,everything happend so fast … she is living with me from sunday.her name is Anezka and she is WANDERFULL,she has amazing big black eyes ,perfect figure and she is so kind, well she is still a little bit shy ,but i think it will work out between us.

yesterday i introdused her to my mother ,she likes her a lot ,she is really super,she is 2 years old and she is perfect mix of german shepherd and rotvailer ;-) ,pretty big dog. whooof!!!!

```
    i saved her against some ugly dog-asylum and i think
she knows that so likes me a lot ;-) ,so puppy has a
puppy …
    anyway ,it is bad news that you will not come over
here,but maybe I will take Anezka to Paris but i think
she doesn't like cats a lot … if you know what i mean ;-)
    have a nice day and write something more one time please
,whoof?
```

He never fails to make me giggle. But I must look at my life plans and focus on that. I look at my list of goals and I realize I have achieved a lot in the last months in Paris. My French is fluent. Also, I have thrown myself into a mix of dance classes – jazz, Afro-Brazilian, and modern expressive dance, and I am feeling much more fit and toned. It has been satisfying to be back exercising and into dancing again. It's something I wanted for such a long time.

Now I can focus on what *I* want to do without wondering what Marek is thinking or doing. I remind myself that I can't be tempted by those plush lips and his playful charm anymore.

I start having a recurring daydream about dancing on stage like when I was fifteen years old. In the daydream, I'm performing in a dance competition to The Cure song, "Never Enough." I'm in a black leotard and see-through black tights. I smile broadly on stage with an air of radiance. Energy is beaming out of my fingers as I swing my outstretched arms. With kicks, leaps, and rolls, I end in a jazz pose, one heel raised behind me and arms in an upside-down V. Photo finish, panting, and still smiling. The adjudicator awards me first prize.

The song title "Never Enough" seems to embody my life. Here I am living in Paris, possibly the most beautiful city in the world. I'm doing dance class each day and have been working regularly in New York, but I am still searching for more. *Will there be a day that it all seems enough?*

I muse, perhaps one day when I'm settled: settled in a loving relationship, settled in a wonderful place I can call home, and settled in a satisfying creative career, perhaps then it will "be enough."

I hold hope that Milan will be my ticket to all three.

CHAPTER 9

Take the first step in faith. You don't have to see the whole staircase. Just take the first step.

- Martin Luther King, Jr.

Before leaving Paris, I purchase my own piece of France: a beautiful silver Peugeot 206 cc – *coupe cabriolet*. Elena had said to me, "Get something sexy, Luna. The next car you have will be like a van or something practical you'll need when you have kids. You're young and single. It must be a convertible!"

I was wary that theft in Milan is meant to be high so a soft-top roof would not be practical. When I heard there was a Peugeot hard-top convertible, I knew that was the car I wanted.

Buying the car is not that easy, but satisfying as the final test of my French language skills; negotiating with arrogant, Parisian car salesmen. I visit ten different Peugeot dealerships before finally scoring the car I want: right color, right price, right delivery date, leather upholstery (lush!), and best of all, they agree to payment on my credit card (yay, frequent-flier miles).

I still wonder what force inside me is drawing me to Milan. I'm so convinced it will be the right place for me, despite the fact I don't speak a word of Italian and I have no connections there. Perhaps I am a little crazy, but that's where I'm at. No job, no boyfriend, no kids, no mortgage

– just a bank account full of savings. I am completely free, so why not give it a whirl?

It seems everyone I know has ganged up to advise me against making the move to Milan. My European friends and acquaintances, including Italians, are so negative.

"It's an industrial city," they say.

"It doesn't have the flair of other Italian cities."

"Why don't you move to Rome or Florence?"

"Milan is very expensive and unattractive."

"You should be moving to Barcelona in Spain, not Milan."

I read in my *Let's Go* Travel Guide to see what it says about Milan: "The pace of life is quick, and *il dolce di fare niente* (the sweetness of doing nothing) is an unfamiliar taste." And that is my point; I don't want to hang around and do nothing, I want to launch into the next phase of my life with a creative endeavor. I hope Milan will hold the key.

As the months pass, I keep the memories of the wonderful weekend in Milan alive so I'm not tempted to change my mind. There's a force behind me, telling me Milan is where I should go.

I bid farewell to my humble abode on Rue de Buci, and drive – taking a long route – across France. I go south to the Cote d'Azur and along to the Italian Riviera, then after a few refreshing beach stops, make my way along the highway toward Milan. I keep at a comfortable 120 kilometers per hour, while cars fly past me at 150.

As I enter the city, there are trams, bicycles, mopeds, pedestrians, motorbikes, cars, and buses to dodge, not to mention uneven cobblestone streets that make it sound like my tires are going to burst at any moment. There are also trolley buses which are mad, huge vehicles that almost sag as they veer sharply, hanging off puppet-like strings. I worry that my precious shiny new vehicle is going to swiftly become an abyss of dents and scratches.

I grip the wheel, heart racing. What am I doing here? Is this the Milan that felt so right from afar?

A passing ambulance scares the hell out of me, then a blue police car comes flying out of nowhere with sirens in full force. I stop my car dead in its tracks, and the police car heads straight for me in my lane. I am petrified and, even after he swerves past me and is far away, I stay frozen at the traffic lights until the cars behind me start beeping. I move tentatively, and then a fire engine comes zooming down another street. *Have I arrived in the land of sheer chaos?*

Milan is a maze of one-way streets, but I eventually find the hotel I booked and park in a nearby parking station. The hotel is rather dingy and in an unattractive part of town, not far from where I stayed with Elena so many months before. I struggle to communicate because no one speaks English. It's very different to the Milan I had in mind.

When I find an apartment, I'm sure my new life here will take off, but the real estate agents show me a slew of shabby, overpriced apartments that make me really worry I have made the wrong move.

I manage to find an agent who speaks English. We make an appointment to see a one-bedroom apartment that he says is in Milan center. We agree to meet on Thursday at two p.m.

On Thursday morning, I'm a bit nervous in anticipation of the meeting with the agent, hopeful it will mean the end of living in a hotel. I have started an Italian course, so I have class every morning. I rush from my lesson, grab a quick sandwich for lunch, reach our rendezvous point, and then wait, wait, and wait. *Where is he? Did he agree to rent the apartment to someone else? Or did I get the date wrong?* I call him.

"I sorry," he explains to me. "I am having lunch with my sister. Can we to meet tomorrow?"

I can't believe it. In New York, it's all go-go-go. People don't just not turn up to meetings. Doesn't he realize he'll get a commission from me? How could he be lunching with his sister?

If Milan is meant to be relatively fast-paced and organized, all I could think is thank goodness I'm not living in another part of this country since it would drive me crazy. I'd heard that in Rome it's normal to be two hours late to a meeting, or just not show up, but I didn't expect this in Milan.

The next day I have a meeting with the agent at the same time and place. This time, quite punctually, a navy blue BMW Z3 pulls up. Behind the wheel is a bronzed, athletic twenty-something with short brown hair – looking more like a tennis pro than a real estate agent.

"Luna?" he calls to me out the window, leaning on his suntanned arm. "*Buongiorno*. I'm Giuseppe."

"You remembered our meeting this time," I say.

"*Si, bellissima*, so sorry but I forget yesterday. We go there now."

He parks at the next block and I wonder why he bothered picking me up in the car. We could have walked in less than two minutes.

"You have such beautiful hands," he says to me. "You play piano?"

What I need is an apartment, not a flirtatious Italian real estate agent. "I played when I was a child," I answer him to be polite. Then, eager to switch the conversation to business, I ask, "Is this the street?"

"*Si! Siamo arrivati*. There are a few apartamentos I can show you, but this is a good choice if you want one bedroom."

Via Carducci is next to my Italian school. I know the street well. A thoroughfare that used to be part of the city's canal system, it's now crowded with cars and buses. He points to the building from outside. It looks like a majestic palace with its regal-looking columns and ornate carved stone sculptures. I can imagine the five-story *palazzo*, as the Italians call them, would have once been one family's home.

"Wow, this building looks lovely. What is the monthly rent on the apartment?"

"I not sure. I must to ask my father."

The ornate wooden door leading off the street has a smaller door built into it. We crouch to enter through what is like a human-sized cat flap. We enter a grand foyer that is clean and spacious with a pastel mosaic tiled floor and baroque-style statue of a naked woman in the corner. At the end of the foyer there is natural light entering from outside. *I love it already.*

There are patterns on the wall that look like wallpaper, but when I touch it, I realize it's stone carved in an intricate design. I lean up to look through the spiral staircase to the ceiling at the top floor. There are white puffy clouds painted on a blue sky reminiscent of Michelangelo.

We take the elevator up to the next floor. It seems a pity not to have walked up the marble staircase. At the apartment door, Giuseppe fumbles between keys and a small device with flashing lights. He pushes some buttons.

"I must to take off the alarm," he says. He then uses two very long and sturdy keys to enter the apartment.

"It's like a fortress," I say.

He flicks the lights, illuminating a huge space. An expanse of dark polished wood floor gleams up at me. The walls are covered with light-gray fabric wallpaper. The high white ceilings have floral plaster decorations. Absolutely no comparison to the atrocities I have been shown so far by real estate agents in Milan.

"This lounge room is huge," I say. "Could you open the shutters?"

As the sun streams in across the floor, I have visions of myself prancing around in my own private dance studio. I had nice apartments in New York and Paris, but they were hardly what you would call spacious. The unblemished floorboards are calling out to me. I plan to erect a large mirror on the far wall of the lounge room with a ballet barre. I can see myself doing stretches and leaps. This place is a dream.

He takes me for a tour. We first visit a spacious bedroom with floor-to-ceiling wardrobes, a chandelier and built-in dresser, and a large modern bathroom. Guiseppe then takes me to what he calls the "maid's quarters" which is a small room with an ensuite bathroom and laundry.

As I admire the view out of the french windows in the kitchen, I notice a balcony to the right. Guiseppe walks me through what looks like a closet, and we land in an oak-paneled room lined with bookshelves. I picture myself on a wintery afternoon, snugly lounging on a bottle-green chaise longue writing poetry in my very own library.

"So you see the apartment only one bedroom, but it big," he says.

What? *Is this guy kidding me?* It's not one, but three bedrooms from what I've calculated. The maid's quarters and library will be guest bedrooms with single beds. I know I want the apartment. Trouble is I don't know the rental rate yet, and there's no furniture. I don't know how long I will be living in Milan, and furnishing a place like this is definitely not a venture I'm willing to undertake.

Then, as if reading my thoughts, he says, "There all antique furniture, it stored downstairs. You use what you need."

I can't believe my luck. Antique is not my usual style, but when in Italy, it sounds divine.

Giuseppe calls his father to say I'm interested and, not to my surprise, the rent is well over what I want to spend. Also, the minimum contract term is one year. *Do I even know I want to stay in Milan that long? I hope so ...* Plus, the clincher is they require a whole year's rental as a deposit. It's a huge amount to have tied up, but I have my savings and remind myself "you only live once." It's a complete splurge, but I know deep down I can afford it.

I take another sweeping look at the apartment and have a great feeling about the coming year. Without any more hesitation I tell Guiseppe, "I'll take it."

I don't know what Milan holds for me, but I know this: I'm ready to find out.

CHAPTER 10

Trust that still, small voice that says, 'This might work and I'll try it'.

- Diane Mariechild

I'm all set up in my gorgeous apartment, and my new Milanese life can't come together fast enough. I spend many a solitary night curled up on my rather decadent, salmon-pink antique couch, watching music television. I wish the phone would ring with an invitation to go somewhere.

I continue my morning Italian classes, and in the afternoons make myself busy "making home" in my apartment, or walk around the old cobblestone streets of Milan's historic center, which is just a stone's throw from where I live.

I relish the fact I don't have to work for New York anymore. I finally have time for myself. In the evenings, I watch Italian television. There are glitzy, big-breasted women and small men rattling on in Italian at incredible speed. Frustrated because I can't understand much, I resort to watching music videos on the All Music channel and MTV. They are both Italian programs, and while I find myself disappointed with the quality of Italian music and video clips, I am intrigued. All the music videos feature solo male artists singing Italian ballads, with long names I can never seem to remember.

Then, one music video really catches my attention. It's a song that they played on the radio all the time the previous summer. There are three attractive girls singing, "Hey, Ha! Bla Bla Bla." I can't make out the words for the life of me because they sing really fast and in Spanish. But it's known as "The Ketchup Song" and the group is called Las Ketchup. The girls do coordinated movements on a beachside bar. It's a dance that everyone got to know over the summer, and despite the incoherent words, the song is super catchy. I record it and watch it again and again. It's so simple, but a huge hit.

The fact that I have free time for the first time in so long has an impact on me. I write in my diary, and lose myself in the moment. I don't have a schedule or have to rush anywhere, so I can write for as long as I wish. I remember back to when I was twelve years old. My dream was to be a published author. I write and write, and savor every moment.

I look back on a previous entry in my journal: it said my goals were to move to Milan, find a great apartment, and immerse myself in a creative career. Here I am in Milan, living in a wonderful apartment, so two of my goals are ticked off my list. Now I have to solve the mystery of the creative career. *What will it be??*

I had thought I would apply for a job in fashion, but with no experience behind me it seems I would be reverted to an entry-level position. With salaries around the 300 euro mark per month, I clear my mind of that as a consideration.

As I write each day and ask myself questions about what I really want, I'm surprised by a recurring answer that comes up. *I want to perform on stage. I want to dance.*

Was there any basis for this desire to perform? I'm not sure if this is going anywhere, but I know if I do have a yearning to be on stage, this is something that I'd better act on NOW. I don't see myself dancing on stage in my forties. This "performance pining" is something that will have to be seized in this moment of time.

I get an email from a friend in Monaco. He tells me I must meet Massimo, his buddy in Milan. He calls Massimo "Mr. Milano." I email Massimo and he immediately calls me and offers to take me out. He says he and his driver will pick me up from my place at seven p.m. the next night.

All I can think of is Carrie from *Sex and The City*. I conjure up images of Mr. Milano as my very own Mr. Big in Milan. I am full of anticipation. I buy myself a padded bra for the occasion. I remember a male model friend from New York was always on at me about the importance of wearing a push-up bra. He said it was like icing on a cake. So, thanks to him, I buy my first black lacey bra with small little pads that sit under the boob – I feel buxom and fabulous. I have on my highest-heeled black leather boots, and I am ready to meet my Big.

The doorbell rings. I give myself one last glance in the mirror and a nod that I am looking suitably elegant, and I grin to ensure there is no food in my teeth. I catch the elevator down and walk outside. A small man in a brown suit wearing dark-rimmed rectangular glasses greets me enthusiastically. *Is this the driver or Mr. Milano?*

"Bellissima! I heard so much of you!" It is Mr. Milano. My Milanese Big is very, very small.

I feel decidedly tall as we lean in to kiss each other's cheeks. Mr. Milano's face comes up to my padded breasts.

"Massimo! So wonderful to meet you finally." We clasp each other's hands and smile widely. He places his right hand on my back as he leads me to his car.

Massimo radiates Italian energy, and I'm sure we are going to have a great time together. I do wish, however, that I wasn't wearing quite such high-heeled boots.

I slide into the back seat of his chauffeur-driven Mercedes. Massimo sits by my side. "You know now this week is the *Salone Internazionale de Mobile?*" he says with a lilting Italian accent. "It the biggest event of the year in Milan."

"I have heard of the fair before, but I didn't know it was this week."

"I am an architect so for me, it very important," he says. He passes me a thick glossy company brochure. "I brought this for you. You can see the projects that my company work on."

"Thank you. It's beautiful." I pass my fingers over the embossing on the front cover. I skim through the pages and see striking buildings that his firm has brought to life – from sleek glass towers to stylish villas.

"And now, we go to an hotel opening of a good friend of mine."

"Sounds great. I'm up for anything." I hear my voice when I speak, and realize how Australian I must sound.

"First we must to pick up my good friend Valentina," says Massimo. "She waiting for us."

We pull up outside Bar Magenta, my somewhat grungy local bar, which is on my street. Massimo makes a call.

"Your friend is in Bar Magenta?" I ask, genuinely surprised that his friend would hang out there.

"*Si*, she say she there," Massimo says.

Soon a girl rocks up in tight jeans and a short blue vinyl jacket. Going by her figure, she looks like she's going on eighteen.

She jumps in the front seat. "*Ciao tutti!*" she says, turning around to show her smiling face midst a head of long, curly black hair.

"Valentina, this is my friend, Luna," he says in English. "She not speak Italian."

"Ah! Are you from America?" she asks and does not wait for my response. "I lived in Miami for ten years. I tell you, people are more normal there. I *love* America. These Italian guys are gonna drive me crazy. I meet young guys, completely gorgeous, but they are *so* screwed up."

"Valentina always like younger men," Massimo says to me.

"They're a real pain in my ass," she continues as our car starts pulling from the curb. "*Aspetta un attimo!*" she yells to the driver. "Massimo, you have to wait for Ilaria, my friend. She wants to come too. You'll love her. She's gorgeous."

"Okay bella, but we must to make hurry a little."

Valentina flicks open her phone to make a call. I understand something about a "*cullo*", which I know means bottom, presumably telling her friend to get her ass into gear. She's waving her arms around and speaks at light speed.

A moment later, a young woman with warm brown skin taps on the car window. Ilaria jumps in the back with us. She's wearing a lollypop-pink letterman-style jacket and tight jeans with a thick chain as a belt around her tiny hips.

"Thank you so much for taking me," Ilaria says in Italian, short of breath.

"You gotta speak English. Luna does not speak Italian," says Valentina.

"Where we go to?" Ilaria asks in slow, broken English.

"The opening party of a new design hotel near the Duomo," says Massimo. "It called The Gray Hotel."

The Gray Hotel. *Not such a great name*, I think to myself, and soon we are there. As we enter, the foyer entices me with its bright pink lounges trimmed with red and chairs suspended on swings. It's a modern paradise with a long white bar set up with sensational hors d'oeuvres and bottles of pink champagne. There is certainly nothing gray about it.

Massimo leaves us at the bar, and Valentina, Ilaria, and I simultaneously dive into the bubbly. Ilaria gives a shy smile and glances toward Valentina, as if looking for permission to speak. Valentina, on the other hand, has already claimed her space at the bar, tossing her hair with the flair of a woman used to being noticed.

"Sorry for my English," says Ilaria, playing with a huge silver ring on her tiny finger.

"Don't worry. It sounds fine," I say. "It's better than my Italian."

"How old are you?" asks Valentina, arching her back and sticking out her full chest as she leans against the bar.

"I wanted to ask the same," I say with a grin. "I'm thirty and I'm Australian, not American."

"I'm thirty-five," Valentina says proudly.

Wow, talk about Italian conservation. "You look so much younger," I say. "What line of work do you do?"

"I used to do some modeling but now I have my own fashion label in Italy and America."

Valentina's an olive Mediterranean beauty with high cheekbones and a tiny, chiseled nose. I'm not surprised she used to be a model.

"Wow, Valentina," I say, genuinely impressed. "And you, Ilaria? Are you from Milan?" I ask, admiring her exotic looks with light-brown wavy hair and coffee-bean complexion.

"I know I not look like from here, but I am," she says proudly. "My papà is from Ivory Coast, and my mamma's Italian. I study communication in the university."

"Ilaria is just a baby, only twenty-seven," says Valentina, ruffling Ilaria's hair. "She's done modeling too."

Massimo approaches us.

"*Bellissimi*," he says. "We've been invited to a private tour of the hotel rooms."

The hotel's managing director takes us all upstairs. He opens his arms in a showy fashion to welcome us into one of the hotel rooms. The bathroom is directly to our right. We see a Jacuzzi bathtub filled with water covered by rose petals. There are bras hanging around, open toiletry bags, used towels on the floor, an open tube of toothpaste oozing on the sink. Then, as we go into the bedroom, there are clothes all over the place and a guy lounging on the bed in a kimono-style dressing gown, remote control in hand, flicking television channels. I'm slightly embarrassed to have intruded, but then the managing director starts to explain in perfect English that the man is an actor.

"The room has been set up as a scene so that you can visualize the use of the room by guests," he says. "Here we have a businessman staying in the room with his girlfriend. The girlfriend goes out shopping and he watches TV."

They certainly have their gender stereotypes down pat.

Next we are taken to see what he calls "the ballet dancer's room." There is a pink leotard-clad dancer doing stretches on a makeshift ballet barre. A Baryshnikov documentary is showing on the TV. The bedspread is covered with long-stemmed fresh roses of assorted pinks and cream. The sweet fragrance consumes the room.

Then we go up a flight of stairs and the hotel's managing director says, "This is the rock star's room. The rock star is out but she left her toddler in the room with a nanny."

There's a blond-haired two-year-old boy sitting playing on the floor and a nanny is dressed in a black and white French maid's uniform including a little bonnet. Madonna plays a guitar live in concert on the TV and there are risqué leather bustiers, skin-like suede pants, and lace bodices strewn around.

This setup seems to thrill Valentina. "This is my room!" Her husky voice raises an octave. "This is *my* room." She stretches out her arms over to Massimo. "I wanna have the rock star's room!"

After we finish at the hotel, Massimo takes us for dinner at a trendy seafood restaurant on a famous Milanese boulevard called Corso Como. After a generous serving of salmon sashimi followed by grilled dorado, we order espressos and sip on grappa. The white grappa is so strong that it makes me wince, but the Italians believe in it as a digestive after a meal. "I am not sure I'll ever get used to grappa!" I admit.

Valentina and Ilaria start singing the famous Eros Ramazzotti song, "*Voglio Volare*" (I want to fly), and sway rhythmically. Customers at nearby tables look over with approving smiles. Massimo and I are rapt and start moving along with them. They are two of the most beautiful and extroverted girls I've ever met, and together they make such an entertaining pair.

I look over to them as they continue singing, their arms moving in a flamenco-style, drawing delighted glances from the other tables. I can't help but think they'd be perfect pop star material. There's an electric energy between them – Valentina's fiery flair and unapologetic sass, Ilaria's effortless charisma and playful charm. I haven't had this much fun in ages, and now here they are, turning a restaurant into a spontaneous stage.

A crazy idea pops into my head: *What if we started a multicultural girl band?* The thought makes me giggle. The three of us, each so different yet somehow strikingly complementary. Ilaria, with her deep-toned complexion, wild curls, and magnetic vibe. Valentina, glowing with Mediterranean confidence and all bold gestures, has star power written all over her. And me – fair, blonde, and bouncing with the kind of wide-eyed enthusiasm only an Aussie abroad can muster. Together, we look like a United Colors of Benetton ad.

Massimo looks at us with pride, as though he's part of something fabulous just by being in our orbit. We stand out, even in this city of fashion and flair. I haven't seen anything like us on Italian MTV.

Later that night, I toss and turn in bed, the idea taking on a life of its own. The creative right side of my brain is working overtime.

Right brain: We'd be like the Spanish group Las Ketchup that took Europe by storm – but bolder, more original. Not just a blend of cultures, but a fusion of spirit and style.

Left brain: Don't be ridiculous. What do you know about the music industry?

Right brain: It's fresh, and it's fun. This is exactly the kind of wild idea you moved to Milan for. How often do you meet two fun and attractive girls, who obviously like to sing?

Left side: You've had too much champagne. How would you ask them? Surely they'll think you're crazy.

Right side: You'll never get this opportunity again. Don't let this pass.

Left side: They are trendy Milanese girls, and you used to do Excel spreadsheets. Why would they team up with you?

Right side: Just ask them! What have you got to lose?

Left side: Don't ask them. They won't agree. Chances are you'll forget about this by the morning.

CHAPTER 11

Every child is an artist. The problem is how to remain an artist once he grows up.

- Pablo Picasso

I receive an unexpected email.

```
October 14, 2002
From: marek@hotmail.cz
Subject: see ya
Ciao Lunio, I want to see you. Puppy needs his Keti.
When will you visit me ??? Please?
```

I am happy to hear from Marek, but the idea of uprooting myself to see him now feels like rewinding to an old episode I've already outgrown. The truth is, I've been swept up in this new Italian chapter of mine.

I've started to fall for the everyday charm here. The locals seem genuinely happy and carefree – chatting with strangers in shops, patiently nodding through my toddler-level Italian like I'm some kind of linguistic prodigy. I still can't believe I chose Milan over Paris, but every day it feels more and more like the right kind of crazy. I'm exercising, eating healthy food (lots of salads with fresh mozzarella and bresaola), and realizing that Italy is greeting me with open arms.

In Paris I lived on the same street for months, and never got a hint of recognition from any of the locals. In Milan, the supermarket checkout girl smiled on day one with a *"Buonasera, come sta?"* and has remembered me ever since. The man at the supermarket fish counter shouts, *"Ciao* Bella!" and waves his arms like I'm a long-lost cousin. He sneakily weighs only half my sea bass so I pay less. Am I being flirted with? Probably. Am I complaining? Not one bit.

My Italian teacher, Graziella, is like a cappuccino – warm and bubbly. There are all women in my beginner class, ranging from their twenties to mid-thirties. Graziella is devoted to making sure we all learn to speak Italian and have fun. During class I ask to go to the *"toiletta"* (as I call it by mistake). Graziella smiles and says, *"Certo bella."* (Of course, beautiful.)

One day a teacher is sick, so another class is merged with ours. Graziella claps her hands like she's announcing a game show.

"I want you to write about *il tipico uomo Italiano* – the typical Italian man," she says, speaking in extra-slow Italian and using enough hand gestures to land a plane. "Use three adjectives from this list." She holds up a sheet like a flight attendant demonstrating safety instructions.

I end up paired with a girl from the other class. She drags her chair over with a graceful swoosh of honey-blonde hair and plops down next to me like she's been doing this all her life. She's tall – like, Amazon tall – with long legs and the kind of confidence that says she's never worried about fitting into European doorways.

"Hi, I'm Shannon," she says with a familiar accent.

"Where are you from?" I ask.

"Sydney," she says.

"Me too!" I say. I gather she is about my age, so I am keen to see if we might know some people in common.

A couple of German girls start the exercise. One says with a thick accent, *"Un tipico uomo Italiano e basso, geloso, and egoisto."*

That exactly mirrors our list. The class erupts with laughter when the Korean and Venezuelan girls chime in – same description, different accents. Apparently, the global consensus is that the average Italian man is short, jealous, and egotistical.

Then the teacher asks us to use three adjectives to describe *un buono amico simpatico,* a nice male friend.

This time it's our turn to give an answer.

"*Alto, sportive, e carino,*" reads out Shannon.

Again, giggles ensue when our answers are much the same as our classmates: tall, sporty, and caring.

"Doesn't sound like we're gonna find our dream men in Italy," I say to Shannon.

"Tell me about it," she says with an all-too-knowing grin.

I am eager to know more. "We'll have to meet for a drink sometime."

"How about *aperitivo* tonight?" she says.

"You're on!"

Aperitivo is a Milanese tradition in bars and cafés between six p.m. and nine p.m. where you can eat buffet-style food for free with any drink order. Going for aperitivo is a social occasion every night of the week.

I meet Shannon at my local bar, Bar Magenta. While certainly not the best *aperitivo* in town, it's a good place to talk.

At the bar, we order *Vodka Limones* from a bartender who looks about twenty-two and is dressed like a GQ version of a waiter in a fresh white shirt. Channeling his inner Tom Cruise from *Cocktail,* he starts tossing bottles and flipping ice cubes, and he goes on and on ...

"When is this going to end?" Shannon mutters, side-eyeing the performance.

"Take it as a compliment. I'm sure he's performing for you," I reply.

"The other day I was driving and a red Alfa Romeo started tailing me.

The guy behind the wheel began honking and waving like my car was on fire. I pulled over, worried something was wrong. He got out, handed me a piece of paper that said 'You are Fantastic', with his phone number."

Shannon laughs. "Italian men sure know how to boost your ego."

"I know!" I say.

"And if a day goes by in Italy and you are not called *bella*, you know it's just *SO* not your day."

"And they start young. A nineteen-year-old asked my mum out for a drink. She's in her sixties!"

"It's true, they are *relentless*," she says. "And I don't think it makes any difference whether a man is married or single, ancient or adolescent, they all love to flirt."

"The most baffling to me are the Italian policemen. They don't seem to do anything but drive around checking out women."

We giggle.

We finally have our *Vodka Limones* in hand and take a seat at one of the long wooden tables in the corner.

"So what brought you to Milan?" I ask Shannon.

"I went to Rome because I fell in love. Unfortunately, the relationship didn't work out. But I still wanted to live in Italy, so I decided to come here."

"Was it a bad ending with the guy?"

"Not great. He cheated on me."

"Do you think all Italians are like that?"

"No, many are harmless. I just chose the wrong guy."

"Okay, and we have to think positive that the men in Milan will be different," I say. "Flirtatious but faithful."

"What's your profession?"

"I used to be a model ..."

"Of course you did." I grin. "Everyone in Milan seems to have a modeling past."

"But here I'm setting up my own company specializing in teaching English. I have my teaching license. What about you, what do you do?"

"I was a banker in New York, and officially as of this month I'm unemployed."

"I heard Milan is great for jobs in finance."

"Actually, I don't want another job in finance. This evening we should celebrate my escape from corporate life." I lift my glass. "It was a long time in the making, and here I am finally *free*."

"What do you plan to do?"

"Definitely something creative. I am getting far-fetched ideas about doing something with music."

Shannon laughs and shakes her head. "Sounds like for you the expression 'career change' should be 'career overhaul.'"

We keep chatting and order another round. Shannon's fun, sharp, and surprisingly grounded. It feels like the start of a real friendship.

We say goodnight, and I stroll home, head a little buzzy from the drinks, but mostly from the possibility. My whole adult life, I've defined myself as "risk-averse." Now, at thirty-one, here I am in Milan, with no plan as to what I will do next, just open to what the world might throw my way. It's probably the most reckless thing I've ever done. Love it.

Back home, I blast Shakira. I let the beat of "Whenever, Wherever" take over, and suddenly I'm trying to emulate Shakira's body rolls. Soon I've completely dimmed the lounge room lights and I'm moving my torso in waves and rippling like a serpent on the ground. I spin and turn, and somewhere between a shimmy and a hair flip, it all comes back – the years of dance training, the feeling of stage lights on my skin. I lose track of time. I sweat. I smile until my cheeks hurt.

Eventually, I collapse on the floor, starfish-style, heart pounding.

"I am an artist again," I whisper, hugging myself. "I'm an artist again!"

I am ecstatic. I haven't felt this alive since the last time I performed on stage – which was in a competition more than a decade ago. It was one of the highlights of my time at university. All those years ago, I remember the show host asking me after my performance, "What are your plans after graduation?"

I had said, "I want to travel, work in finance, and learn languages."

"And your performing career?"

Good question.

"Oh," I shrugged, "I just do it because I love it."

And now? Ten years later, I'm in Milan at a crossroads, sweaty from a solo dance party, dreaming of music and reinvention.

Could performing be more than just something I love? Could it be my next career?

CHAPTER 12

Life is a great big canvas, and you should throw all the paint on it you can.

- Danny Kaye

I'm learning that in Italy, "I'll call you tomorrow" might mean next week – or never. It's part of the charm (and chaos) of this place, but a real test of my Type-A tendencies. When I say I will do something, I do it. So, I'm extra grateful that Massimo and Shannon are both reliable.

Massimo's been inviting me out twice a week, and he's always surrounded by beautiful, well-educated women. There's rarely a man in sight – unfortunately for me – but the food is always exquisite, and the conversation never fails to entertain.

I'm invited to a *singles party* hosted by Isabella Maria Margherita Lombardo della Rochetta di Savoia, a thirty-seven-year-old countess I met through Massimo. She's a fascinating character: works in fashion, has a black belt in karate, and throws parties that sound like something out of an Italian Vogue editorial.

I really enjoyed meeting Isabella a few weeks ago, and I was thrilled when she extended the invitation for me to join her party. She said I was welcome to invite Shannon.

Having another Aussie around to banter with in English is priceless. Shannon and I giggle like teenagers as we ever-so-elegantly step off a

68

city bus, just as a few guests arrive in Porsches and Saabs. Classic Milan. We go upstairs and buzz the door.

A petite woman opens it with a warm smile, and we step inside to be greeted by Isabella with air kisses and flair. She's wearing a sleek black dress with a high slit beaded in diamantes. We hand over a lush bouquet, which she graciously accepts and promptly delegates to a nearby assistant.

We move into the large expanse of her regal lounge room. An antique oak dining table has a selection of mini-quiches, caviar, and smoked salmon canapés next to a huge glass bowl filled with sangria. We hover near the table and start mingling when Isabella introduces us to some of her friends who've recently returned from Sydney.

When Massimo arrives, with Valentina and Ilaria in tow, the party is already in full swing. There are at least fifty guests, all impeccably dressed, radiating Milanese glamour.

"There are so many good-looking men here," Shannon says.

"Tell me about it," I reply. "And genius move – only inviting singles."

"Our hostess seems to have the right approach," Shannon whispers, nodding toward Isabella.

With tan legs exposed, countess Isabella traverses the room. Her full breasts lead her, as if they are suspended in mid-air, and she throws her blonde head back in delighted conversation with a tall, sporty guy who's clearly smitten.

A group is seated at a large table outside on the terrace. "Shall we join them?" I ask. Shannon nods, and we make our way over. Ilaria, Valentina, and Massimo are also there.

We join the group in a bizarre debate – something about toes and intelligence.

"Take off your shoes and look at your second toe," one American guy says, "If it's longer than your other toes, it's a sign of great intelligence."

"I must be intelligent," I say to Shannon jokingly. "I know my second toe is longer."

The group starts taking off their shoes to study their feet.

"Oh, you have such a wonderfully long second toe," says Valentina flirtatiously to the American guy. "I think I *have* to marry you."

She looks stunning in a red dress, which is set off perfectly against her olive skin and mass of waist-length black curls.

Her potential suitor blushes. "We will talk about this further, my lovely," he says.

Massimo puts his black leather moccasin back on and leans over to hug me. "*Mia cara bella,*" he says affectionately so the group can hear. However, he can't seem to keep his eyes off Valentina, constantly glancing in her direction.

A Middle-Eastern-style buffet dinner is served, boasting fragrant curries of beef, chicken, and fish. There's a deep silver dish filled with steamed saffron rice and open wine bottles lie on ice-packed carafes. A line forms so Shannon and I decide to wait to the side. Valentina and Ilaria come over to chat.

"We had fun the other night, no?" says Ilaria.

"Yes! I really enjoyed meeting you," I say. "I wanted to see you both again. I'm so glad you're here tonight."

"*Si*, we have to take you out sometime and show you the real Milan," says Ilaria.

"Enough stuffy parties," says Valentina. "But actually, this one's not so bad at all."

"I agree it's a great crowd, and such perfect weather for it," I say, glancing at the warm evening sky. But my mind is racing. *Instead of making small talk, why not try to ask them about the girl band?*

As if reading my mind, Shannon whispers to me, "Just mention it, Luna. What have you got to lose?"

I give her a grateful smile. I love Shannon's energy and support. As soon as I had mentioned the idea to her, she was so enthusiastic. She doesn't think I'm completely off the wall. But I still can't help thinking Valentina and Ilaria might not take it so positively.

Will they just laugh at me and think I'm a weirdo?

I inhale deeply, wink at Shannon, and take a big swig of sangria. I turn to Ilaria and Valentina.

"I had an idea the other night after we were out together," I say and then pause.

Both girls' gazes are fixed on me and Ilaria tilts her head. She looks at me like Bambi with her big deep-brown eyes. "An idea?" she asks.

"What idea?" Valentina chimes in.

They seem such nice girls, I shouldn't be scared to ask, so I quickly blurt it out. "What about the three of us starting a girl band together?"

Two confused faces stare back at me.

I continue, "You know, like Las Ketchup, the Spanish group, but better because we all look so different."

They both giggle. "Wait – are you serious?" Valentina asks, intrigued.

"Completely. There doesn't seem to be any girl bands in Italy. Do you know of any?"

"There was one, years ago," Ilaria says. "They had the summer song. Five girls, name 'Lollypop.' *Ma sono sparite.*" (But they disappeared.)

"What do you know about starting up a girl band?" asks Valentina. "I thought you were a banker?"

"I was," I say, "but I used to perform a lot when I was younger. C'mon, you guys have done modeling before and you seem to like to sing. We'll improvise. Think how much fun it will be."

"I've been a stylist for loads of music videos in LA," says Valentina.

"I was in music clip once," says Ilaria. "I had to drive a car with singer in it. It fun. Like a little movie."

"See," I say, clapping my hands together. "So both of you even have some experience. C'mon, this'll be great."

"But the people that make it in the music industry have loads of connections and they're incredibly talented," says Valentina.

"Last summer, Europe went wild for 'The Ketchup Song,'" I say. "The name was unusual, the lyrics made no sense, but the girls were cute and had a catchy dance. Boom – summer hit."

"We can to make a lot of money?" asks Ilaria.

"We could," I say. "And we can definitely have a lot of fun. The Ketchup girls came out of nowhere, had one hit, and that was it. We don't need a lifetime career – just one unforgettable song."

"I not sure I sing so well," says Ilaria, twirling one of her brown curls between her fingers.

"I heard you both singing at the restaurant," I say. "You sounded great."

"She can totally sing," says Valentina. "She never stops singing along to the radio."

"*Forse,*" (maybe) says Ilaria with a little knowing grin.

"You don't have to have the best voice," I say. "Some famous artists aren't the greatest singers technically, but they have a unique sound and songs that have really catchy lyrics. I think the song is key."

"But what do you know about the industry?" asks Valentina. "It's not that easy."

"I know it won't be easy, but we can try. If we're original and have good energy, we can do it."

"But I haven't even finish my university," says Ilaria.

"I have a full-time job running my fashion company," says Valentina.

"Of course. But guys, we're in charge of our own schedules. We'll just play it by ear."

After a quick glance between them, something clicks, and suddenly we're all bouncing with excitement. Between bursts of teenage-like squeals, we launch into a flurry of ideas: where we could film a video, who to talk to for music, and which photographers they know.

"I'm stylist!" says Valentina. "I'll design our clothes. We have to look amazing."

"What will we be called?" asks Ilaria. She looks at me for the answer.

I look at her blankly and shake my head. "No idea. I haven't thought that far."

"We need a really good name," Valentina persists. "C'mon guys, we need to think of something."

"It has to be easy to remember," I say. "The name Spice Girls is clever. Sugababes is ideal, love that. Destiny's Child is more obscure, but iconic. Atomic Kitten is a really cute name." They nod in agreement. "But I'm not good at coming up with names."

"We have to have something that represents the three of us." Valentina puts out her hands as if calling to spirits in a séance and freezes for a split second. "I've got it. I know. I know! Blonde, brunette, and black, like the color of our hair." She grabs a handful of her black locks then points to our heads. "B-B-B!"

I think back to the day in New York when Mario, the Italian hairdresser, insisted that I go blonde. Ironic how I'm now living in Italy, and my hair color is suddenly relevant to what seems to be the start of my next venture. Ironic, or maybe not. Maybe the new Luna was destined for this moment ...

"Hey, that's excellent," I say, glad I'd been streaking my hair even blonder as of late. "And the name BBB works in every language. I want us to be super-international."

Ilaria nods in approval. "BBB. *Bella, bella!*"

"I've always been really good with names," says Valentina, putting one hand on her hip and using the other to flick her hair behind her shoulders. "It's my thing."

Massimo is close by and Valentina waves him over to join us. Without delay, Valentina asks him directly, "Wanna be our investor?"

I cringe at her straightforwardness, but at the same time, I really admire it.

"What you girls talking about? So much noise and laughing," Massimo says, smiling.

"We're gonna start a girl band," Valentina says, "and we really want *you* as our investor. We'll be called BBB. Great name, no?" She tilts her head toward him and affectionately puts her arm around his waist. "C'mon Massimo!" Valentina jumps a little on the spot in anticipation of his answer.

"But music is not my business," he says.

Valentina persists. "Pleeeeeeaase Massimo. It's gonna be *fab*ulous, you'll love it. Don't you want us to be your girls?" She jumps between me and Ilaria and the three of us smile broadly as if for a camera.

Massimo has an expression of being far from convinced but nods in agreement. "Okay, you are my girls."

More squeals of joy ensue on our part. I am in complete awe of Valentina's skill of asking for something and getting it. I can see she'll be a strong asset to the group.

Shannon seems thrilled that Valentina and Ilaria plunged into it with such gusto. "They're perfect, Luna."

"I won't look like a hippo in the middle?" I ask her. I've been doing regular exercise as of late, but I still feel far from fit pop star material.

"Not at all. Ilaria's a stick, but Valentina has more curves. Honestly, you all look so different, it's the ideal combination."

Throughout the evening, Ilaria comes up to me with questions. "How will we know what to do if you never done this before?" she asks.

"We'll work it out as we go along." I try to assure her. "Don't worry."

"You completely crazy," she laughs. "Think of all the gorgeous guys we'll meet."

That night I get home at after three a.m. but it feels like only midnight. I'm utterly exhilarated and can't wait to see how this venture unfolds.

CHAPTER 13

Follow your bliss and the universe will open doors for you where there were only walls.

- Joseph Campbell

Over the following weeks, Valentina and Ilaria come over regularly. I'm blown away by their enthusiasm. We're always on the phone to each other, go out at night, and they introduce me to their friends. I am drawn into their world.

One night they come over to watch MTV.

"The Madonna special starts in a few minutes," I say.

"You and your Madonna special," says Valentina.

"I think we can learn from it," I reply. "I'm gonna record it."

"You're obsessed!" she says, hitting my upper arm in a joking manner.

"Of course. Next, it has to be us. BBB on MTV," I say. "I have some prosecco in the fridge. You want a glass?"

"*Si, certo*," says Ilaria. "I think you do not need ask."

"We should be called AA not BBB," says Valentina. "I've never drunk this much before. What are you girls doing to me!"

We all laugh. It is true though, each of our "BBB Brainstorming" meetings have inevitably turned into late-night drinking fests.

"It's just early days and we're having fun. We won't always have this freedom," I say.

"Are we still having a photo shoot tomorrow?" asks Valentina.

"*Si*, your cousin from London will photo us?" asks Ilaria.

My cousin, Lachlan, who has a good-quality camera, has agreed to take the first BBB photos while he's visiting this weekend.

"He's on his way. His train from the airport is arriving" – I look at my watch – "in about half an hour or so. Who wants to walk with me to the station?"

"I come!" says Ilaria.

The station is at the end of my street, less than ten minutes away. Ilaria and I walk to greet Lachlan in style with champagne flutes of prosecco in hand. We arrive to see him leaning on his oversized chrome suitcase. He's chugging on a cigarette, wearing his loudest Hawaiian shirt that is a shocking electric blue. I can hear him singing along to the song "Absolutely Flawless" as it plays on his iPod. I have to laugh, he's always so retro.

Lachlan is in his mid-twenties and loves to party. I have an inkling we're in for a big weekend. *Oh please let us have a good photo shoot tomorrow.* I don't want it to turn into a wasted opportunity to get some photos of the group.

"Smelly!" I yell out at him in excitement.

"Hi Smell-smell!" he says and hugs me.

"Smelly?" asks Ilaria, looking at me in confusion. "Like *puzza*?"

"Yes," I say. "When we shared a room in London, the name just grew."

"And this must be the lovely Ilaria." Lachlan kisses her left cheek. "Pleasure to meet you," he says as he kisses her right cheek. "You may call me Lachy."

"*Benvenuto a Milano*, Lachy."

"So, you going to show me the whole of Milan tonight?" he asks us. "I'm up for action!"

"*Si*, we take you to Porta di Ticinese for sure," says Ilaria. "There our favorite bar. And you must to see the ancient columns."

"But remember we have the photo shoot at one p.m. tomorrow," I say. "No all-nighter, guys."

Later that evening, after the Madonna special has finished and we have drunk a lot of prosecco, we follow the tram lines up the crowded street toward the old, graying city walls. Ilaria and Valentina have their arms around each other as if to hold each other up straight. They jointly swagger from side to side, stopping to say, "Ciao!" to almost everyone we pass.

Ilaria's wavy brown hair is hanging around her face like a rag doll. She is wearing a pink frilly G-string that peeks out of her very low-waisted jeans. The pink is fluorescent against her skin and no matter how many times Valentina pushes it down for her, it exposes itself for all to see.

Valentina and Ilaria start singing loudly in Italian as we make our way through the crowds to the main square. We join a group of guys playing guitars to the tune of "Yesterday." The girls start to sing along, not sure of the words, and their voices are by no means sweet additions to the music. The guitarists don't seem to mind, however, soaking up the attention of these two beautiful women as they play.

"Way to go, Smell-smell," says Lachlan. "Your band members are super cool."

"They have great energy."

"*Amazing* energy. Not sure they can sing though."

I am a bit disgruntled by his comment. We'll have to start singing lessons as soon as possible.

The next day, I shower, wash and blow dry my hair, then enter my room to look at what to wear. Suddenly, my ceiling-to-floor wardrobe is completely daunting. *So many clothes, but what to wear?* I'm in my bathrobe while looking through piles in my closet. Today is our photo shoot and I have no idea what to put on. Summer? Winter? Mid-season? *What does a pop star wear?*

I pick out a purple long-sleeved off-the-shoulder Diesel top that I bought in New York ages ago but have never worn. I put it on with some favorite long black MaxMara dress pants and sexy black imitation snakeskin heels. While not completely convinced with my outfit, I think I look okay.

Valentina arrives punctually at one p.m. She's in her usual attire, looking sporty in trendy red and white trainers, red three-quarter pants, white T-shirt, and a hooded red sweatshirt around her waist.

"What are you wearing?" she says.

"I had no idea what to put on. This okay?"

"Nah-ah. I have to see your wardrobe – all of it."

Valentina begins sliding the hangers around and scrimmaging through wads of clothes, leaving them disheveled. She has a desperate look as she can't seem to find anything she likes.

"Put this on," she finally says and throws a skirt at me. It's short and gray with florescent white edges and a big blue plastic star on the back. I bought it at Byron Bay in Australia years ago but have only ever worn it once at a dance party in Ibiza.

She finds a wool lace top that I didn't even know I had and passes it to me. It looks like an old lady's singlet. *She expects me to wear that?* Then, she rumbles through my shoes, rejecting them all with grunts of distaste until she finds a pair of black leather basketball-type boots.

"I can't wear those with a skirt," I insist. But she's in another world that happens to be my underwear drawer, and she pulls out a pair of black opaque stockings that I soon realize she wants to cut up.

"I need scissors," she says. "Now."

"Those stockings are my favorites. I'll find you another pair. Just give me a moment," I say. "The scissors are in the kitchen, top drawer."

I'm calm when I talk to her, but my patience is pushed. Surely I'm going to look like an absolute idiot in this gear, and now I'm also down a pair of stockings. I eventually find some old stockings that have a hole in the toe and I hand them to Valentina so she can start hacking away at them with the scissors.

I put everything on. I am conscious that my legs are glowing white and I'm not used to wearing heel-less, chunky boots with skirts. To top it all off, she puts a section of black stocking on one of my arms. I feel like a regurgitation of a bad-rapper look left over from the eighties. She finds a big floppy black hat, one thing that I do like, and passes it to me.

"Your hair's a mess. Cover it," she says. I just washed my hair and thought it looked great. *She's the stylist*, I keep on repeating to myself, but truth is I feel ridiculous.

I don't want to leave my bedroom, let alone venture onto the streets of Milan. *Is she kidding me?* I move precariously toward the hallway and call out to Lachlan.

He comes over, snickering when he sees my disgruntled expression. He looks at me thoroughly and is noticeably impressed. "Awesome, Smell," he says. "Though, the glove is a little Michael Jacksonesque."

It's already past two p.m. Ilaria's over an hour late. I call her to remind her we need bright daylight for the photo shoot. When she arrives, she's much more elegant than usual, wearing a gold knitted halter-neck top, tight dark jeans, and brown slip-on sandals with a jewel at the big toe.

"You look beautiful," I say.

Valentina joins us at the door. "No, no, no, no, no!" she says, looking at Ilaria.

Then they rattle on in Italian. Ilaria is resistant, but Valentina says she should go back home and she instructs her exactly what to wear. Ilaria lives a good twenty-minute drive away, but Valentina insists she change her clothes.

Ilaria and I catch each other's eyes and shrug. She's the stylist. What else can we do? I presume since Valentina's worked fifteen years in the fashion industry and been a stylist for music videos in America, she knows what she's doing.

While we wait, Lachlan, Valentina, and I perch on antique-style dining chairs in my lounge room and look out the window onto Via Carducci. It's a brilliant sunny day and I watch the bronzed Italians passing by. I look down at my exposed white legs and realize I haven't had a proper suntan since I left Australia ten years ago. And now, here I am, a moon-like beacon in Milan – and today we have a photo shoot. I'm not in my element in these clothes.

Ilaria eventually comes back dressed in baggy jeans, Converse boots, a long-sleeved American football T-shirt with large numbers in blue on the front and back, and her keys dangling on a strap around her neck.

"Perfect," Valentina says and gives her a big hug.

I'm not sure the look does her justice, but I hold back – Valentina seems thrilled with the result.

We clearly look like a female rapper band ... is this in line with my vision for the group?

Ilaria and Valentina are chatting with Lachlan in the lounge room.

"The day's almost gone, guys," I say. "Let's start. How about some photos here as a warm-up, and then we'll head outside for some outdoor shots. Lachlan, you ready?"

"Am indeedy. Cool McGool, let's get to it. Ladies, move over here. Valentina, you sit on this armchair, Ilaria you lean here, and Smell you stand behind."

As he starts snapping away, we break into different poses, varying between serious shots and smiling.

"Great. Awesome," says Lachlan. "Move your heads closer now – no teeth this time. I want a sexy look. Imagine I'm Robbie Williams and you really want to bonk me."

"Yuck! You're my cousin," I say. We all giggle.

After Lachlan takes a few more shots, Valentina jumps up to look at the photos on the camera screen. Obviously there's something wrong. Valentina stares at me with a serious expression on her face.

"Luna," she says, and I anticipate her chastising me for my lack of modeling ability. "The hat has to go." She reaches for a piece of the leftover stocking that is on the floor and ties a knot in one end. "Here, put this on instead."

My floppy black hat is actually the only thing I like out of my whole outfit, and now she is taking that off me?

"What?" I say to her as she passes me the slither of stocking. I hold it as if it is a dead fish hanging from its tail. "It's tiny. It'll make me look like a pinhead."

"Just try it and we'll check it out," she says with confidence.

I go to the mirror and stretch the stocking over my head. My long hair falls dead straight as the skin-tight contraption that Valentina created pushes against the sides of my head. It looks like something pulled out of a hip-hop video gone wrong. I look at my reflection in the full-length mirror and cringe. It isn't me.

Lachlan takes a few more photos. This time, we download them to view on my computer.

I'm relieved to see that I blend in well with my new "hat."

"Valentina, you are good!" I say. "I can't believe it really does look so much better."

"Too right," says Lachlan. "It gives Smelly here a certain 'bad girl' edge that fits well with you two. It's a strong look you've got goin' girls."

I can't believe that not so long ago in the office in New York my basic attire was a navy blue pin-striped suit. Then I felt I was dressed for a conservative role that didn't really suit me. And from one complete extreme to the other, now I am well and truly playing dress-up.

We go to the nearby Porta di Ticinese to continue the photo shoot. It's a historic part of town with huge ancient Roman columns lined up along the piazza providing us with a typical Italian backdrop. A group of bongo players happens to be playing in the square. Ilaria, Valentina, and I dance around like crazy while Lachlan snaps away. It's so good to dance and let out the tension of getting to this stage in the shoot today.

Finally, I can relax and feel the reward that I am doing something in line with my dream of a creative career.

Creative Luna: I can't believe I actually consider this my "work" now. Good on you, Luna. This is a great new phase: live to work, not work to live.

At high school and in my twenties, I would have seen myself married and having children by now. Who would ever have imagined I'd be living in Milan, learning to speak Italian, and starting up a girl band? I wouldn't trade it for the world.

I walk down my street from Cadorna train station. It's almost nine p.m. and the sun is setting. Summer is on its way. There's not a cloud and the sky is a radiant blue. The majestic buildings lined along the street have a pinkish hue and the scattered trees are huge and lush. A bright orange tram rattles past and all I can think is how wonderful it is to be in Milan.

An old man is selling flowers on the street corner. He has such a kind face that reminds me of the roadside vendors in Warsaw, where my mother is from. I ask him how much they cost, and he responds, *"Dieci euros per tutti."* I tell him that I will just buy a small bunch.

A man passing the curb on his Vespa stops next to us. He hears the conversation and says that he'll buy all the flowers for me. He swiftly hands over a ten-euro note to the old man and it's a done deal. The old man wraps up the flowers, putting in some extra greenery, and passes me the sweet-scented bunch.

The guy on the Vespa doesn't call me *"Bella"* or ask my name. I have the impression he genuinely wants to help the old flower seller, and I just happen to be at the right place at the right time to receive the gift.

"Moltissime grazie," I say and he continues on his way.

I carry on walking, drenched in the last rays of the setting sun. The city has opened itself up to me. Or have I opened myself up to it?

CHAPTER 14

Obstacles cannot crush me. Every obstacle yields to firm resolve.

- Leonardo da Vinci

The following week we show a selection of photos around to friends and contacts. The pictures are vibrant and fun. We get extremely positive feedback.

"That's so great that people like us," says Ilaria next time when we meet at my place.

"They like the way we look together, but it's time we find a song," I say. "I feel it's a bit of a joke that we are a girl band without any music."

"What kind of songs will we do?" asks Ilaria.

"Hip-hop," says Valentina. "It's so popular right now – everyone's into it. You know, like Eminem."

"Eminem?" I say. "I think he swears a lot. I like retro and dance music. I don't even own one hip-hop CD."

"I like all music," says Ilaria, "but I like de idea of singing of peace and love. I don't to like to swear."

I look over to Valentina, my eyes pleading. "I agree, no swearing," I say, "but we do need an original sound, so we stand out."

"We'll stand out because we're old," says Valentina. "All these artists are babies."

"It's true, they so young," says Ilaria, looking over at me. She has disappointment on her face, as if our girl band venture is over.

"I think we can use our age to our complete advantage," I say. "We're not teenagers, but a group of intelligent, educated women. Not your stereotypical packaged girl band."

"*Si, certo*," says Ilaria, nodding in approval.

Valentina doesn't seem convinced. "If anyone asks, just tell them we're in our twenties." She points to us one by one. "Ilaria, you can be twenty-one, Luna you be twenty-six, and I'll be twenty-eight."

Not thrilled with the idea of fudging our age, I go along to keep our brainstorming session alive.

"Just remember," I say, "we're not only singers and dancers, but the stylist, PR, and organizer. We have to sell ourselves as a multi-talented, unique group."

Valentina chimes in on another unexpected note. "Guys, I'm not singing."

Silence. Ilaria and I exchange perplexed looks.

"Do you play an instrument?" I ask.

"No."

"Then you have to sing," I say. "We're a girl band. The three of us sing and dance together."

"Seriously, Luna. I love the band idea, but trust me – no one wants to hear me sing." Valentina moves her mass of black curls from one shoulder to the other and then looks at me, her brown almond-shaped eyes piercing. "I'll style us and dance, but leave the vocals to you two."

The concept of a non-singing girl band member leaves me bewildered. "I thought singing was the fun part," I say.

"I'm not singing." Valentina shakes her head.

"Equipment for mixing of voices in studios is so high-tech," I insist. "You'll sound amazing, I promise."

"No way. I'm not singing."

"If she say no, she mean it," says Ilaria with a knowing look.

I have a vision for our group – an extreme eighties theme that suits the disco tune that plays in my head. We're dressed in short, electric-blue fur jackets, red vinyl miniskirts, and long, shiny silver platform boots. Thick fake eyelashes, full crimson lips that sparkle, and big hair. Assorted bright feather boas might be strewn around the stage, and we're rocking it up with huge mics in one hand, waving our other arms in the air as the crowd goes wild, dancing with us.

Back to the reality of my lounge room. This conversation with Valentina worries me. She not only dressed us in the photo shoot as female rappers, but she thinks we need to be twenty-year-old Eminems in order to succeed. And she won't sing! My girl band dream is going completely off track.

So, fix it. A familiar inner voice pipes up. Corporate Luna!

Corporate Luna: Admit it, Creative Luna, you haven't got this all sorted. You need me. I'm organized, disciplined, and business-minded. You've got a potential new venture here and we need to optimize it. Stop drinking and partying so hard and face the music. The reality is that your girl band needs music!

Creative Luna: Stop being so pushy, Corporate Luna. We will work this out …

Corporate Luna: It's time to get serious about having fun. Want to perform on stage? Want a real band behind those pretty pictures? Put down that champagne glass, and pick up a planner. It's time to rehearse.

Corporate Luna is right. I've tried to leave my corporate self behind but now it seems I need her help. If I'm going to make this work, I need a real band. I need to be a boss and put these girls to work.

CHAPTER 15

If you can't fly then run, if you can't run then walk, if you can't walk then crawl, but whatever you do you have to keep moving forward.

- Martin Luther King Jr.

Ilaria and I sing together as the teacher plays up the scale on the piano. It's our first BBB singing lesson and I'm so pleased that Ilaria is confident.

"Ilaria, you have a naturally lovely voice," the Argentinean singing teacher tells her.

"Thank you," Ilaria says, obviously happy.

"You two are very lucky," the teacher says with a gentle Argentinean lilt. "Your voices blend beautifully. That doesn't always happen."

Boosted with enthusiasm following the approval of our singing voices, I decide it's time to step into the spotlight and get things moving.

I seek out any and all contacts I can through friends of friends, and send out BBB presentations. I have put together elegant folders of information about BBB including six large print photos. I listen to songs that are proposed to us that we could possibly use, but none gel, so I pitch a wonderful friend of mine in London, Olivia Madden, who is a songwriter. I had not approached her previously because I knew Valentina wanted hip-hop, but as none of my connections create that kind of music, we might as well explore different music options.

Optimistic, I prepare myself for pop stardom. Picking up my exercise routine, I start jogging with Shannon, do yoga class, and kickboxing. I buy a bicycle and meet friends in the park for rides. For years I have worn predominantly black clothes because I found it easy and they suited a conservative look, but now I'm getting the confidence to venture into colors. I treat myself to some Milanese clothes – oh what a joy to shop at MaxMara and Armani!

I continue regular lessons with the singing teacher, but Ilaria's interest in the lessons waivers. She usually doesn't join me. I also get the details of a dance instructor. However, always lingering in the back of my mind is a fear that both girls will decide to pull out. Impostor syndrome creeps in, in a big way.

Corporate Luna: What do you know about managing and being in a girl band?

Creative Luna: You can soooooo do this!!! You're doing great. Keep on going!

Thank goodness for Creative Luna.

Valentina calls me. "You wouldn't believe it," she says. "I have the best contact for us."

I'm relieved to hear her voice sound so enthusiastic. "Great. Tell me, tell me."

"I got the phone number for Rocco. I worked on a music video with him in LA, and he now works in Rome. He's a record producer!"

"That's great. Have you spoken to him?"

"Yes, he's totally cool and totally into us. He's just a baby, maybe twenty-four, but on the fast track. He's already produced some hits."

I don't dare to ask what his hits were – hip-hop? Whatever the music type, however, this Rocco character sounds exactly what we need.

"Fabulous!" I say. "We should go to Rome to see him."

"No, I'm too busy to go there," says Valentina.

Damn. I would jump on a train to see him in a flash.

"Let him come to us," she continues. "Rocco told me he comes to Milan most weeks anyway."

"Okay, arrange a meeting with him next time he's in Milan. We can meet him at my place if you like."

It's a Monday night and we have a nine p.m. meeting with Rocco at my place. Valentina, Ilaria, and I are dressed up with makeup on, sitting on the couch in my living room, a photo presentation for Rocco lying on the coffee table in front of us. We wait.

"It's nine thirty. Are you sure he's coming?" I ask Valentina.

"This is Italy remember. And he's from Rome. I'll call him, but he's probably on his way." She calls him on her cell phone but he doesn't answer. She leaves him a message, repeating the address.

By ten p.m. she calls again, and gets through. She says, "See, I told you. He's on his way. He's really near."

By eleven p.m. there's still no sign. She calls again to see what's happening. He answers, they have a brief chat but then she hangs up on him, sounding really annoyed. "*Merda*. He's not coming."

"What did he say?"

"That he'll be back next week, we can meet then. Yadda yadda."

"I don't mind," I say, "just a pity we lost the whole evening waiting around. Next week is fine. No worries, Val."

"Fine with me too," says Ilaria.

"I'm not meeting him next time," Valentina says. "He's missed his chance with this."

"Look. I agree he's a complete shit for standing us up," I say. "But, reality is, he's a really great contact to have. He works for one of the biggest record companies. We should try to meet him."

"Yes, we should to try," says Ilaria.

"I don't know." Valentina tucks her long dark curls behind her ears. She shakes her head while looking down at her cell phone in her hands.

"Honestly, let's just give him the benefit of the doubt," I say. "Anything could have come up tonight."

"Something came up all right," Valentina says. "It's white and was snorted up his nose. He's off his face, partying around town, and can't be bothered to meet us. Luna, I tell you, this is all a big waste of time. I have a business to run."

Her words echo in my head, louder than I'd like: *All a big waste of time. Am I wasting my time?*

But I still believe we're onto something with this group. I am certainly not ready to give up.

I'm still in regular contact with my ex-boss, Bob. He always asks me when I'll be going back to New York to work for his company again. I tell him I won't be. But if this girl band doesn't take off, I might have to.

I consider what it would be like back in New York, living a banker's life and going to the office each day. I just can't imagine myself going back. It gives me extra impetus to make this girl band a success.

Ilaria comes to pick me up one day after she had a week's holiday away with friends.

"Look at the photos," she says, steering the wheel, opening the glove box to take out a small album, changing gears, and attempting to light up a Marlboro Red at the same time. "You won't believe this guy!"

I keep one eye on the road while I start to flip through the photos.

I stop flicking pages when one photo takes my attention. It's of Ilaria, spread out across the sand with a to-die-for hunk lying beside her. He's completely naked. He has a mane of blond hair and piercing blue eyes that seem to penetrate the camera. His arms are wrapped around Ilaria in a spooning position, his golden tan against Ilaria's sun-kissed skin makes for quite a dramatic photo.

"He from Barcelona! I want to live there. It the best city in the world."

"But you cannot move to Barcelona yet," I say. "I'm just glad you're back in Milan!"

"Me too, I happy I'm back," she says, giggling. "Oh. I still have to tell the best thing. My good friend, you know Eduardo, he wonderful, gay and really rich?"

I shake my head. I don't think I have ever heard of Eduardo before. Ilaria has so many friends, it's hard to keep up.

"I tell you about him for sure," she continues. "He invite me for sail in his yacht. We had amazing time, and I met this girl, Jia."

I look over at her. Is she just about to tell me that she has a crush on a girl? There was something in her tone.

"Jia is so funny, Chinese from Hong Kong. We was the only girls on board. So sick and tired of gay bars in St. Tropez and always with good-looking mens we cannot to kiss, Jia and me get along so well. Always laughing."

"And?"

"Jia is bigger drinker than me. Seriously!"

I look at her with disbelief. "You drink *a lot*." I'm still wondering where this conversation is leading.

"But I think she will be great for BBB."

Oh wow, I didn't expect that. I hope Ilaria's statement about Jia's consumption of alcohol has nothing to do with why she thinks she would make a good member of our group.

Ilaria continues, "At night when everyone ready for bed, Jia make strong cocktails and tell stories in perfect Italian with her Chinese accent. Then Jia go to sleep with arms crossed over chest like mamma from Egypt." Ilaria puts her arms across her chest to show me. I wish she'd keep her hands on the wheel. "I would find her there, exactly the same position, in the morning."

"What a character," I say, genuinely intrigued by this idea of an Asian girl band member.

"And she speak five languages."

"Wow."

"She doing a master in Bologna but I don't remember what she study."

"How far away is Bologna?"

"It close. *Forse* two hours. Me and Jia we catch a train back to Italy together and it unbelievable," Ilaria says. "Jia know all words to classic Italian songs. We singing together on the train. You will like her so much. She really cute and so funny."

I think about Valentina's flailing energy to be a part of the band and not wanting to sing. Having a fourth member would be a great buffer, and even better with Asian heritage to add to the mix.

"I really like the idea of her joining," I say. "I never thought of having a fourth B, but she sounds perfect."

"Okay, I call her," Ilaria says.

The next day, I phone Ilaria. "You must come over! A CD with Olivia Madden's songs has arrived in the mail."

"*Si! Certo!* I finish to lunch with my parents and I come just now."

"I listened to the CD once already, and it's great."

I call Valentina. "Hey, we have some music that arrived from London. It's more like dance music, not hip-hop, but I think it could work really well. Ilaria's going to come over to listen to it, can you join us?"

"No. I'm busy." She doesn't explain.

I've been in touch with Valentina intermittently over the past weeks, and when we see each other out at parties we always have a great time, but we have not had a BBB meeting for weeks.

"Okay, we'll talk soon," I say. "*Ciao.*" I hang up the phone. *What's up with her?* Her abruptness really gets me down. Is she upset we got the music from one of my contacts? I really don't know.

Ilaria comes over, beaming with excitement to hear the music. She immediately reenergizes me.

We listen to the CD together. There's one song in particular that we like. The song starts, "We are elements ..." and has an uplifting Ibiza-style beat behind it. Ilaria and I start bopping along to the music.

"What are the words?" she asks.

"It's talking about the elements – earth, water, fire, and air," I say.

"Nooo ... That incredible. If we are four, we *are* the elements! We can be one each. I like it!"

"I really like it too." I smile and soak in relief. After months of meetings and no action, disappointments and frustrations, finally we might break through to the next level.

"This so great," Ilaria says, giggling. "BBB has a song! Finally!" She opens her arms and gives me a hug.

"But the next step is to show it to Valentina," I say. "I doubt it's her type of music. I honestly tried to find hip-hop. I hope she understands."

"*Non preoccupare.*" (Don't worry.) "Valentina be fine."

I call Valentina. No response. I call her again the next day. No response. The following day, she answers.

"We listened to the music," I tell her. "We've found a couple of songs that we like."

"I really don't have time to talk about this now."

"I can make a copy for you and send it in the mail."

"Okay."

"Also, we're going to Bologna to meet Jia – she's a friend of Ilaria's who might be a great fit for the group. She's from Hong Kong."

Silence.

"What do you think if there are four of us?"

"Do what you want."

"Wanna come with us?"

"Can't."

She's in a bad mood and I don't know why. She's loosened her grip, letting me call all the shots with BBB. I want the freedom to manage things and to move things forward, but I don't like the way it's happening. Something's wrong.

"Is everything okay?" I ask.

"I don't have time to talk. Ciao."

I chat with Massimo and he admits she's been rather offhand with him too lately. I hope it's just work stress and it will pass.

CHAPTER 16

To every disadvantage there is a corresponding advantage.

- W. Clement Stone

Ilaria and I take my car and drive to Bologna to meet Jia. The possibility of her joining the group gives me hope. I like the idea of there being four of us and it might ease the pressure on Valentina. A fourth member, and a fresh perspective, could be exactly what we need.

Jia's apartment is in the middle of the old town. Wide walkways hug the buildings lined with tall Roman-style columns. We enter and go up a small elevator. Jia welcomes us into her spacious duplex with a modern open kitchen, loft bed, and a small balcony.

I'm struck by her looks. Jia has the delicate, flawless beauty of a porcelain doll. She's elegant and willowy, has a fair complexion with straight, shoulder-length hair.

"Just make yourselves at home here in the living room," she says to us in Italian. "This couch works as a bed. Tonight we can go for dinner and later I'd like to show you a few of my favorite bars."

"All sounds great," I say in English. "Thanks for having us."

"Si, grazie mille, Jia," says Ilaria.

"How come you speak Italian so well?" I ask Jia.

"I've lived in Italy for almost three years. I was in Florence before, working with a fashion house."

"What are you studying in Bologna?"

"I'm doing an MBA with a concentration in fashion."

Jia seems completely relaxed, walking around the room tidying things. She starts to unpack the dishwasher. She moves easily around her apartment, wearing Levi's and a cropped white tee. There's something effortless about her – stylish and self-assured. Her limbs are long and thin, and she's likely taller than me and Ilaria.

"Ilaria tells me you love to sing," I say.

"I'll tell you honestly," Jia says, "I never thought about singing before, let alone joining a girl band. I just sing for myself." She giggles. "You know, nothing serious at all."

Well, that certainly isn't the most convincing answer I've heard. I remember back to how Ilaria was raving about Jia singing Italian songs during their train ride. I am sure her voice will be fine.

"Would you have time to come to Milan for rehearsals?" I ask.

"I have a lot of friends in Milan, so I am there often for parties. I can always study on the train, so that's no big deal."

"Listen to the songs we chose," I say, handing her a CD.

She puts on the music and turns up the volume. Ilaria and I start singing along to "Elements" and dancing together. Jia smiles at us and it seems she wants to join in on the fun.

We continue to talk over the music.

"The plan is," I say, "in mid-October, the songwriter, Olivia Madden, will come to Milan for an intensive weekend of training. Then, we're booked to record in a studio in London at the beginning of November."

"Who covers the expenses?"

"The cost of the recording should be paid by a friend, Massimo, who's agreed to be our investor. I sent him a letter a few days ago, giving an outline of the studio and training costs. But I said that we'd pay our own travel expenses. Flights are cheap and we can all stay at my aunt's house in London."

"How often do you guys rehearse?"

"We try to get together as often as possible. I've started regular singing lessons, and Ilaria will start coming too."

"Isn't there another B in the BBBs?" she asks.

"*Si*, Valentina," says Ilaria. "But she don't want sing."

"Yeah, no singing lessons for her," I say. "She's a great girl though, also into fashion. I have no doubt you'll get along perfectly."

"And my work?" says Ilaria. "And the photos. Tell her."

"Oh yes. Important. Ilaria has a job working in Paris for a few months, so we must have a photo shoot before she leaves."

"Hey, Pari!" says Jia. "That's exciting, Ilaria."

"*Si. Grazie*. I so happy."

"And who's the photographer for our shoot?" Jia asks.

"*Mi ex, Lorenzo*," says Ilaria. "He really talented."

"He has a professional studio," I say, "and he's not charging us a cent. Couldn't be a better deal."

"This all sounds wonderful, but just so you know I have a lot on my plate with my studies." She looks at me with an apologetic look on her face. "I committed to do the honors program so now I also have a thesis to write on top of my usual workload. If I join, I don't want to let you guys down. Seems like you've got a full schedule ahead."

It's great that she's thoughtful and takes the decision seriously.

"No worries," I say. "Let's just enjoy tonight and you can think about it. I'll leave the CD with you. Ask any questions you want, and let us know soon as you can."

The song "Elements" finishes, and the second song from Olivia that we selected for BBB starts playing. Ilaria and I sing along, "*Come get naked with me, baby. Come get naked with me, aaahhh.*"

"It's cheeky, I know," I say, "but it totally sticks in your head."

"This is racy," says Jia. "I like the songs you've chosen."

"We only have two songs at this stage," I say, "but I think they both have good potential."

Jia takes us to a home-style restaurant near her apartment. She says it's typically Bolognese. We enter a large space dotted with red and white checkered table clothes. It's really crowded and noisy, possibly not the best place for getting to know each other, but we have a great time, eat Parma ham, buffalo mozzarella, handmade pasta with Bolognese ragu, and drink lots of red wine.

"My brother's in a band," says Jia. "They haven't done a recording, but he writes songs and plays the guitar. He's kind of the rebel of the family."

"And you?"

"I'm the do-gooder. My parents have high expectations."

"With BBB," I say, wanting to pump up the pep talk, "the way I see it, we all have other careers and interests we want to pursue afterward, but we'll have an amazing experience, and this will be an excellent springboard for the future."

"It's really tempting," she says.

"Just think, by this time next year you would have graduated with your master's and you might also be a pop star."

"Well, if I do decide to join the group, I would do it because it's a challenge. My resume is pretty education and work-oriented, and I think doing something like this would make it more diverse."

Considering Valentina's wavering enthusiasm of late, I really like that it seems Jia would be a dedicated trooper who is driven to succeed.

Corporate Luna: I really want Jia to join BBB. I'm impressed that she's a high achiever. I think she'll be great to have on board.

We go to different bars around the tangerine university town with endless piazzas and marbled archways. We end up drinking sambuca back at Jia's place. Jia surprises me again – one minute academic, the next rolling sambuca shots like a champ. I like that about her.

Ilaria performs for us on the floor – she's on all fours doing movements on par with a cat stretching its spine.

"Have you seen Ilaria do this before?" I ask Jia.

"No, and just as well. I think she would have rolled off the yacht." We all laugh and are in good spirits.

"If you join the group, you'll no doubt get to know it well," I say. "It's her three a.m. special."

"I've made up my mind," says Jia. I look over to her and she raises her sambuca shot. "I really want to do the BBBs with you girls."

I'm surprised she made the decision so fast. "You sure it's not just the cocktails talking?"

"No. I've thought about it enough," she says, "and there's no way I want to miss out on this adventure."

"C'mon Ilaria, come over here," I say. "Jia's joining the group!"

"Really? Oh! I so happy," Ilaria says, bouncing toward us.

Ilaria and I lift up our shot glasses to join Jia's. "Yay, BBB!" we say in perfect unison.

I am thrilled.

"Pronto." Valentina answers her phone.

"Hi Val, it's Luna."

"I'm driving. Can we talk another day?"

"This afternoon? It's already October and we have to make some plans."

"Okay, talk to me now."

"Did you get the CD?" I ask.

"Yes."

"And?"

"I hate that kind of music. You have to find something else."

Hates it? I didn't think she'd absolutely love it, but her reaction seems a bit extreme.

"I already organized so much," I say. "And we have the money from Massimo. He's agreed to give us funding for the recording of the demo. I already set the dates for the studio in London."

"I can't stand that music. I like anything – rock, rap – anything at all, but not that."

"It's too late to change it now. You said I could go ahead." I knew Valentina wasn't a big dance music fan, but I didn't expect this at all.

"How did it go with Ilaria's friend?" she asks.

"Jia's on board. She's really fun, you'll like her."

"Look, if I'm not in the group, there's still three of you. Count me out."

"But Val, it won't be the same without you." I don't want her to leave the group. I remember our meetings in my lounge room and think of all the time we've spent on this venture so far. *She's going to let that all go to waste?*

"You don't need me," she says.

"We started this together. C'mon, what's up, Val?"

"I just have other priorities in my life now."

"Really? I thought you wanted this?" I think back to her excitement in the Rock Star room at The Gray Hotel so many months before on the first night we met with Massimo. All those BBB meetings, and the enthusiasm she had put into being our stylist for our first shoot, asking Massimo to be our investor ... Will BBB survive without her?

"Don't fuss, okay? You girls are going to be fine," she says.

We both hold on the line, silent and unsure. My mind races, searching for something to say – anything that might make her stay. She, I imagine, is sitting with her own disappointment that this is the end of the popstar dream for her.

I watch MTV that night and it suddenly seems so uninteresting. I'm worried about BBB's future. I was counting on Valentina's know-how and charisma to help make it all work. I don't think Massimo will pull out the promised money, but I'm certainly doubtful of his continued support. I want to forget the phone call with Valentina ever happened.

I close my eyes and try to erase the call from my mind. But it lingers like a song I can't skip. I open my diary and write:

You have your days – some good, some bad, but today is best forgotten.

Then I close the journal, hoping tomorrow feels lighter.

CHAPTER 17

To escape criticism – do nothing, say nothing, be nothing.

- Elbert Hubbard

My hair is so long and blonde these days that people start asking me if I'm Swedish. We soon come to realize that the idea of the girl band without Valentina is almost comical, in a positive way. None of us fit the usual mold of what people expect from an Italian girl group – and that's exactly what makes us stand out.

"I can't wait to see you three together," our Argentinean singing teacher says. "What a fabulous international mix."

"We the no-look-Italian, Italian girl band," Ilaria says laughing.

Word gets back to friends in New York and beyond that I started up a girl group.

```
To: luna@yahoo.it
From: charles@nylawfirm.com
Subject: Milan
Hey! Know of a girl band playing in Milan next Saturday
night? I'll be in town.
Charlie
```

```
To: luna@yahoo.it
From: gen@brussels.be
Subject: To my favorite pop star!
You're IN the group??? OMG! I thought you were managing.
Go girl!
Bisous.
```

It's all action. Ilaria has even stopped partying to keep her vocal cords in order. I also try to look after my voice. I don't go out much, and I'm only an occasional smoker, but I find that now I have a reason not to smoke, it makes me think of smoking. It's like being on a diet – it actually makes you think of food more than usual.

I sit on my windowsill one night and look at the full moon. I listen to our song, "Elements," focusing on the lyrics.

We are elements

We sit and watch the sun go down

And we can't imagine anyone we'd rather be with here and now

The lyrics seem perfect for my situation – I'm doing exactly what I love with two great girls with wonderful energy.

At the house where I grew up in Sydney, I had a little garden off my bedroom. As a teenager, I used to sit on a rock in the middle of that garden whenever I was feeling particularly emotional. I would stare out into the night sky and it seemed each time I sat on that rock, it happened to be a full moon. I found its presence soothing – it was as if the moon was waiting for me when I needed it.

I always wondered if I had a special connection with the moon because of my name. In French, *la lune* is the moon and *la luna* is the moon in Italian – exactly my name! I sit still, letting the moonlight wash over me like quiet reassurance. I get a rush of feelings that I'm here doing exactly what I'm meant to be doing.

The day of our photo shoot is nearing and we still have no plan what to wear. Now that Valentina has left, we don't have an in-house stylist, so we have to make some decisions about our look and clothes. I wonder if I should try to get Valentina on board, just to style us, but deep down, I know it's now our chance to branch out of the rapper look and embrace a more pop image that is in line with our music.

"We need to know what we're wearing in advance," I say to Ilaria many times over the weeks. "So we know what to bring to the shoot and so we don't waste time in the studio."

It's the day before the shoot and I can't believe I'm explaining it to her again. "We really need to have an idea of what we are wearing. The shoot is tomorrow. Jia will be arriving soon and I need you here so the three of us can try on some outfits together."

"I must to see my family tonight," Ilaria says. "My parents never see me, and they angry."

"They should understand if you explain it to them. We've all made sacrifices. Jia's coming all the way from Bologna, missing her evening lecture, and I sold my tickets to the David Bowie concert. Can't you come just for a while? I really want to make sure we all look good."

"You tell me what to take and I see you *domani.*"

"Okay," I say, defeated. "I'll call you later tonight once we've worked it out. Oh, and please don't be late to the shoot." I've realized that Ilaria is notoriously tardy.

Jia soon arrives to my place and we have a productive session working out some outfits with Shannon there to advise us. Fortunately, I know Ilaria's wardrobe quite well by now so I let her know what to bring.

The photographer, Lorenzo, Ilaria's ex-boyfriend, originally asked for us to come to the studio at nine o'clock, but I insisted it couldn't be earlier than eleven. I have to wake up early to go to the hairdresser, and I know Jia and Ilaria are hardly morning people. Shannon agreed to join us for moral support and to help out at the shoot.

Jia, Shannon, and I arrive at the studio in the center of Milan punctually. Lorenzo greets us and I can't believe it's him.

"Lorenzo? I'm Luna."

"I know," he says with a deep voice and kisses my cheeks.

I was expecting some towering, brooding heartthrob. Instead, Lorenzo turns out to be short, with soft curls and a calm energy.

He takes us around his large studio, explaining the equipment and complex lighting, and shows us where we should change. We have a look through his portfolio, showing some clients he works for. The photos are impressive. He clearly knows what he's doing.

Shannon modeled for years and has experience with putting on professional makeup. I never wear foundation, but she emphasizes how important it is to wear more makeup than usual for a photo shoot because the color gets soaked up by the lights.

"Where's Ilaria?" asks Shannon as she packs on to my face what feels like layers of foundation.

I shrug. "No idea."

Ilaria arrives at 11.40 a.m. Not bad.

We start by wearing jeans with white T-shirts for a simple Calvin Klein look. Jia has a red rose on the front of her T-shirt and I asked Ilaria to bring along one that is similar. It seems to work well, but when we look at a preview of the photos it's clear that the roses are clashing.

"Here, I brought a selection of white T-shirts," I say to Ilaria. "Can you put on one of these?"

"But I like my T-shirt. What's wrong with it?"

"Look at the photos. The rose is so big it overtakes our faces. Can you try a white one?" I say.

"But you told me to bring this T-shirt. I want wear it."

"A white one will look better."

Ilaria throws her hands up. "Stop telling me what to do. This is me. My body, my face."

"Of course you have to be happy, but we also have to look good like a group. Try this on?" I take a T-shirt from my bag.

"You can't push me what to wear!"

I never anticipated this. There might be added stress because her ex-boyfriend is the photographer. I know she still has feelings for him, but I thought she'd be submissive as a kitten. Instead, she's feisty.

"Ilaria," says Jia. "Please. We're losing time. Just try it."

I go to the change room with Ilaria and take various T-shirts with me. She tries on a few, complaining that they are either too big or too small. One looks excellent. It's just a simple white singlet, and hugs her figure nicely.

"That's it," I say. "Keep that one on. Looks great."

"I don't like it."

"You look fabulous. Can we just try it?"

Ilaria finally submits.

As we continue with the shoot, Shannon steps in from time to time to fix our hair and comment on our expressions.

We change into evening dresses with fur jackets for a "movie star" look. Jia has a Russian-style fur hat. She looks amazing in a tight gold cocktail dress with a big furry head – Queen Nefertiti hits Moscow.

We then do another look in all black. When I asked Ilaria to bring something in black, she went for a bondage theme with a tight patent leather bodice and a whip. She doesn't match Jia's and my more elegant look, but we don't have any alternative, so we have to make do. I have a black scarf that I wrap around my head so I look more unusual, and Jia puts on extra chunky jewelry and a black bob wig. Somewhere between edgy, glam, S&M, and vintage kitsch – not exactly coordinated, but strangely it works.

While we are still dressed in our black clothes, we use some fluorescent pink props for a different, more playful theme. I have brought some things from my fancy-dress box – including pink feathery fans, pink sunglasses, and pink boas. Ilaria has brought a pink-feathered notebook with matching pen. She pretends to take notes in a few shots, looking like an intellectual bondage master. We then put on the oversized pink sunglasses and pout for the camera.

Finally, Jia has a large piece of rusty light-beige lace that she thought we could do something creative with. We put on nude underwear and wrap the material around us. As we look at the preview shots, I realize the contrast of our skin tones against the lace is striking, but also somehow subtle and artistic.

When I quickly review a selection of photos from the whole shoot, I'm relieved to see there are some really great shots of us as a group. The shoot has been a success.

After hugging, Ilaria and I both say, "So sorry." Then we rush to the airport to pick up Olivia Madden who is arriving for our weekend of intensive singing lessons.

"I love your energy, Ilaria," Olivia says. "Luna, how did you find her? She's got that spark – total star quality."

"*Come get naked with me, baby*," we sing in the car on the way home. Olivia instructs us how to do harmonies. She gives me the soprano part while Ilaria sings the main tune.

"Sounding good, girls," she says.

That night, I have a full house. Ilaria, Jia, and Olivia stay at my place so we can get up for some intensive singing training the next day.

Olivia goes to sleep early. It's the first break from her two-year-old daughter for months and she's exhausted.

I work out how to use the video function on my digital camera and take some footage of Ilaria and Jia dancing. Ilaria gyrates on the floor like a lion in heat, and then Jia and Ilaria pose in some sensual positions together.

"That's amazing! I love it," I say. "You two have incredible chemistry – it looks amazing on camera."

I want the moment to last forever. We're getting along so well and I don't want to think back to the photo shoot when I lost the fun-loving, gregarious Ilaria.

I receive a text from a guy in a band that I met a while back:

```
Hey blondy spice! Are you coming to Plastic tonight?
I'll go there!  Mauro 22.11
```

```
No, sorry. we have to rehearse early tomorrow morning
but I hope to see you soon.  Luna 22.23
```

"I'd love to go to Plastic actually," Jia says later as we finish off a bottle of prosecco. "I've always heard so much about it."

"We could have gone," I say, "but I thought you girls said you were tired and wanted to rest."

"No, we say we not want go because of you," Ilaria says.

"Well." I look at my watch. "It's only midnight. It's not too late. We could just go for a quick boogie?"

Ilaria's and Jia's faces light up.

```
We're on our way!  Luna 00.01
```

We go to Plastic and dance with Mauro's all-male band members. We have a great time feeling like pop stars with our hair still styled and makeup on from the photo shoot.

When I was working in New York as a banker, I always felt reserved and uninteresting, but here I am, a wannabe pop star rocking around with a bunch of hunky musos in Milan. What a blast!

The next morning Olivia wakes us up with cups of tea, and then we eventually start our lesson. It's the first time I've heard Jia sing.

Olivia sets us a few exercises for our vocal cords, but also mixed with some acting, which she explains should help us feel at ease on stage.

"Okay, now sing like you're a cat," says Olivia. "Meow meow meow, and make some catlike body movements."

Jia attacks the exercise with such gusto and determination – we can see the heavy concentration on her face.

Jia gives it her all, arms stretching like a prowling cat, and her face laser-focused. The sound she makes – "Meu, meu, meu" ... somewhere between a meow and a melody – sends us all into fits of laughter. She's so funny that I have to run out of the room because I wet my pants. What I would have done to capture that on video! Jia was priceless!

Overall, I love Jia's diligence. She sticks with the exercises that Olivia throws at her, despite not quite hitting the notes, and despite requests that are far too challenging for her. Her voice is very meek, but I gather nerves have a lot to do with it.

The singing training weekend over, Jia goes back to Bologna and Ilaria leaves for her stint working for a fashion house in Paris. I have a lot of work to do to prepare for the recording of our demo CD in London. I rehearse the songs every day and have singing lessons every second day. At times I want to pull the plug on the dates we set for early November and postpone it all so we have more time to practice, but I think it's one of those things you never feel ready for. We need a demo to show around to record companies so I just have to make the best of the dates we have.

Meanwhile, quotes for doing promotional videos, logo designs, and the like don't get back to me when promised. I start to feel like everything's stuck in second gear. People seem genuinely interested, but deadlines float by. When I vent to an Italian friend, he shrugs. "It's not about being in Italy," he says. "Like you are blonde, some people are hopeless."

I'm happy to be heading over to London for a few days – I need a break. Little do I realize, I am bringing a little Italian chaos with me ...

CHAPTER 18

"What day is it?" "It's today," squeaked Piglet. "My favorite day," said Pooh.

- A.A. Milne

I arrive in London feeling like a musician. I have Olivia's keyboard that she left in Milan, a big bag full of clothes, my computer, and another bag full of toiletries – without a trolley I can barely move under the weight. I look like a completely overloaded donkey. I'm trying to get into an elevator at Liverpool Street station and I can't fit.

"Can I help you?" a middle-aged man with a jolly face asks me. He has his son who looks about six years old with him.

"I don't think I'll get up the escalator with all this," I say. "Would you mind helping me get this into the lift?"

"Of course. And tell me, are you a one-man band?"

I search his expression. I'm not sure if he's serious or not. "Almost!" I say. I hadn't seen Jia or Ilaria since Olivia's visit to Milan, which was close to three weeks ago, so I really do feel like a one-man band.

When I'm finally outside the station, I get into a black cab and within minutes London's majestic beauty surrounds me. It's so pristine compared to the Milan that I know, and at dusk the light has a deep-yellow tinge. The city seems to glow.

Ilaria gets the dates mixed up. She booked her train from Paris to arrive in London on the Saturday rather than the Friday. I can't believe it when she tells me. I'm so disappointed, and can only describe it as "astonishing" because we have been talking about this recording in the studio for nearly two months.

Jia arrives in London Friday evening and we go over to Olivia's house to rehearse so she can give us some last-minute singing tips. Olivia prepares us dinner with wine and we watch the MTV Music Awards.

"Talking about singing," says Jia, "it's almost eleven p.m."

"Okay. Let's do it," says Olivia, turning off the telly and sitting behind her keyboard. "Do this warm-up scale together. *Ah-ah-ah*," she sings.

Then we rehearse our songs. Jia sings, "*Touch of a feather, I'm gonna make your body fly.*"

"Wow, Jia," Olivia says. "You've *really* improved."

"I've worked a lot these past weeks," she explains. "I've been recording my voice and repeating the verses over and over until I got them right. I think my boyfriend was ready to thump me."

Before we know it, it's Saturday, and Jia and I are on the other side of London, in Crouch Hill, just about to record our songs.

Olivia had warned us that the studio facilities are rather basic. The music producer has the studio set up in his apartment. A bachelor pad to the extreme with thinning, green carpet and a moldy bathroom. The lounge room turned studio, however, is state of the art. It's completely decked out with impressive mixers, keyboards, and flashing equipment. Olivia takes us through some scales and breathing exercises to warm up our voices. Then I'm sent into a smaller separate room, and I'm facing a large oval microphone that has a grandma-style beige stocking over it. It looks like something makeshift from the fifties.

Jitters run up and down my tummy. I'm so excited to start our first recording. I stand there with a large black leather headset on. I can hear everything that Olivia and the music producer are saying from the other room through the headphones.

"Keep one ear free so that you can hear yourself sing," instructs Olivia.

I expose my left ear.

"Take a breath now. You ready?" asks Olivia.

"Yes." Breath. Breath.

The music plays and I start to sing:

"*We are elements,*

We sit and watch the sun go down ..."

"Luna, your pitch is off," says Olivia.

"Okay. Let me try again." They start the music. "*We are elements,*" I sing, trying my best to hit the right note.

"No, still not right. Listen to me ... ah ... we ... that's the note you need to hit. If you get the first note wrong, you'll be flat the whole way through the song."

"*Ah ... we,*" I sing.

"Almost, once more," says Olivia.

"*Weeeeeeeee ...*"

"Nearly."

"*Weeeee.*"

"Better."

They continue to give me advice as to expression and tone, and we do retakes of certain parts of the song over and over, and over and over again until they hear something they're happy with.

Although it's totally exhausting, I love the experience. It's added confirmation that singing is a vocation I could pursue with a passion.

"Okay, you're done. Jia's on!" says the producer.

"Shouldn't Ilaria be here by now?" asks Olivia.

I look at the time. "She should have arrived a while ago," I say. "I'll call her now."

Where is Ilaria?

"She's missed her train so she had to catch a later one," I relay to them after I get off the phone with her. "And now it seems she's lost somewhere in London."

Ilaria arrives at the studio at 5.30 p.m. after Jia and I have finished singing for the day. With hardly a moment to breathe, Ilaria manages to inhale a quick cigarette and then hits the recording room.

"*Element, we seet and watch de sun go dauwn,*" she sings with her usual confidence.

Despite forgetting the words because she hasn't practiced, and even admitting that she hasn't listened to the songs at all in Paris, she's a natural. Ilaria loves the microphone and sings much better than in the lessons. She knows this is the real thing and she's giving it her all. We have to do many takes to help her with the words and pronunciation, but she's in tune and her voice is full of energy.

Overall, I'm really proud of both girls. We're so fresh at this – we don't know what we are doing in the studio, but we do well. The music producer is patient and it's wonderful to have Olivia to support us.

That night, Lachlan comes over to my aunt's place to film us dressing up and dancing around. I hire a good-quality video camera for the occasion. It's so rare that we are all together and I want to take the opportunity to get some video footage for a promotional DVD.

My aunt is away, so we have the house to ourselves and even my aunt's big Labrador-bulldog cross, Brutus, is excited by all the action. We start with some "BBB behind the scenes" footage, with Jia blow-drying my hair, and me putting Ilaria's makeup on. Then Olivia comes over and interviews us for the camera, pretending to be Simon Cowell from *America's Got Talent*.

Jia's wearing her china-doll wig with bangs and bob. She has a lilac feather boa wrapped around her shoulders, looking very diva-like. Olivia is sitting on a chair opposite her like a television interview.

"Jia, if you could be any living creature, what would it be?" asks Olivia.

There's a pause then Jia says, "I'd be an eagle, so I can fly around, looking at everything from above and dip down when I feel like it."

"Olivia, what you smokin'?" Lachlan says, laughing.

"Yeh," I say, "what's with all the animal references? You had Jia being a cat in singing class in Milan, and now a bird. How about some questions related to the music industry?"

"Okay." Olivia clears her throat and then asks in a professional tone, "Jia, how long have you been singing and dancing for?"

Jia looks at Olivia intently. "Three weeks."

We crack up laughing.

"No," I say. "Disaster! Jia, at least say three years. Livi, why don't you ask Jia about how many languages she speaks. Not music related, but very impressive."

"All right," says Olivia.

Pause.

"Jia," she asks. "I've heard you're a woman of many tongues. What languages do you speak?"

We all try not to crack up again. I look at the floor and by concentrating on a small gap in the parquet I manage to suppress my giggles.

Jia stays very serious. "I speak English, *Italiano, Espanol, Francais, Zhongguo* – that's Chinese – and I took a semester of Arabic at college."

"And what do you think of the Spice Girls?" asks Olivia.

Jia says, "The Spice Girls? Sorry, but who are they?"

I stop in my tracks in disbelief, then burst out all the hysteria I have been keeping inside me. I sound like a wounded hyena, but I can't stop laughing. Jia is completely serious. She doesn't have a clue who the Spice Girls are.

"Well, you'd certainly be 'Intellectual Spice,'" says Lachlan, continuing to film this rather extraordinary girl band event. "Who in the world hasn't heard of the Spice Girls?"

Jia seems somewhat pleased she's been the stir of so much entertainment. I'm crying from laughter. What kind of girl band member have I managed to recruit?

"But who are they?" Jia persists. "I spend all my time studying, I don't know any girl bands."

I'm stunned. I mean, how has someone managed to avoid the Spice Girls? But it's also kind of refreshing.

"Where did we find her?" Ilaria asks me, raising her arms and moving toward Jia for a big hug. "Where did we find you? I love you, Jia – you are amazing."

After the interviews, Olivia directs some dance moves. The three of us attempt to do some coordinated body rolls, but we never seem to get it right. Help! Starting BBB dance classes has been pushed to the top of my agenda.

We finally finish at about three a.m. The next day we are going to have another full day in the studio, but it's like we're running on air, and nothing matters except for the very moment that we're together.

I go upstairs to say goodnight to the girls who are sharing a room. They're lying on either side of the double bed in white nightshirts with a red cherry design. My aunt's dog has strategically placed himself in the middle of them both. He's furiously wagging his tail in excitement. I can almost see the mischievous smile on his face – he knows he's in a prime spot.

"Are they matching nighties?" I ask.

"Almost. Just a coincidence," says Jia.

"Well, Brutus seems to be in heaven," I say. "Do you mind him sleeping on your bed?"

"It's fine for now," says Jia. "We'll move him if he's a nuisance. Don't worry. Night, Luna."

"Buona notte," says Ilaria.

In the morning, the girls tell me how they could barely sleep because Brutus was a huge snoring lump in the middle of the bed. They tried to push him off without success.

Nevertheless, we go back to the studio with gusto. Jia has to leave early because she has an exam the next morning in Bologna, but Ilaria and I stay late, singing retakes of certain lines that the producer isn't happy with. We stay on in London for another day, and have a wonderful time together out and about.

A friend introduces us to a singer and songwriter called Harrison who has performed in America and the UK. Ilaria and I are both impressed by him, and he agrees to come to Milan when Ilaria returns from Paris to give BBB singing training.

Back in Milan, I go downstairs to collect my mail. I've been checking frantically every day, waiting for our demo CD to arrive. Finally, it's here.

My stomach is in jitters. My fingers shaking, I take the CD out of the padded envelope, and – admiring how "BBB Demo" is typewritten in red on the front – I put the disc in the CD player. I press play to hear the first song, cringing with anticipation.

"*We are elements – we sit and watch the sun go down ...*" Oh my goodness, it's my voice. Wow, it actually sounds okay. My voice! I sound slightly husky? It's just so weird to hear myself.

I listen to "Elements" through to the end and overall I'm really pleased. I like the way the music producer has distributed the parts so that each of us sings a solo verse, and then we sing the chorus together. Ilaria's accent is quite noticeable, but I don't see that as a huge downfall, and Jia's voice blends in beautifully – soft but clear. The producer's done wonders, and the balance between us really works. It's definitely polished enough to show to record companies.

It moves on to the next song, "Come Get Naked With Me."

"*Hello, let me introduce myself to you,*" my voice sings through the stereo speakers.

Again I freak out that it's my voice, but I think the song sounds good! I listen to the songs over and over, not believing it's really our group with our own demo CD.

I play it to Shannon and others, and everyone says it sounds particularly professional, like songs you would hear on the radio. I carry a copy of the CD with me everywhere I go and even convince the DJs in some bars to play it.

"Could you play this?" I ask a friendly-looking DJ one evening at a party at Plastic.

"What?"

"It's two songs that my girl band, BBB, recorded."

"I don't have time. I have many requests." Seems he's not as friendly as I thought.

"Just have a listen and see if you like it. Please," I say. "I'm here with friends and we'd love to dance to our songs."

He puts on the disc and listens to it through his headset. He gives me a quick nod, indicating to leave the CD with him. I go back to the sofas where Shannon and a group of friends are sitting.

About five songs later, I hear my voice. "*Hello let me introduce myself to you ...*" Wow! For a second, I freeze – hearing my voice blast through the speakers is surreal. People are dancing on the floor and we all run there to join them.

"Get Naked" finishes and the DJ immediately follows with our second song, "Elements." How great! There we are, boogying away to BBB's very own music.

When I go back to pick up my CD and thank the DJ, he says, "No problem," and gives a small smile. I consider it a good sign that he played both tracks.

CHAPTER 19

Luck is what happens when preparation meets with opportunity.

- Seneca the Younger

I put together a BBB presentation with a careful selection of the best photos from our shoot. I show the photos around, finding that people look at them intently and are intrigued. They love how we look together, and everyone says Jia photographs particularly well. There's something about her elegance and quiet confidence that draws people in. I'm thrilled the feedback is so positive. I've got added motivation that we have something which could work.

As a result of sending around our semi-professional BBB packages along with a copy of our demo CD, I'm put in touch with a friend of a friend who owns the biggest record company in Milan – Foscolo Vittorini. I am beyond excited.

I call Carlo Vittorini's office the next day, and arrange a meeting through his secretary who seems to know who I am.

I meet him alone, because Ilaria is still in Paris and Jia is busy in Bologna. The office is in a historic building. My heart is racing as I enter. The walls boast an array of frames with albums that have gone gold, platinum, and the like. The secretary immediately shows me through to Signor Vittorini's office.

Carlo Vittorini is perched behind his desk in his immense office and brushes back his gray hair with his hand. He has the air of a very important man, and he reminds me of the old-school Board of Directors I dealt with regularly in New York.

He takes me into a spacious conference room where we have a chat in Italian over coffee and listen to the music.

He taps his foot while it plays. "It reminds me of ABBA," he says to me in Italian.

He listens through to the end of the two songs.

"My record labels are only for Italian artists," he says, "and they all sing in Italian. You are too international."

I sink. I want to say that being international is exactly what makes us special – but I keep quiet.

Then he says, "I'll call my friend who has a well-known dance music label, he could be interested."

"That would be wonderful."

He makes a call to his friend. He then hands me a small white piece of paper with the contact details for Dario Gravano.

I call Dario Gravano later that afternoon and it's easy to set up a meeting. I'm surprised by how powerful word of mouth is in Italy. I feel like everyone is laying out the red carpet for us just because we know someone in common.

"*Signor Gravano, sono Luna,*" I say to the forty-something guy dressed in a long-sleeved black T-shirt and jeans on the other side of the desk. It's a stark contrast to Signor Vittorini's conservative office and demeanor.

"We can speak in English if you like," he says. "And call me Dario."

"Sure, Dario. Great to meet you."

He indicates with his arm for me to sit down on one of the chairs on the other side of his desk.

"So," he says, taking a long breath as if it's the first time he's breathed all day. "I know nothing. What are you about?"

"I have some photos here so I can walk you through. We're called BBB and we're a multicultural girl band."

"Very interesting," he says, rubbing his finger over the first A4-size photo of us in the presentation – our movie-star look in fur.

"This is Ilaria who is Italian, but half-Somalian." I feel I should stress our Italian edge. "She grew up in Milan. And this is Jia," I continue. "She's lived in Italy for about five years. She's from Hong Kong and speaks fluent Italian and English."

He works his way through the photos, stopping to laugh at the one with the pink props. "Nice," he says. "And the music?"

I pass him a CD and he goes to the other side of his rather small modern office and puts the CD into a large stereo. The humungous black speakers start pounding with the bass.

He listens to both songs. "I like the second one," he says.

"It's called 'Come Get Naked With Me.'"

"I could guess that," he says with a smirk. "It's quite pop and original. Reminds me a bit of Kylie Minogue – did you hear her latest album?"

Lachlan recently sent me the *Body Language* CD and I have been listening to it nonstop. The whole of England had gone crazy over Kylie's hit, "Slow," and Lachlan insists that the song is so damn sexy it has increased the amount of procreation in the UK threefold.

"Yes, I know it well," I say.

Dario continues, "We can launch a single and see how it goes. If it goes well, we can consider an album, but if not, the only outlay for us is the distribution of a single and a bit of promo."

"Sounds fair," I say, almost ready to explode with excitement.

"Times are tough in the music industry. CD sales are down due to people downloading songs from the internet. It's getting hard to make ends meet."

"I understand completely," I say, trying to knock the look of sheer ecstasy off my face and look compassionate.

He goes on, "My company has launched many famous Italian artists. We partner with 300 foreign record labels for international distribution. I'll send your single abroad to countries like the Netherlands, Germany, and Sweden. They're all places with a big dance music market and we'll see whether anyone picks it up."

"Wow," I say. We really are going to be international!

"There's a very limited dance music market in Italy, so abroad is usually the best way to go," he says. "But, there are always a few hits a year in Italy in the pop-dance genre, so we can be hopeful that the Italian public will like it."

I waltz out of the meeting feeling like angels are flapping at my shoulders. I first heard the song "Come Get Naked With Me" a few years ago when Olivia visited me in New York. I always loved the song, but how could I have ever possibly envisioned it might one day be the key to the success of my very own girl group.

I call Ilaria in Paris to share the news.

"Ilaria, you won't believe it," I say. "We're gonna have a record deal for 'Get Naked.'"

"*Che?*" she screams into the phone. "*Incredibile.*"

"I have another meeting with the head of the company next week to go through finer details, but they want to release our single!"

"*Veramente in-cre-dibile,*" she says, sounding like she might burst. "I have news too. I be back in Milan next week so I will come with you to meet him."

Before we know it, we are at the meeting with Dario. Ilaria's punctual. So far so good.

"I want to re-record the song," he says, "and revamp the background music. No huge changes, but fix it up. You'll work with Enrico in the studio. He's one of our in-house producers."

"No problem." I expected Dario to have outrageous suggestions to do with our image, but I'm pleasantly surprised he's keeping the discussion around music. I find him very professional and reasonable.

"We'll prepare one contract for BBB," he continues, "and a separate contract for the songwriter."

Dario's assistant comes in with a written message, and then a guy comes to the door. He's tall and dark with slicked black hair like from a vampire movie.

"This is DJ Ballo, my partner," says Dario. I know the name, he's a famous DJ in Italy. "And this is BBB," Dario says. "Well, two members of the group."

"*Ciao tutti!*" he says with a broad mouth full of huge teeth. He passes Dario a CD and slinks off, raising his peaked eyebrows at us as he closes the door. Meanwhile, another guy slips into the office and sits on a stool beside Dario.

"Ah, good. This is Enrico, the producer who'll do your music," Dario says. "You speak English, Rici?"

"Sí," he says, a little nervously. Enrique is tall and lean, with tousled brown hair and the casual-cool air of someone in his late twenties. He's dressed in black jeans and red sneakers, a matching long-sleeved T-shirt stamped with the company logo in crisp white – like he walked straight out of a startup ad campaign.

My mind is boggling at the thought that this is really happening. Ilaria just keeps nodding – her usual chattiness is always curbed when the conversation is in English.

"Okay, so we'll email you the contract once it's translated into English," says Dario. And that's our cue that the meeting is over.

"I'm so surprised that he never asked us questions like how many years singing experience we have, or how old we are," I say to Ilaria in the elevator.

"It good like this. He like us, you can see."

We only got our demo a few weeks ago, and we're already seriously discussing a record deal. I still can hardly believe it's real.

CHAPTER 20

Desire, ask, believe, receive.

- Stella Terrill Man

It's February and BBB is settled like a happy little family in my apartment in Milan. The girls have moved into my place for the month, and we're set for four weeks of intensive singing and dancing training. If we are soon going to be promoting our single, we need to be ready to perform live on stage.

Bob called about a month back to see if there was any chance I would consider going back to New York to work for him. When I told him the girl band was becoming a serious venture, he seemed quite intrigued and asked me if he could help in any way. I let him know we needed equipment for our rehearsals: a keyboard, microphones, microphone stands, and an amplifier. Bob said I should buy them and send him the bill. I'm blown away by his generosity and support.

I still see Massimo regularly and he likes to take the BBB girls and me out to dinner from time to time, but since he's already paid for the recording of our demo and Valentina has left the group, I haven't had the courage to ask him for any more money. My savings account is gradually going down, and I just hope the investment will be worth it. I'm making sure I arrange everything on as tight a budget as possible.

I buy a selection of DVDs for us to watch in the evenings as part of our "girl band education." I have *Raw Spice*, *A Year with Atomic Kitten*, and *Destiny's Child: World Tour*, to name just a few.

Harrison, the singer-songwriter we met in London, has flown over for the first week to be our singing teacher. To save costs, he's staying with us. He seems to like the idea of living with a girl band for six nights.

"The music world is tough," he says on his first night. "But from what Luna tells me, it sounds like you're halfway there."

Harrison's regal British accent, juxtaposed against a head of unruly strawberry-blond locks and deep-blue eyes, brings color to all our cheeks.

"Congratulations on your record deal," he continues. "There's many a talented music artist out there who would want to be in your shoes. Let's rest up tonight, and we'll start at midday tomorrow after your dance class. Right, Luna?"

"Bianca will be here at ten a.m.," I say. "We'll have two hours of dance, shower, and a quick break. So let's aim for a one p.m. start for the singing lesson, okay?"

Ilaria and Jia nod. I gather we're all a bit jittery, wondering what surprises this month is going to bring.

That night we open a bottle of wine, which soon becomes two, and well, like us, our singing coach enjoys his booze. He also happens to be a very heavy smoker. I wish I'd banned smoking from my apartment for the month, but how could I? I'm in the minority.

Not a very good beginning to our week of vocal lessons.

"Wake up! It's ten to ten!" I call out the next morning. "Bianca's gonna be here any moment. Get your dance gear on."

"My head is sore," says Jia. "How much wine did we drink?"

"Not loads, but we sat in a smoke-filled room all night and didn't drink water. I feel like crap too."

"Where's Ilaria?" she asks.

"She won't get up," I say. "She's superglued to the bed."

I go back into my room where Ilaria's sleeping. "C'mon. We're gonna start any moment. Please wake up."

"No, I can't," she says.

She seriously doesn't plan on getting up. "You have to," I say. "We have a dance lesson in six minutes."

I run to the stereo and blare music at full bore. There's no way Ilaria will sleep through that. I knock gently on Harrison's door, apologizing to him that I have no choice, and warn him that the music from our dance class will start soon anyway. He's not impressed.

"Turn it down a tad," he says, sounding edgy. "No need to exaggerate."

"You don't know what I'm dealing with here," I say through the door. "Ilaria has to get up."

"Okay, okay – I'm up," Ilaria mumbles from the end of the hall.

I turn down the volume and the doorbell rings. I buzz in our dance instructor, Bianca. She arrives looking fresh – 4'10'" and full of presence, her dreadlocks pulled back neatly. I suddenly realize what a disheveled mess I must look. Instead of getting myself together, I was worrying about waking up the girls. Although I'd brushed my teeth, I'm sure I reek of wine and smoke. I feel it in my skin.

Ilaria and Jia join us in the lounge room in their tracksuit pants. I have a huge mirror that's turned sideways for the class so we can see ourselves. Bianca stands in front of the mirror ready to start and I can see all our reflections perfectly. We look at each other and grin.

Bianca passes me a CD to put on. All the songs on Bianca's compilation are excellent, ranging from soft rock to chill house. It's great to move, to really feel the music soaking into my limbs. It reminds me why we're doing all this.

We go over basic dance postures, and she instructs us how to hold our hands and where to place our feet. We do some hip-popping and small routines, laughing when we can't keep up. I consider it the ideal dance class. I can't believe we're going to do this every day for the next month – I'm thrilled at the thought. Our own BBB dance class in the comfort of my beautiful living room. When I first saw this lounge room, I'd imagined it as a dance studio with a big mirror, and now it is a reality.

"Put on your music," Bianca instructs me.

"Okay. Should we start with 'Elements'?"

"Sure. We can work with that song first. I have some ideas," she says in impeccable English. "Hear this beginning part? It's more dreamy, so you could try this." She shows us how we should run around in circles flapping our arms.

I certainly don't consider the movements appropriate for a pop group, but I bite my tongue and hesitantly follow suit.

Harrison walks in, observing us intently. "Looking good, girls," he says with approving nod.

I don't agree. I feel like we're participating in a modern dance recital. Bianca is obviously an experienced teacher, but I have to take her aside after class.

"That dance you showed us is lovely, but we won't be able to do it and sing at the same time."

"I need to get you all moving. You have done a lot of dance classes before, but Ilaria and Jia are new to this."

I get her point, but we just need some sexy pop moves that we can coordinate. We're not preparing for *Swan Lake*.

"We need to dance with the microphone stands in front of us, and have movements that we can do while we sing. You know, like the Spice Girls or Britney Spears. We only have one month, so we might as well get straight into it."

"Okay, I'll think of some other choreography."

"Great, thanks," I say.

"*Na*," I sing.

"*Na*," sings Harrison, pressing down a key. "Luna, listen to the note. Your pitch is off."

"*Na*," I sing.

"No, you don't have it," he says. "Jia, you try."

"*Na*," sings Jia.

"No. Ilaria?"

"*Na*," she sings.

"Yes, she's got it. Luna and Jia, you're both tone-deaf. Ilaria's the only one who has it right."

"Harrison, tone-deaf is a very strong statement," I say. "It's not right."

I've had many singing lessons, was always selected for choirs at school, and was in musicals for many years up to my early twenties. I know I'm a reasonable singer who can hold a tune. I feel strong enough to handle Harrison's words, but Jia? She's new to this. I want her to believe in herself and her ability, not be told she's tone-deaf!

"Well, maybe tone-deaf isn't the right term," he says, fumbling for words. "Your pitch is off, that's what I want to say."

"So are you going to teach us?" I ask. "You'll show us how to get our pitch right?"

"Of course I will," he says. "That's what I'm here for. Luna, follow me in this scale."

"*Na, na, na, na, na*," I sing up. "*Na, na, na, na, na*," I sing down.

"Better. Now Jia."

By day three of our intensive month, I'm absolutely exhausted. My muscles ache and I can hardly move. I'm sure the other girls feel the same. However, I'm not going to budge on our schedule. We're going to have singing and dancing every weekday of this month, without fail.

The first five days fly by.

"Okay girls, I know it's been a tough week," says Harrison, "and I just want to say to you all, congratulations. You've done really well and worked really hard. I know we've had our ups and downs, but that's what the music industry is all about."

"Thanks for coming," I say.

"It's been great to have you here," says Jia.

Ilaria gives a clap, and we give a short round of applause for Harrison.

"Harrison, I can't believe it's your last night already," Jia says. "I think you've been such a help. Can you come back?"

"Well, that's up to Luna," he says, looking over my way.

"Sure," I say. "You're welcome any time."

"What about when we sing at the studio for the record company?" Jia asks me. "I think it would be great if Harrison could join us. I'd feel better, knowing he was there."

"Good idea," I say, then look over to Harrison. "As soon as I know the dates, I'll let you know. It'll be mid-March sometime."

"I should be free. I'd be happy to be there," he says, lighting a cigarette and leaning back on the sofa in a stately fashion. "And considering tonight is my last night, I want you girls to do another exercise. This is a fun one."

"Okay," says Ilaria. "What you want?"

If I'm not mistaken, Harrison blushes. "Put on your favorite music," he says, "and lip-sync in front of the mics."

"Easily done," I say. Then I ask the girls, "What do you think? Should we do Miss Kittin?"

We giggle – all three of us love this. Miss Kittin is a French DJ and singer. Her lyrics are repetitive and powerful. The song we put on is called "Frank Sinatra," and she states a few obscenities and then says, "Frank Sinatra is dead." The song is very edgy and has a clubby beat.

As Harrison uses the trusty video function on my camera, we stand in front of the mics and go wild, dancing and singing along with Miss Kittin blaring in the background.

"This is good," he says, looking very pleased with himself. "I wanted to know if you are confident performers, and the answer is affirmative."

We don't want to stop. The next CD I put on is The Rolling Stones. We listen to "Satisfaction" on repeat, and go full diva with total rockstar energy. I have a cheapo guitar that's more for show than anything, and Jia takes it, pretending to play. Ilaria does some microphone-stand grinding and I toss my blonde hair in spurts while doing some of my favorite Shakira-style body rolls.

Harrison is the perfect audience, completely engaged in us, and we are lapping it up.

The month progresses and I finally feel we are a real group. Singing and dancing at the same time is a challenge. Concentrating on posture, breathing, steps, timing, music, lyrics, arms, legs, head, where to look, and smiling at the audience in just the right way is not an easy task by any means. It's a completely new level of coordination that I learn this month, and it gives me a heightened respect for pop artists.

Ilaria loves the idea of potentially making money doing something that's so much fun. Meantime, Jia receives a very lucrative job offer with a great international fashion company, but she tells them she isn't available because of BBB. I'm thrilled by their dedication. It's a new phase for the girl band. We are three women from three different cultures, powering through exhaustion and self-doubt in pursuit of a shared dream, and finding joy in every messy, magical step.

To put all our hard work into practice, we arrange for friends and contacts to come over to my apartment on the last Saturday night of the month to be our first real audience.

CHAPTER 21

I am always doing things I can't do, that's how I get to do them.

- Pablo Picasso

The day of our debut show is here. We have our microphones, stands, and amplifier set up in my lounge room. We move all the furniture to the side so people can either sit on the floor or stand.

Massimo was first on the invitation list, but he's traveling so can't make it. We are expecting some fashion contacts of Jia's who might be potential sponsors. Other than that, we limit the invitations to close friends, as well as our singing and dancing teachers. We expect about thirty people.

I'm with Ilaria and Jia in my bedroom getting ready. We don't want to talk to anyone before the show. We've been instructed by our dance teacher, Bianca, that we should stick together as a group and not get distracted by other people before a performance.

Shannon, who's in charge of lighting and sound, comes in regularly, giving us updates.

"How many people are out there?" asks Jia. "It's getting really noisy."

"At least forty," Shannon says. "It's packed and the crowd's getting restless. You have to start."

"I'm going to have an *infart*," says Ilaria. "I'm going to have an *infart!*"

Infarto means "heart attack" in Italian, and the way Ilaria mixes the Italian with English I find hilarious, relieving my nerves a little, but I'm too preoccupied to laugh.

Inside my body is screaming, *No!! Noooooooooooooo!!!!!!!!* I suddenly don't think I even want to perform. I can't help but wonder why in all hell I'm putting myself through this. Wouldn't it be easier to go to an office each day rather than experience such awful nerves? How did I get myself into this? *What was I thinking?* I can't remember ever feeling quite so nervous before going on stage before.

The three of us huddle in a circle and have a group hug.

We enter the lounge room dressed in gold tops, jeans, and high heels. The room is filled with smoke and everyone starts yelling, "*Woouuw, woouuw,*" and clapping. We stand behind our microphones and Jia gives a short introduction. I asked her to do it, as I feel too nervous to talk.

"Hi everyone and thank you for joining us this evening. First, we'd like to perform for you an original song that was written for us by our contacts in London. It's called 'Elements.'"

We turn around to face the wall behind us. The mirror is there, and I bow my head so as not to see the other girls' reflections. I try to zone out and just focus on what I'm supposed to be doing. I nod to give Shannon the okay, and the music starts.

As we stand on the spot with our backs to the audience, we do some of the balletic arm movements that Bianca was so keen on. We then turn around one by one as we sing in Italian, "*Fuoco,*" "*Agua,*" and "*Aria.*"

Then I sing the opening verse, concentrating on breathing where the teachers instructed.

"*We are elements*" (breath) "*we sit and watch the sun go down ...*" (breath) "*And we can't imagine*" (breath) "*anyone we'd rather be with here and now ...*" (breath)

The music picks up and we start our coordinated moves with the beat. It's surreal to be performing. I scan our audience. Everyone is sitting on the floor or standing near the walls, looking at us with no particular expression. They are kind of open-mouthed and blank. What's wrong? Don't they like our show? *Why aren't they tapping their feet or smiling?*

Bianca told us not to make eye contact with the audience. She said it's best to look just above head level, so it looks like you are looking at them, but you're actually looking into a void. I redirect my vision to perform and smile to the window at the back of the room, so as not to get distracted.

When the song finishes, the audience breaks into a huge round of applause. We leave the "stage" and go back into my bedroom to change our clothes for our next song.

One of Ilaria's friends comes flying in. "That was amazing! Everyone loves you!" She has a cigarette in her hand and Ilaria and Jia go over to her for a puff.

"No smoking in here please," I say. "We have to change as quickly as possible. It'll all be over soon. Come on guys, keep focused, we're only part way there."

Jia puts on black leather pants, long suede boots, and a fitted black strapless top. I'm wearing a tight black dress with a full-length silver zipper down the front, a lacy bodice peeping out with shoestring straps. Ilaria wears a flimsy black miniskirt that gently lifts as she moves, and suspender-type opaque tights that show off her bronzed thighs.

We have another group hug and go back out again, this time to sing "Come Get Naked With Me." I'm still nervous as hell, but the adrenaline is so powerful that I can't wait to perform again.

I start singing as flirtatiously as possible, again concentrating on my breathing.

"Hello, let me introduce myself to you ..." (breath) *"You know who I am"* (breath) *"I'll show you something new ... ah ah"* (breath)

The crowd is silent throughout, watching us intently. Although they are observing us like stunned mullets, I feel more at ease this time, knowing they enjoyed the first song. As we continued with "Get Naked," our choreography is impeccably timed, better than in rehearsals. Again, there's thunderous applause at the end.

We leave the stage, promptly coming back in wearing humungous, multicolored afro wigs that Jia bought in Hong Kong, and bright feather boas. Everyone laughs, and we sing a cover of the song "Kiss Me" as an encore. We don't sing solos since we aren't confident enough for that, but we sing all together and everyone seems to enjoy it.

Most people stay on after the show to drink and dance. I love how everyone is so animated. Friends put on our wigs and mimic BBB moves. It's like the whole audience is sharing our post-performance high.

I go up to one of Ilaria's friends who's about twenty-two and ask her, "So, how did you like it?"

"*Complimenti! Complimenti!* I don't expect it be so good. You are so professional!"

That's exactly what I want to hear.

"What d'ya think of the show?" I ask an Australian friend who's in her mid-twenties.

"Well, couldn't believe it was you. All of you looked so glamorous, like a real group. For the first time I believe this could really work. Well done, matey," she says and gives me a hug.

Shannon videos the crowd. I approach as she interviews her Italian boyfriend. They've been together quite a few months now and he has met the BBB girls before. He's a successful, international businessman in his early thirties, and I'm so interested to hear his impression.

"How do you like BBB?" she asks him in English.

"I like that you can see three very different personalities on the stage," he says. "Luna is the confident one, Jia is the shy one, and Ilaria is the wild one. But I think Ilaria was holding back a little. She should be even wilder because it suits her."

It's true – we each bring something completely different. Different cultures, different energies. Maybe that's what makes us work. This wasn't a stadium. This wasn't MTV. But for the first time, I see a glimpse of the pop stars we could become.

Since our hectic February schedule is over, I finally have a moment to collect my thoughts and recalibrate. What a whirlwind! Singing and dancing every day for a month! And like a wonderful big cherry on the cake, a successful debut show. We are on a roll now, and I cannot wait to perform again.

I look back on my previous goals, and yes, I performed! I want to take this further. I revise my goals:

1. *More exposure for BBB*
2. *Find a top singing teacher*
3. *Meet a lovely guy*

Meantime, the record company has been very slow in producing the contract. Dario explains that their lawyer has been on holiday, which delayed the translation into English. Time is ticking – it's early March and we want "Come Get Naked With Me" to be released for the European summer.

I use my spare time to pick up my Italian skills. More and more, managing the group requires that I speak Italian fluently. I have private lessons most days to rehash all the grammar, and I start reading articles in Italian. It goes well, but I'm still stuck in the habit of speaking English with most of my friends, so I don't practice as much as I should.

I put my feelers out for gigs. People who organize paid gigs ask me where we have performed previously. A show in my living room doesn't fit the bill. They want us to have a public performance, and moreover, to see a video of it. So I set my focus on that as the next step.

Ilaria is the expert on venues in Milan.

"There one place just near your *appartamento*," she says in her usual endearing mix of English and Italian. "I think it be perfect for BBB."

"Okay, great, let's go check it out."

We walk along Corso Magenta, a beautiful old street filled with chic boutiques and an old-world feel. I struggle on the slippery cobblestones in my heeled boots, wondering how the Milanese women elegantly prance along the same street in stilettos. A yellow tram rumbles toward us and we throw ourselves onto a narrow piece of footpath that is half-filled with mud. We enter a café. It has a long L-shaped bar, wooden tables and chairs. This is the venue.

The manager, a lady in her late 40s, only speaks Italian. "You won't perform up here," she says. "Come, follow me, I'll show you."

We go down a small spiral staircase into the dark. She flicks on some lights, illuminating a decent-sized rectangular room filled with tables and chairs. There's a stage at one end and a mirrored disco ball hanging from the center of the ceiling.

"It small," says Ilaria to me in English, "but it okay, no?"

"Well, I don't know how many people would come, so smaller the better. Nothing worse than an empty venue."

"*Certo*," says Ilaria in agreement.

"Here," I say, "if we have forty people in the audience, it will be good."

We book a date in two weeks' time, a Tuesday night in March. We don't think to ask for any money from the lady, we're just pleased that she agreed to have us perform here, and I am happy we don't have to pay rent to use the space.

Ilaria suggests we call our show "BBB LAIV." It's how Italians pronounce 'live,' and we all think it's funny – kitsch, ironic, and perfectly us, so that's what we name it.

With the help of Jia, who's savvy with graphic design, I prepare the flyer. It's a simple design with a large photo of us in the middle. We're all in a row, flirting with the camera, hands resting on each others' shoulders. Ilaria is leaning forward, blowing a kiss.

I send the flyer by email to everyone I know and anyone who I've collected business cards from during my time in Milan. Ilaria and Jia also send it to everybody they know. I print some of the flyers and we post them up at the venue and put some up at the most famous music store in Milan.

```
To: ilaria@milan.net; jia@bologna.edu
From: luna@yahoo.it
Hi guys,
We don't have much time before the show. Can we rehearse
this weekend? I think we should do a different third song
other than Kiss Me. I gather most of our audience will be
the same friends so it won't be so fun this time putting
on the wigs and singing the same song. Do you agree?
BBBaci xoxox
```

```
To: luna@yahoo.it; ilaria@milan.net
From: jia@bologna.edu
Hey girlies!
I have bad news. I'm completely behind with my studies.
I have a mid-term this week, and my professor wants to
see the first 10,000 words of my thesis, which I still
haven't finished. I can make it for the gig but will only
come a few days before to rehearse. Agree we shouldn't
do Kiss Me again.
Kiss
```

```
To: luna@yahoo.it; jia@bologna.edu
From: ilaria@milan.net
i have news. i just got accept new job. assistant booker
at E modeling!!! so now I busy all days. i come to rehearse
when i can. ciao bellas
```

We have our first public performance lined up and it seems BBB is like rice paper again, capable of being torn apart any second.

Meantime, the record company tells me they want us to record soon, even before signing the contract. I'm so pleased it's moving forward, but they book us into the studio for Tuesday afternoon, which is the afternoon right before our show. They seem to have no flexibility with dates. The flyers for our show are out and it's too late to change the date. What awful timing.

It is like the universe is testing whether we can hold it together, or whether we'll unravel before the curtain even rises.

CHAPTER 22

Surround yourself only with people who are going to lift you higher.

- Oprah Winfrey

"Hey, hey, hey!" says Harrison, hugging me when I pick him up from the airport.

He's so cheery, but I'm furious. We have the recording in the studio the next day, as well as our debut public show, and he arrives two days later than promised.

"The other girls haven't shown up yet because you didn't arrive," I say. "I hate leaving it all to the last minute."

That night the girls come over and for the first time since the show at my place, we start rehearsing.

The next day, Harrison joins Jia and me in the studio. Ilaria can't join us because she's at work so they'll have to record her voice another day.

Harrison insisted on putting his guitar in the trunk of my car, and now he wants to take it up to the studios.

"Why do you need your guitar?" I ask him.

"I always like to bring it along. You never know."

I wish he would remember that this is our day and we have a rushed schedule. I imagine he has visions of playing some of his own music to the music producer. It doesn't fit. It's a dance music label and while

139

Harrison is talented, his repertoire consists of melancholy ballads. I just don't see a place at our recording session for his music or his guitar.

"Okay, but please focus on getting us singing right?"

"Bella!" says Enrico, the music producer, as I enter. We kiss each other's cheeks like old friends.

"This is Jia," I say.

"Hey! So good to meet you, Jia," he says warmly and kisses her too.

"Enrico, this is Harrison. He's one of our singing teachers."

"Good to meet you," says Enrico, shaking his hand.

Jia excuses herself and goes into the next room to warm up her voice.

"It's a pity Ilaria isn't here," says Harrison to Enrico. "She has the strongest voice."

I give Harrison a look of death. "As we agreed," I say to Enrico, "she'll come one night after work that's convenient to you."

Harrison persists. "You likely want to rearrange the vocals of the song to make Ilaria the lead singer, and Jia and Luna backing singers."

"Harrison," I say as calmly as possible, "please, just leave it to Enrico."

"I thought Enrico would want my honest opinion," he says. "Ilaria's like Beyoncé in Destiny's Child."

"Enrico, you do what you want with the song. We've never considered having a lead singer. At the moment, as you know, we all sing equally, one verse each."

Fortunately, Enrico is called over by the mixing guy so I have a chance to give a piece of my mind to Harrison. I'm livid.

"What do you think you are doing?"

"Nothing, just telling him what I think."

"Well just remember that I'm the manager," I say. "If we're going to have a lead singer, BBB will discuss it as a group. Stop putting your ideas into Enrico's head."

"Ilaria's the only one of you with a natural singing voice," he says. "It's the way it's going to have to be."

"Well, if it's going to have to be that way, Enrico will decide that for himself," I say. "You are not our manager."

"But I know a lot more about singing than you do."

"True, but I know the girls' personalities better than you do. Believe me, it wouldn't be right to put that much responsibility on Ilaria right now. I can't get her to rehearsals or singing lessons, she's just started a full-time job at a modeling agency, she's always late, and here you are influencing the record producer to make her our lead vocal? What are you trying to do to me? I can't imagine having to rely on her more than I do already."

I feel flushed. I could almost cry. It's so unfair of Harrison to put himself in the middle of our record deal. Why did we invite him back? It's been six weeks since we saw him last, and a lot has happened. He can't just slip back over from London and act like the king of BBB.

Enrico comes back over and I'm sure he heard us arguing. I feel completely unprofessional. I invited Harrison along to our recording as our teacher, and now, instead of helping us, he's just stressing me out.

"Who's up first?" says Enrico.

"I'll go," I say. "Just give me a moment while I warm up." My voice is cracking from being near tears.

In the studio, I am taken to a soundproof room with a microphone. I sing through the song a few times. Suddenly, my inexperience feels blatant. Here I am in the swankiest of swanky studios, surrounded by hundreds of thousands of dollars' worth of equipment. I feel my voice isn't strong enough to carry through the whole song powerfully.

"Can I sing just one part at a time?" I ask Enrico. "You know, focus on a section and get it right before we move to the next."

He doesn't seem impressed. "Put the microphone up a bit higher," he advises. "You need to lengthen your neck."

My throat hurts, that's the truth of it. And mentally I'm not all there. I keep thinking over everything rather than focusing on hitting the right notes. My mind wanders to the conversation with Harrison, and then I think about what I have to do for the show that night. My thoughts keep swirling like a whirlpool. I still haven't even picked up our T-shirts with big Bs printed on the front of them and we need them for tonight's gig. I keep singing, breathing with my diaphragm – in, out, in, out. I could almost faint.

Enrico pastes all the best takes together and plays it back.

"I think it's really fine, Luna," says Jia through the microphone to me in the soundproof room.

"Where's Harrison?" I ask. "I'd like his opinion too."

"Not sure," she says. "I think he's in the stairwell smoking a cigarette."

I give up on Harrison. I ask Enrico to play it once more. I'm not sure if the "final cut" is great, but one thing is clear, I'm much better than I was at the studio in London. The singing lessons have paid off.

Jia goes next and I get out the video camera to record the moment. She attacks the song with confidence. We manage to enjoy the rest of the afternoon, working with the music crew, and then have to rush off to get ready for our show.

"Remember the show is at ten p.m.!" I say to Enrico as we run out.

"I don't think I can make it, but I try," he says.

On the way home, I make a detour to pick up the BBB T-shirts.

"Hi, I'm back!" I say, coming through the door of my apartment.

Jia comes out of the bathroom, her hair wrapped in a towel. "How do the T-shirts look?"

"Great. Come here, I'll show you." I lay out two rows of T-shirts on the dining table. Three are white, with big red Bs written on the front, the other three are tight, strapless black tops with the Bs printed in silver.

"They're really cool," says Jia. "Which are mine? I'll try them on."

"There's a size small for you in the white ones," I say, checking the tags. "Here it is." I pass it to her. "With the black ones, it's one size fits all, so take whichever."

Jia goes to her room to try on the tops. She comes back wearing jeans and the black strapless *B* top. She starts doing some of the "Come Get Naked With Me" choreography in front of the big mirror.

"Do you have a needle and thread?" she asks. "I'm afraid it's going to fall down."

"Sure, and please sew it as tight as you need," I say.

"Where's Ilaria?" asks Jia. "She should try on hers too."

"I'm gonna call her. She promised to be here by now."

By the time Jia and I are warming up our voices, dressed in jeans and the white T-shirts for the opening number with makeup and hair done, Ilaria arrives.

"You're so late," I say to her. "Try these on quickly, and we'll have to go straight to the venue."

"It fit fine," she says. "The black okay too."

I've hired a top-quality video camera for this evening and Shannon has agreed to film us. After all our hard work and expense, we have to start making money from this venture. A good video of us performing live is key to start securing paid gigs.

It's only our second show, and our first performance open to the public, but I feel excited and not nearly as nervous as last time.

"Let's go," I say. We have a brisk five-minute walk from my place to the venue. As we approach, we see there are people spilling out onto the street.

"*Cazzo!*" says Ilaria. "They all come to see us?"

"Try to ignore them." I give her a quick hug to show my excitement. "Remember we're meant to stay focused before we perform."

The venue is so jammed with people that we can hardly get through the door. Everyone is greeting us as we push through the crowd. Ilaria, Jia, and I hold each others' hands and we gradually make our way down the cramped spiral staircase. We enter the small room near the stage where we leave our change of clothes. We can hear the loud buzz outside, like a huge swarm of bees.

"You ready, guys?" I make a quick last check of our T-shirts, makeup, and hair.

"I think so," says Jia.

"*Merda*," says Ilaria. "Why we do this to ourselves?"

"It's gonna be great," I reply.

We walk on stage and Ilaria and Jia nod. They are ready to go. The music for "Elements" starts, and we perform the number without a hiccup. The crowd is completely animated, and dances along with us, especially when we do our synchronized hand movements during the chorus. Friends in the front row egg us on. I feel great up on the stage, not hesitating to make direct eye contact with the dark forest of faces before me. It seems like the whole of Milan is here.

Shannon is standing on a chair on the right-hand side of the stage, holding up the video camera. She gives me a huge grin as we finish the first number.

We leave the stage, and go to get changed for the next song. It still bothers me that we only have two songs to perform, but at least with the costume change we stretch out the show and provide some variety.

"I think that went great," I say once we're back in our changing room.

"Yeah, I really enjoyed it!" says Jia.

"Me too," says Ilaria. "You see how many people come to see us?"

"There must be about a hundred people," says Jia.

"We should have booked a bigger venue after all," I say. "Next time."

We put on the black strapless *B* tops with short black skirts and long black boots.

"The black BBB tops look really good, guys!" I say. "Ready?"

"*Si*," says Ilaria.

"Okay, but first, group hug." Jia puts her arms around me and Ilaria.

We huddle in a circle and shout, "Yay BBB!"

We wade through the crowd to the stage. The heat is stifling. The air feels thick. I see hands attached to arms reaching past a mob of bodies to touch us.

Up on stage, we hardly have our bearings when the music starts blaring. I sing the opening verse for "Get Naked."

"Hello, let me introduce myself to you ..." Adrenaline burns like acid as I propel myself into the number. The crowd is alive and pumping with everyone trying to get to the front, jumping up to see over each other's heads. I feel like a superstar.

The mirrored disco ball in the center of the ceiling is turning, leaving a patchwork of moving light across the walls of the room. Suddenly I feel dizzy. The air is steamy and smoky, but I continue to power through the motions.

We reach the chorus where we do our choreography in unison. We move our hands along the forms of our torsos, as we repeat the words, *"Come get naked with me, baby."*

The crowd's energy must be rubbing off on us, as we all put more and more gusto into our singing, *"Come get naked with me, baby, Come get naked with me, ah-ah-ah."*

I catch a glimpse of Ilaria's friends in the front row. Their dancing has slowed and they have a disturbed look. They start to point at Ilaria and make faces as if wanting to show something to her. Meanwhile, I continue to sing, trying to coordinate the slinky moves and keep a sexy smile on my face while attempting to work out what's going wrong. We hit the right notes and our dancing is fluid, but the crowd grows wild.

"Ilaria! Ilaria!" her friends in the front begin to chant.

I keep on glancing down at them and they look increasingly anxious. I make eye contact with a friend and she points to Ilaria and then points to her chest. She then covers her eyes with her hand.

I look over at Ilaria on the stage next to me.

Ilaria's black strapless top had slipped down. Her perfect breasts exposed to the crowd, like chocolate cupcakes. *Oh my goodness!*

For a split second, the world stopped. No music, no movement. I thought I'd feel panic.

The crowd whooped. Jia laughed. I shrugged and kept singing.

Maybe I was finally letting go.

— ele —

"Where's Harrison?" asks Jia. We're sitting in my lounge room, the evening after the show.

"I took him to the airport this afternoon," I say. "He apologized."

"I'm sorry that he came back," says Jia. "I know it was stressful for you."

"No worries," I say. "I got the name of a new singing teacher in Milan and she's meant to be really excellent."

"Luna, I so sorry," says Ilaria, breaking her silence. "For my top falling."

"What?" I say with a laugh. "Everyone thought we arranged it on purpose. It was like free publicity."

"*Veramente?*" she asks.

"Completely. You handled it so well. I was worried you were going to miss your solo, but you didn't."

"You managed to reach for the mic just in time," says Jia. "I would have been mortified, but you just pulled up your top and got back into it."

"Yeah," I say, "I think you were in your element. After our first show, many people said they wanted you more wild and so this time they certainly got it!"

"It only my bosom," says Ilaria, shrugging. She lifts her skinny arms and ruffles her curly brown hair.

"The cafe owner told me it's the last time we should perform for free," I say. "She thinks we're too good."

"My friends told me they had to pay five euros to enter," says Jia. "With that plus all the drinks they sold, the café must have made a killing because of us."

"They must to give us money," says Ilaria.

"That wasn't the deal," I say, "but I agree it was totally cheeky of them to charge everyone without telling us. Listen to this though – the cafe owner says we have serious interest from a lady who works with

146

television. She runs an agency that places entertainers on various TV shows and wants us to do a spot on" – I check my phone messages for the exact name – "*Top of the Pops*. Hang on, that is a British show."

"*Top of the Pops*?" says Ilaria in an almost screech. "We have Italian Top of the Pops, it on Mediaset. It the most popular music show. It on each Saturday. Everybody watch it."

"Wow, and we're set to have our TV debut on it!" I say.

"This is all moving so quickly," says Jia. "I still haven't even told my parents I'm doing the BBBs yet."

"Sounds like the time to tell them is approaching," I say. I can gather from Jia's expression that she doesn't think telling her parents will be an easy conversation.

If her parents don't approve of the band … would she have to walk away? I don't ask. I don't think I want to know.

CHAPTER 23

Life shrinks or expands in proportion with one's courage.

- Anais Nin

We are in the studios of Mediaset, the largest Italian national TV station. We're taken into a spacious dressing room where two makeup artists are waiting for us.

"So Ilaria, tell me what do we have to do?" I say, eager to find out what lies ahead for us. The agent who booked this gig for us couldn't understand my Italian over the phone and insisted on calling Ilaria.

"Something to do with Costantino," she says.

"Who is Costantino?" asks Jia.

"I've never heard of him," I say.

"He famous, like from reality show," says Ilaria.

"What does he have to do with us?" Jia asks me.

"I have no idea," I say, and show my palms up defensively. I turn to Ilaria, "I still don't know who Costantino is and what he has to do with our performance." Extracting any useful information out of Ilaria is like juicing a dried peach.

A man shouts in Italian to us through the dressing-room door.

"Music," says Jia. "He wants our music."

"Okay, I'll give it to him." I go to pass him the CD and he indicates for me to follow him. We walk along a gray corridor, passing numerous identical doors, and then reach what looks like a recording studio.

He gives the CD to a sound technician who places it in a disc drive.

"There's two songs here, which one?" the technician asks me in very fast Italian.

"*La prima canzone*," I say, dreading that they too might have trouble understanding me.

"Okay," he says, listening to the track. "Which thirty seconds do you want to use?"

I quickly go over the choreography and song breakdown of "Elements" in my head. I ask him to start at the chorus toward the end when we are all singing together. He edits it and plays it back to me for my okay. It sounds good.

I make my way back down the corridor to the other girls. They greet me, faces covered with what seems to be half an inch of heavy makeup.

"Wow," I say. "Looking amazing."

"It feels awful," says Jia. "I wish I could scratch it off."

"These makeup artists know what they're doing," I say. "I'm sure it'll look really great on TV."

"The show coordinator gave us these scripts," says Jia. "I'm really not sure about it."

"Script? We have to say something?" I ask.

"We sure do," says Jia. "They said that first we will sing in what looks like a rehearsal studio, and then the show host will enter to ask us about a product."

"It's an advertisement?"

"Yes, it's for cards with photos of Costantino on them. I think it's really cheesy," says Jia. "I'm really not sure we should be doing this."

I look over at Jia, seeing her disappointment. For her, this segment probably feels like a betrayal of all the serious ambitions her parents have for her. I don't blame her.

149

"But we're here now," I say, "and they're counting on us. I think it's too late to pull out."

"I know, but it seems so tacky," says Jia.

"Let me see the script," I say and Jia passes one of the pages to me.

"*Com'e bello Costantino...*" I read. "We have to say how good-looking this guy is? We sound like teenagers."

"And what is *la fanastica Maxibusta di Costantino?*" asks Jia, reading her copy.

"Sounds like a type of bra," I say.

"Maxibusta is the cards, with his pictures," says Ilaria. "I see them on TV before."

"Well, what do *you* think?" I ask Ilaria. "You're Italian. Is this as bad as it seems?"

"He a huge Italian heartthrob. It not so bad."

"Okay, it might not be the best exposure for BBB," I say, "but it's better than none. Right?"

"I'll do it if you want to," says Jia.

We are taken to the studio. There are three cameramen, light technicians, and sound technicians already waiting for us. As soon as I enter the set, I feel the heat – the lights are brutal. I begin to sweat. There's a woman with a makeup compact in hand who regularly comes up to us to dab powder on our faces.

There are glossy, life-sized photographs of Costantino erected behind our microphone stands. He seems to have a permanent two-day growth, and wears a thick silver chain around his neck. In one picture, he's lying on a zebra-skin sofa with a pumped-up bicep behind his head. His white shirt is open, exposing a tan, hairless chest. His generous crotch is bulging.

HOST: *E chi e la piu innamorata di Costantino* [And who is the most in love with Costantino?]

LUNA (eagerly): *Io! Ho 68 photocards e 92 ministickers!* [I have 68 photocards and 92 stickers!]

ILARIA (defiantly): *Hupf! Io di photocards di Costantino ne ho 120 ... e di stickers 97!* [Ha! I have 120 photocards and 97 stickers!]

JIA (disappointed): *Io ho solo 4 photocards e 12 ministickers ...* [I only have 4 photocards and 12 ministickers ...]

Argghhhh!!! All I can do is cringe.

As the hours pass, I get used to the idea. At least it isn't in English. Doing it in Italian makes it more bearable. Also, we find out we'll be paid 300 euros, which is a small start, but a big step as BBB's first earnings.

We agree to do takes for two commercials. We do our thirty seconds of dancing and lip-syncing and they tell us it's fine after the second take. Then we end up in the studio for about another five hours, painfully standing in heels, recording the advertisements.

When it's over, I say, "Thanks, guys, for sticking it out and doing it."

"Yeah, it wasn't so bad," says Jia.

"At least we had our BBB T-shirts on, and the host introduced us as BBB, so who knows, something might come of it."

"And we get our first BBB money!" says Ilaria.

"Exactly," I say. "Let's catch a taxi home to celebrate."

"Yay BBB!" Ilaria and Jia shout.

I laugh to myself, chalking the day up as yet another entry in our ever-growing list of BBB Bloopers. Jia is heading back to Bologna the next morning, and in a few days, Ilaria and I are booked in for our first lesson with Fabiola, one of the most respected vocal coaches in Milan.

One thing is crystal clear: if I want to avoid more mix-ups, I need to level up my Italian.

I take a moment to jot down my next goals:

1. Book more gigs in Milan – paid only.
2. Start putting together a great summer tour.
3. Finally become fluent in Italian – time to invest in private lessons.

Romance is on the back burner. I have a girl band to hold together.

Fabiola enters the room, striding in her khaki pants toward the keyboard. She puts down her lime-green plastic handbag and starts playing around with the switches on my keyboard mixer.

"I'll get that for you. You just want regular piano sound, right?" I ask.

"Yes, thanks. Nice place," she says, looking around at the microphones and speaker system. "You got it all set up here, don't you?" She rolls a fair hand through her short bright-orange hair. She definitely doesn't look like any of the Milanese girls I have encountered before, and her English is impeccable.

"There'll be some shows coming up," I say. "We need to sing live confidently. That's what we're working toward."

"And the other group members?"

"Jia lives in Bologna, but Ilaria should be here any moment." *Perhaps I'm too optimistic that Ilaria will be punctual.*

She looks at her watch. "Well, let's start. I can do a warm-up with her when she arrives." Fabiola tries out a scale on the keyboard, adjusting the volume. She then asks me to sing along.

"*Ah-ah-ah-ah-ah-ah-ah-ah.*" Our voices rise in unison.

"Now, on your own."

"*Ah-ah-ah-ah-ah-ah-ah-ah.*"

"Good." She plays the scale again, this time a note higher.

"*Ah-ah-ah-ah-ah-ah-ah-ah.*" I go on, singing higher and higher. "*Ah-ah-ah-ah-ah-ah-ah-ahaaa.*" My voice breaks on the last note.

"It's not too high," Fabiola insists. "You have to be more clever than the note. Just pretend you're going to sing lower, but trick your voice and actually sing higher. So your brain says lower, but your voice is going higher. Okay? Try again."

"*Ah-ah-ah-ah-ah-ah-ah-ah.*" I'm shocked. "It worked! That's crazy." We finish the scales.

"I need to check your breathing," says Fabiola, getting very close. She puts one hand on the small of my back and the other on my stomach. I know singing teachers often need to touch your diaphragm or posture, but her face is rammed up against mine and her breath caresses my cheek. I wish Ilaria would arrive. I'm not used to this kind of body contact.

"Breathe!" she yells at me. "I'm not doing this because I enjoy it. I need to teach you how to respirate properly. Now push that diaphragm. Your lungs should be full of air when you are singing. Your stomach might not look so good sticking out, but it should be out. Now push."

She then gives me a series of exercises that I have to do lying on the floor. She asks me to put the heaviest book I own on my stomach. The book happens to be the English-Italian dictionary, and I'm supposed to make it rise and fall.

I have officially entered the world of singing boot camp.

"Get up now. I want you to sing a song for me," she says.

"I have no idea where Ilaria is," I say. "Just a moment, I'll call her."

Ilaria answers the phone. It sounds like she's still at home.

"She says she's on her way," I tell Fabiola.

"*Va bene*. Now, which song would you like to sing? I have many to choose from."

I flick through the pages of her huge, alphabetized binder. "What about Christina Aguilera's 'Beautiful'? But it's hard, no?"

"Let's try," she says. "It should be fine." She puts the backing track into the CD player, gives me a cue, and I start singing.

"*Every day is so wonderful* ..."

I hate listening to my voice. It sounds muted like it's on low volume and there's no strength. I kick myself that I chose this song. How could I even hope to sing a song sung by Christina Aguilera?

"We have a problem here," says Fabiola.

"I know, my pitch."

"Luna, you hit the notes fine. Pitch is not the problem. You're making the most common of all mistakes. You're singing like a little girl – without confidence. You need to sing like a woman." She goes back to the keyboard and we're back to doing scales.

"*Ma ma ma ma ma!*" Fabiola sings loudly along with the notes. "Okay, now you do the same. You are shouting to your mother. Ma!"

"Ma," I say.

"No, really shout it out. It has to come from inside," she says. "Shout – Ma!"

"Ma."

"More!"

"Ma!"

"That's better but now louder. Imagine she's at the other end of the house and you want her to hear. Ma!"

"MA!"

"Perfect. That is your voice. Follow after me, *Ma-ma-ma-ma-ma!*"

"*Ma-ma-ma-ma-ma.*"

"No. Louder!"

"*Ma-ma-ma-ma-MA!*"

This is the most physically challenging singing lesson I have ever done. I don't know if I like the sound of my voice when it's shouting, but it feels satisfying. The voice is really coming from within me. We continue practicing the "Ma" and then go back to the song.

"You have to concentrate to keep that voice we just found. Sing loud. Sing confident. You can reach all the notes – you did in the scales."

"Okay."

"Stand very tall, feet apart, take a deep breath, and focus on your diaphragm. Breathe regularly when you sing and get that voice out. Keep shouting to your mother, but use the words of the song. Ready?"

"Yes," I say, completely nervous, trying to concentrate on everything at the same time.

The doorbell rings. Ilaria! It's the worst timing. I was so focused to try out the song, and now she's ruined the momentum. I look at my watch, surprised to see there's only ten minutes of the two-hour lesson left. *Why did Ilaria bother coming so late?*

I open the door to let her in, but I don't kiss her hello or crack a smile. I run back to my post next to Fabiola and the keyboard, ready to sing.

"I so sorry. My parent—" she starts.

"Sit there," Fabiola says, pointing to a chair. "You've missed the whole class. Don't say a word. Luna, would you prefer her in another room?"

Fabiola's reaction makes me grin. Fabiola's such a character, treating Ilaria as if she's in primary school. "No, it's okay," I say. "She can stay."

The music starts. Fabiola nods – my cue to start.

I sing, "*Every day is so wonderful* ..."

Ilaria looks at me open-mouthed. I am belting it out. My voice sounds rather forced in parts and I miss some notes, but I'm actually singing with power. I am singing like a woman who knows she has something to say.

We go through the song twice and the lesson is over. I thank Fabiola, schedule a lesson with her for the following week, and she leaves.

"You sound so different," says Ilaria, obviously impressed.

"Yeah, I think Fabiola is amazing. I've tapped into my voice – finally."

"I want to sing like that too," says Ilaria. "Next week I be on time to the class."

Despite the record company not having returned my calls for a few weeks, now I am feeling more confident about the future for BBB.

CHAPTER 24

Failure is only a temporary change in direction to set you straight for your next success.

- Denis Waitely

Just as I finally stopped chasing romance, it started chasing me. The girl band was finding its rhythm again, and I couldn't remember feeling this good about my love life in a long time. Italian men are a curious mix: intense one minute, vanish the next, then they reappear. Completely unreliable, but so disarmingly charming with "Bella," "Bellissima," "Cara," and other gorgeous expressions that it makes it easy to forgive them if they disappear for a while. Honestly, with the number of men calling me these days, it's the only way I can fit them all in.

There's a handsome university professor, an American masseuse, and a Sicilian lawyer called Salvatore who makes me laugh, and when in Italy ... why not see an Italian? Salvatore loves Milan's cocktail bars and clubs. We enjoy many evenings out together. His friends are effortlessly charming, always with a joke or a toast, and I am happy to drift along for the ride.

My life is a good mix of work and play. And, as if with a radar that can sense when I am getting other male attention, I get a text from Marek:

```
I am thinking about you, great memories, sending you
million kisses, puppy ;-) Come see me? Wooof  Marek 20:19
```

I pause, staring at the message. A part of me still feels the tug, but I don't answer. Not tonight. I'm meeting Salvatore.

Salvatore looks unmistakably Italian – tanned skin, expressive brown eyes, and thick dark hair that never seems out of place, even after a night out. He's originally from Sicily, and it shows in the way he gestures when he talks, in the music of his voice, and in the poetry he brings to each message he writes me.

He dresses conservatively with well-cut shirts, polished shoes, and always a neat blazer – but there's a lightness about him that softens the edges. He has a sharp legal mind and a solid, comfortable job, but you'd never know it from the way he tells a story. Salvatore is always smiling, always joking, always ready to turn an ordinary evening into a celebration. He's the kind of man who dances without shame, orders tequila shots for the table, and somehow knows the name of every bartender in Milan.

We are at Cavalli Café, and seek refuge outside on the lounges. The evening is warm and soft, the kind that makes you forget cities can be loud. Salvatore leans back on his elbows, grinning.

"Have I ever told you about Vulcano?" he asks, raising an eyebrow like he's about to deliver a bedtime story and a sales pitch all at once.

"No," I say. "Sounds intense."

He laughs. "Vulcano is one of the Aeolian Islands, near where I grew up. Black sand beaches, sulfur baths that make your skin feel like you were to be born yesterday."

"Tempting," I say.

"The ancient Romans thought Vulcano was the chimney of the god of fire. People still go there to sit in bubbling mud and come out glowing."

I love the way he tells stories.

"Vulcano has character. Drama," Salvatore says, lifting his glass. "Like that Sicilian cousin you can't quite trust, but wouldn't dream of throwing a party without."

I clink his glass. "Sounds like you."

"Ilaria is great," says Shannon as we watch *Top of the Pops* on TV the following Saturday. "She's a talented actress."

"I agree – she's a natural, and she looks fabulous. They did a great job on her makeup."

"Why isn't she here?"

"She's got her whole family coming over to her place to watch the show. They're even wheeling in her ninety-year-old grandmother who just got out of hospital. She said all her aunts and uncles are coming and they're going to have a meal together afterward."

"Being on TV is such a big deal in Italy. It's part of the '*bella figura.*' The Italians say that only the most attractive women are on television so it's considered a big compliment."

"I'm just glad Ilaria's parents seem to support BBB," I say. "Meanwhile, Jia is pleased her parents are in China so there's no chance they'll see her on TV."

"She still hasn't told them?" Shannon's eyebrows lift up toward her hairline.

"She wants this venture as far away from their conservative Chinese values as possible. She's behind in her thesis and might have to extend her studies an extra semester. Jia certainly doesn't want them to have BBB to blame."

Bing. A text message comes in.

Allora grande amica di costantino … quando mi firmi un
autografo?? Mauro 14:08 (So, great friend of Costantino, when
will you sign your autograph for me?)

"The cheek!" I pass Shannon the phone to read it. "He's the guy from
the band I told you about."

I get a flood of similar messages.

"Well, at least we did the TV show," I say. "A bit of fun and recognition.
Since that, things have fallen completely flat. The only thing we have
lined up is an unpaid gig in Bologna at Jia's university ball."

"Have you had any luck getting in touch with the record company?"

"I called the music producer, and he said he has no idea why Dario
isn't returning my calls. Likely too busy."

"That's promising," Shannon says. "At least he didn't say the record
deal was off …"

"But we had our last proper conversation six weeks ago when he said
he was sending over a summary contract. That's a long time … I want
some kind of explanation."

"Of course you do, but isn't it just typical Italy?"

"I suppose so, but I tell you, I hate being on the receiving end."

"No worries, Luna, things will improve," she says. "Just remember, to
every low there's a high."

I hope she's right.

It's late April and we're in Bologna. We have the gig at Jia's university
ball. It'll be the first time we perform four songs.

The night of the ball, we have an early dinner with friends, then drive
up a long, winding road. The venue is a castle just outside Bologna, with
a stunning yellow facade and immaculate grounds.

The ball has already begun and we start mingling.

"It's ten thirty, guys. We better go and get ready," says Jia.

"Yeah," I reply. "We better hurry if they want us to perform at eleven."

"*In bocca al lupo!*" our friends say in unison. It's the Italian expression for good luck, but it means literally "in the mouth of the wolf."

When we get on stage, the crowd is completely animated, singing along to the songs and dancing.

We do a version of ABBA's "Gimme Gimme" as our fourth and final song. We put on wigs and feather boas and go wild on the stage. We have a great time laughing and sweating under the heat of the lights and wigs. This song captures BBB at its best. When I think back to my original visions for a girl band with boas and big hair, it could not be closer than our interpretation of this song.

As I look out at the animated crowd, I drink in the feeling. The show is a huge success.

To every low, there's a high. Shannon was right.

CHAPTER 25

There is one thing that gives radiance to everything.
It's the idea of something around the corner.

- G. K. Chesterton

The record company still hasn't shown us a contract, and we can only assume the deal is off. The record deal falling through is a big blow to Ilaria. She seems disillusioned with BBB and doesn't show up to singing lessons again. My savings are dwindling and I start to wonder whether this whole Milan experience is worth it. Something is crying out to me that it's time to make some financial and personal changes, if not for my sanity then for the future of my bank account.

Corporate Luna: Go back to New York already! You're done.

Creative Luna: Keep your dream alive, but make some positive changes. You can do this!!

I've gone this far with BBB, and I resolve to make this work.

Bob calls me from New York.

"How've you been?" he asks. Although he is in his late sixties, his voice always sounds so young and steadfast. "We miss you here."

161

He's so adorably paternal. Who else would have an ex-boss like this? I feel so fortunate. How could I have left such a great boss to then deal with this unstable girl band and fickle music industry?

"How's the band going?" he asks.

"Good. We've done quite a few shows."

"There's an opening for you in our new London office. We'd love to have you back working for us. They really need you there."

"Bob, that's such a lovely offer." I hesitate. "I'll consider."

"You could do the girl band on the side? I saw the photos you sent. It's a very nice looking, multicultural group you have there."

"Thanks."

"You know we have our annual party in London next month. Why don't you girls perform?"

Now he's talking! "That would be amazing."

What a break for BBB! A gig in London will be a great experience. Also, I know Bob well enough that even with no mention of money this means our first properly paid show, as well as expenses. I feel a huge rush of excitement.

He continues, "We have the renowned professor in global finance, Michael Goldstein, giving a speech. I can introduce you as a new twist on the international economy."

"Bob, that sounds perfect," I say, loving his idea to leverage our diverse backgrounds. I start trying to picture our show in my head. "How many songs should we do?"

He thinks for a moment. "Just two. It's a cocktail party and we always have a string quartet. I don't want to smother the business talk with live music, so just do something short, fun, and colorful."

Short, fun, and colorful. Okay. I repeat the words in my head. Short, fun, and colorful.

CHAPTER 26

A good goal is like a strenuous exercise – it makes you stretch.

- Mary Kay Ash

The reality of us doing the show in London sinks in. We're going to have to perform live in front of around four hundred people and prepare two new suitable songs. This will be a conservative event and there's no way we can do any of the songs we've previously performed – they're either too camp or would be more suited to a party in Ibiza.

I call Fabiola immediately, and the next day she brings over a selection of songs. Jia also starts brainstorming and sends me songs to download and listen to. We finally decide on two well-known Italian songs from the eighties, "Tropicana" and "Primavera." We're an Italian group after all, so in London it will be something original if we sing in Italian. Also, they are both songs with a great summer feel, so they'll be handy to have in our repertoire for the summer tour I plan to arrange.

Jia comes to Milan so we can start practicing the new songs. I send Ilaria a message letting her know what's going on.

"Ilaria still hasn't replied to me," I say to Jia as we go over the songs in my apartment.

"Don't worry. She knows about the show and she's on board," says Jia. "We still have weeks."

163

"I know we have some time, but it's a paid show and we're getting flown all the way to London for it. It's going to be a serious business crowd that expects a quality act."

"She'll be fine."

"Jia, the thought of relying on Ilaria makes me feel uneasy," I admit. "You know I adore her, but this show means a lot to me. All the top executives I used to work with in New York are going to be there. Also, I'm really keen to get our summer tour organized, and I just don't think Ilaria's serious about BBB."

"She needs to be a part of the group. She'll get it together."

"I know. I really want her in the group too," I say. "But I need her to communicate and come to singing lessons."

Over the last days, I had conjured up Corporate Luna's help.

Corporate Luna: Make a change, and do it now. This gig means a lot to you and BBB. You don't have time to waste.

"I've been thinking a lot about it and I have a solution," I say. "We have to find a fourth member before this London gig. We need someone with a good voice who can carry the vocals and who's a confident performer."

Jia doesn't look pleased.

"Think," I continue. "If there are four up on the stage, it's going to take the pressure off all of us. So it might actually make things easier."

"Yes, but more difficult when we have four schedules to work around," says Jia, in her usual, practical way.

"It needs to be someone who's really committed and definitely some-one who lives in Milan," I say. "I'm here all alone doing BBB stuff, and it just doesn't feel like I'm part of a group."

"I can understand, Luna," says Jia. "But we always prided ourselves on our special energy and being friends. With a new person it would all change. With another girl, it might not be so good."

"I totally agree that it needs to be someone who we all gel with, but I need a fourth girl or I know I'm going to be too nervous wondering if Ilaria is going to be late, or refuse to rehearse."

"Okay," she says. "I support your decision."

I'm on a serious hunt for some talent to join BBB. I spread the word through friends and our singing and dancing teachers that we're looking for someone with a Mediterranean vibe. A girl who will blend naturally into our multicultural group and who is a confident singer. The plan is that I do the first round of auditions, and then on a Saturday in two weeks' time Jia will come back to Milan and we'll hold final auditions that day together.

This is Italy, so I thought finding a dark-haired, olive-skinned candidate would be easy, but the auditions are officially a nightmare.

Margarita

From Spain – great

Looks – not very Mediterranean – not great

Recommended by my singing teacher as having a strong voice – great

Knows how to dance flamenco – great

Described as having a free spirit – not so great

Canceled the first date set for the audition – not so great at all

We reschedule and then she was late – bad

Personality – dynamite

Dorota

Looks – cute

Voice – meek but good

Professional dancer – great

Personality – shy

Do I see her in the group? – possibly not

Olga

Looks – okay

Figure – great

Personality – really nice

Voice – operatic

Do I see her in the group? – no

Filomena

Looks – good

Dancer – yes!

Voice – flat

Enthusiasm – zero

Scrap

Gina

Recommended through our dancing teacher – great

Wants to meet in three weeks' time – no good

Scrap

Finding someone who would blend well with us is a difficult feat. Ilaria oozes raw talent, Jia is simply adorable, and while the girls I audition are more technically trained, they don't seem to have the right personality. Or, like Margarita, they are completely unreliable before they've even begun.

I haven't heard from Jia in days but it seems that she's been doing her own work behind the scenes. She calls me.

"Luna, my good friend in Sicily has a cousin who lives in Milan. Her name is Antonella – she's pretty and apparently a really good singer. She used to be in a band, so she's got experience."

"That sounds great!" The idea of a friend of a friend, especially a friend of Jia's, sounds ideal.

"We should still meet the other girls," she says. "But why don't I ask Antonella to come on Saturday to meet us?"

"Can she come here to meet me before?" I'm dying to meet this girl. It sounds like she could be the answer.

"No, she wants to meet you when I'm there. She doesn't speak English, but she says she can sing in English if needed so that's no problem."

"Even better," I say. "We're supposed to be Italian anyway. Arrange to meet her at the time that suits and if we have other auditions I'll work around it."

"What do you mean, *if* we have other auditions? I thought you'd have ten people lined up by now. What's happening?"

"Only a few slight possibilities so far, but I have a few more to come."

"Okay. Well, good luck with it all. I'll email you what time Antonella will be there. Oh, and did Ilaria call you yet?"

"No."

"She told me she would. Don't worry. I'll make sure she's there on Saturday," says Jia.

Jia arrives at my apartment at midday on Saturday. Then, soon after, Ilaria arrives in her usual bounding fashion.

Wearing tight jeans and a hot pink T-shirt, Ilaria looks as effortlessly fabulous as ever – her hair perfectly tousled and lips glossed.

"I haven't seen you in ages, Ilaria," I say, giving her an awkward hug.

There is an unusual silence.

"With the group, can you commit?" I ask.

"*Sì*, I still want be in BBB."

"You know I've been auditioning for a fourth member."

"*Sì*."

"Are you prepared to learn new songs and rehearse for the show in London?"

"*Sì*," she says and nods her head several times as if to convince me. "I know the songs. They in Italian. It be fine. I will come to all rehearsing."

The doorbell rings.

"That must be Antonella," Jia says and gets up to go to the door.

"What she like?" Ilaria asks me.

"I've never met her before," I say.

Antonella and Jia walk in.

"This is Antonella," Jia says in Italian.

Antonella says, *"Piacere."* (Pleased to meet you.). She looks at me and nods with a big white grin.

She has a beautiful face with large features, long straight black hair, and baggy, low-waisted jeans weighed down by a chunky black leather and metal belt. She has a striking figure with a tomboy swagger that works perfectly with her bold look. She's tall, but I can see she's not as tall as Jia. Antonella sits down in an armchair and they all start rattling on in Italian as Jia and Ilaria ask Antonella how long she's been in Milan, where she lives, and where she's from in Sicily.

"Are you following with us speaking Italian okay?" Jia asks me.

"I am understanding well," I say. "Antonella speaks very clearly." I presume the last months of intensive private Italian lessons have finally paid off. Then I direct a question to Antonella in Italian. "What's your singing experience?"

I remember back to Jia's "interview." I had asked her this question when I first met her in Bologna over six months ago. As much as I love Jia, the group certainly isn't at the stage anymore where I would accept the answer that she likes singing for herself. We need someone who has performed previously.

"I did shows with a band at parties," she answers me in Italian. "I was the lead singer. I love performing."

Bingo!

"And have you done any dance classes?" I ask.

"No. I like to dance, but I never did lessons."

"That's fine," I say. "Our dance moves are simple. Did you prepare a song for us?"

"Just in Italian."

"Great, I look forward to hearing it," I say.

She hands me a disc that I put in the player and she stands up facing us with the CD cover in hand, reading the words as she sings. She has a powerful voice that resonates over the CD, and I can see by the way she moves and sings in time that she has great rhythm. I like her gutsy style. She certainly has a Sicilian flair that will complement the group.

"She's been rehearsing all week," says Jia to me in a whisper. "She really wants to be a part of BBB."

I look over to Ilaria and I can see she too is impressed by Antonella.

"Such a good voice," she says.

Antonella certainly is very attractive with her large eyes, full lips, and rosy cheeks. Her voice is very strong and that's the trait we need for BBB most imminently.

Antonella sings two songs and then sits down again, breathing deeply. I can see the girls have warmed to her, and I know having the cousin of Jia's good friend join the group would allay any fears of the group losing that "special energy."

"Luna, when will we be able to tell Antonella the decision?" asks Jia. "You need a few days to think it over?"

"If you guys agree, I'm happy to take her on now," I say.

Ilaria nods and Jia translates the news to Antonella.

"*Si! Grazie, Luna,*" says Antonella standing up and giving me a hug. "*Grazie, grazie!*"

We all stay around chatting and in the excitement we decide that our summer tour is going to be in Sicily. Antonella has many contacts there, Jia has friends, and I'm sure Salvatore's Sicilian crowd would help us out. It seems to be the ideal place to go.

Antonella said her cousin could do some PR for us in Palermo. Also, as Sicily is rather compact, we wouldn't have to move far. So, logistically it seems to be a relatively easy place for us to get started, and best of all, it's a cheap destination. Even if we don't get many gigs, we're cutting our losses by going there rather than somewhere more expensive. Everyone seems thrilled by the idea. So am I. *Summer tour in Sicily, yay!*

After Antonella leaves, Jia, Ilaria, and I chat. It's like nothing ever changed – Ilaria's back to her bubbly, fun self.

We have two more auditions scheduled for that afternoon, but neither of the girls shows up. Italy! Only time will tell whether Antonella is reliable, but having her on board immediately makes me feel so much more relaxed. New days ahead for BBB.

"I'm really glad you like Antonella," says Jia.

"Thank you for the great introduction."

"I don't know how photogenic she is though. I've never seen any photos of her."

"She's very pretty. She'll be fine," I say. "That reminds me, let's work out a date for the next photo shoot. We need photos, and quick."

"Who'll take them?" asks Jia.

We both look at Ilaria. Perhaps Lorenzo again?

"It a very long story," says Ilaria, "but no, it completely over with him. I cannot to ask him."

So that's what was going on. Suddenly, her flakiness over the last weeks made sense. I can imagine Ilaria would have been distraught if her and Lorenzo had a falling out.

"No problem," I say. "Why don't I just ask Shannon to take them? We can go back to Porta di Ticinese. It's a fun spot for photos like that first shoot with Valentina."

"Okay," says Jia. "Good idea."

Yay! BBB!

170

CHAPTER 27

Do not fear mistakes – there are none.

- Miles Davis

Antonella is great to have on board. Rehearsals are going well with her and we spend an afternoon looking in shops, getting some ideas for a dress theme for the London show.

I soon realize, however, that even Antonella is a very free Italian spirit and not always available when she says she is. Both Antonella and Ilaria turn up to rehearsals intermittently.

"It's the Italian way, Luna, nothing personal," Shannon reassures me. I'm grateful to have Shannon around. "Isn't it your birthday next week?" she asks.

"Yes," I confirm. "It's my thirty-second birthday." Thirty-two already? The number felt surreal, like I'd skipped a few chapters without noticing. *Where is time going?*

I decide on a tropical theme for my party, so everyone comes looking festive in brightly colored clothes. I've decorated the house with flowers, moved all the furniture so there's a large open space in the living area, and rolled up the rugs. I have a kind of surfer-beach girl look going on with long and wavy blonde hair, a short aqua skirt with a multicolored hibiscus print, skimpy white T-shirt, and a frangipani behind my ear. As people enter, I put Hawaiian leis around their necks.

I've placed a blender and stacks of cocktail ingredients on a large table in the living room, letting anyone who wishes to make a concoction play bartender. All kinds of fresh fruit mixed with alcohol is going into the blender. I have also pre-made two huge bowls of a very dangerously strong vodka punch.

Ilaria is on form and I'm so glad she's there in her top party spirit. Pink is the fashionable color this season, so she is pink-pink-pink. She wears a short pink tulle tutu skirt and a bright -pink top. She even has little pink shoes that look like ballet slippers, and a tiny pink handbag.

Ilaria immediately gets the party warmed up by dancing. Shannon and I sip cocktails as we watch her move around the floor. We admire her high energy, as always, she is so extraverted and entertaining.

Soon Ilaria and I perform our new song, "Tropicana," although it's a pity Antonella is away, and Jia couldn't come from Bologna as she has classes. Throughout the evening, Ilaria and I keep coming back to our little "show." I'm happy – at least it's an indirect way to get Ilaria rehearsing. I love her on nights like this in full party mode, but still in the back of my mind I'm thinking about how we need to prepare for our first serious paid gig, and we need to get our performance right.

By three a.m. my whole apartment has run dry of food and alcohol. There are still masses of people dancing and the parquet floor is covered with a layer of dirt. I'm barefoot and there's a thick black crust embedded into the soles of my feet. My once-tidy apartment has fully transformed into a grungy nightclub – pulsing music, and sticky cocktails spilling into corners.

More people keep arriving after three a.m., even though it's a Wednesday night. They bring more alcohol with them so everyone else stays. I have been dating Salvatore from Sicily on and off for a few months. I don't see him leaving, but soon I know he's gone because his younger brother tries to kiss me. "That's not right," I say to him. "Italy!" I think to myself, laughing. Everyone else stays drinking and dancing until six o'clock in the morning.

Ilaria starts turning up to rehearsals again and helps Antonella with the dance moves. The BBB girls are all in great spirits, and I couldn't be happier. I buy myself a bicycle and I cycle about in the sun. It is the best way to get around the city, and I regularly ride through Parco Sempione, thoroughly enjoying its leafy paths and soaking up the majestic beauty of Milan.

For our new BBB flyers, we go with a very simple theme: colored T-shirts and jeans. Shannon does a great job at the photo shoot and we have some surprisingly fabulous photos together outside in the sun in front of some bright but tattered posters at Porta di Ticinese. It's a very urban look.

We previously used a red logo of three Bs in a circle on our promotional material. I start using a version with a big yellow ball, like the sun, behind the red Bs. After all, summer is on its way, and the red and yellow together is very eye-catching.

We have many fun performances lined up for the summer, and all are paid gigs. Massimo asks us to perform at his fortieth birthday party in Como, and my uncle at his sixtieth birthday party in Provence. I line up a couple of shows at a local bar, Le Trottoir, which is famous in Milan for live music. Two other very cool and well-known Milanese venues, Executive Lounge and The Rocket, also express interest to have us perform. July is going to be busy. Then we plan to be on tour in Sicily for most of the month of August.

Before we know it, we're in London. It's a very hot June afternoon. We enter the traditional English-style palace that has been rented for Bob's business cocktail party. It's an incredibly elegant sandstone building with frescos covering the high ceilings, original eighteenth-century tapestries and artwork lining the walls, and a large terrace outside overlooking an enormous park.

The rehearsal goes well, and I'm very pleased. There's a guy who helps us with the sound, and he assures me he'll be there for us later when we do the show. Lachlan and some other members of my family watch us rehearse, and they all give us the big thumbs-up.

We go to our spacious dressing room where Olivia is waiting to help us out and to give us a proper vocal warm-up before the show. We put on our clothes and I study our reflection in the mirror.

"I think our outfits look like a mishmash. What do you think, Olivia?" I ask.

"Well," she says, not looking convinced at all by our attire, "Luna, you are the only one who is wearing a dress, so you stick out."

During a rushed shopping trip before the show, we couldn't find a suitable and affordable white dress for Ilaria. She's wearing a white miniskirt and white top.

"What can I do?" I ask. "I have no other clothes with me except jeans."

"You could all wear jeans," Olivia offers.

"Have you seen this venue? No way!" I cry. "It's going to be full of conservative business people in suits. There is absolutely no way we're wearing jeans."

"I don't want to wear this white top," Ilaria exclaims. "It ugly." She reaches into her bag and takes out a lacy, dusty-pink camisole.

"None of what we are wearing looks particularly good together, but the white top is much better than the camisole," I say, trying my best to keep calm.

"I not care. I wear this," she says, putting on the lacy camisole.

I look at our reflection in the mirror, and our supposedly coordinated outfits just went from "not great" to a "real jumble."

"Please, Ilaria," I beg, holding up the discarded white top.

"You not tell me what to wear," she says.

A saving grace – a waiter comes in with a silver platter loaded with delicious nibbles, a bottle of French champagne, and five elegant champagne flutes. I usually have a policy of no alcohol before a show, but this evening I think we all need it. We open the bottle at seven thirty p.m. and use the last half hour to take some deep breaths and regroup.

"I so sorry," says Ilaria, giving me a hug. She is still wearing her lace camisole and seems happy again.

It is eight p.m. and the speeches start. The staff ask us to wait near the stage. All my present and past lives are in the room – banking Luna, creative Luna, and ambitious Luna. If there was ever a moment to prove this dream was worth chasing, it's now.

The speeches go on and on and on and on. A Professor Emeritus Chair in Global Finance who must be ninety-something years old is mumbling, and I'd be surprised if anyone can understand a word he's saying. We've been standing in heels for close to an hour. Our nerves are escalating with every extra moment. Finally, I hear our cue.

Bob, the party host, says, "And now for an alternative twist on the international economy, we have very special guests – BBB, a girl group from Milan."

We are called up onto the stage and simultaneously, much to my dismay, most of the four-hundred-strong audience run outside to the bar area on the large terrace to fill up on champagne and food because they've been stuck in the hot room for so long listening to the speeches.

Our backing track music for "Primavera" starts and the sound levels seem all wrong. We can hardly hear the music. The guy in charge of the sound isn't there. *Damn!* Antonella is meant to do some ohhhhs and ahhhhs, to start the song, but her microphone doesn't seem to be working. I can't hear her. Then Ilaria who is meant to be singing the first verse doesn't start to sing when she is supposed to.

I'd told Antonella before we went on stage that if Ilaria forgot to sing, it was best if Antonella sang since the song is in Italian and she is confident with the words. When I realize Ilaria isn't going to sing, I nudge Antonella, but she doesn't seem to realize what is going on, so I start to sing. Then, realizing what has happened, Antonella starts to sing and then Ilaria starts to sing too. So suddenly there are three of us singing the verse that is meant to be a solo, not that anyone can hear Antonella anyway, and Jia is left to do the dance movements alone. This is turning into BBB's bloopiest of bloopers.

There is a ring of people, with about thirty familiar faces, all looking at us. They are my ex-colleagues from New York. More than colleagues, however, they are some of the highest-level executives and some board members of Bob's company. I know I have no choice but to ignore the chaos around me and just make sure it's the best performance I can give.

The guy in charge of the sound never appears, and no one presses "stop" after the backing music to the first song finishes. We're still singing our a cappella end to "Primavera" when the music for the second song starts. What an absolute disaster. Antonella's microphone still isn't working and Lachlan, realizing what's going on and knowing she's the one with the strongest voice, comes up on stage to swap Antonella's microphone with Jia's. I'm grateful for his help.

By the time we are halfway through the second song, we've overcome our hurdles and all is going fine. At least our finale is strong. To my astonishment, Bob beams and makes his way to the stage. "Can you do one more song?"

"I only brought a backing track with the two songs on there," I say. "We can do the first song again?"

I'm unsure whether he is afraid to revisit the antics of the first song, but he says, "No thanks, it's okay. But you girls were great!"

"You are too kind," I say, cringing inside.

Four girls from four corners of the world – singing in Italian at a palace in London. Maybe our messiness was part of the magic.

The next day, we leave London and I send around a text message to the girls to let them know about our upcoming rehearsal schedule. Ilaria texts back to the group:

```
I don't want to be a part of BBB anymore. I want it to
be fun, not so serious. That show was not good for us,
and I don't have time to rehearse so much anyway.
```

I'm shattered. I'd let Corporate Luna step in – to organize, to strategize, to help – but maybe I'd gone too far. Had I squeezed the joy out of something that was meant to be light and creative?

Still, a part of me pushes back. I do want to make this work. I never saw this as a side project or a phase. I was never just playing.

The London gig was well-paid and exciting – a real challenge and an adventure. I don't want to look back with regrets. But now I'm scared. If Ilaria's leaving the group, will the others follow? Jia joined through Ilaria, and Antonella came on board through Jia. *Is my girl band dream already over?*

The wait until our next meeting is excruciating. A week after the London show, Antonella and Jia finally come over to my place.

"Luna, don't take Ilaria leaving too personally," Jia says gently. "You know this has been coming for a while. Honestly, I think it might be for the best. She was never fully in it."

"Sì," Antonella agrees. "Ilaria was never that serious about the group. We'll be fine without her."

A wave of relief washes over me. They're still in. Phew. BBB isn't over – it's just evolving.

We turn our attention to what's next.

"I really liked it when there were four of us in BBB," I say. "The photos looked amazing with such a mix of backgrounds: Asian, African heritage, Mediterranean, and Australian. It also took the pressure off having just three of us on stage, and the choreography felt more balanced."

The girls agree and we decide we are on a mission to find a replacement for Ilaria. I know from my last search that this is not going to be easy. However, I soon realize with Ilaria gone, it's like the rain clouds have parted. I have renewed hope and determination.

Perhaps seeing all my corporate ex-colleagues in London made me appreciate what I have going on here. They are very cushy with their full bank accounts, but their lives are the same. Here I am making plans for girl band shows in Milan and beyond, and a summer tour in Sicily!

I write in my diary. This time, I want to get really clear about what I want from the new BBB member:

1. *Enthusiastic*
2. *Talented dancer*
3. *Excellent singer*

Corporate Luna is fully supporting me now. The internal battle is finally dissipating.

Corporate Luna: You can do this!

We start preparing for our next show which is in a few weeks' time.

CHAPTER 28

A strong positive attitude will create more miracles than any wonder drug.

- Patricia Neal

I convert some BBB flyers into advertisements for a new band member and put them up in the main performing arts schools in Milan. It's a flyer with one of the urban-look photos of the four of us that we took before the London show. I white-out Ilaria's face and put a large question mark in its place, then add the words "Could this be you?" in large letters. I also ask Olivia in London to put the word out to all her contacts that we are looking for a new recruit. Through friends of Shannon, we advertise in Paris as well. There are so many talented singers in the world, and now we have a performance schedule ahead and plans for a summer tour in Sicily, someone will surely jump at the chance to join us.

Antonella arranges for me to audition her friend, Sacha. She's of mixed heritage, predominantly Filipina, with long, glossy black hair and a petite frame. There's something electric about her – a huge and contagious smile, and coffee-colored eyes that sparkle with mischief.

We hit it off immediately and I thoroughly enjoy meeting her. It's clear she comes from a dance background, as she is constantly moving, almost spinning on the spot in a pirouette fashion. This girl is high-energy!

"I love your spark," I say to her, "but we don't need another Asian-looking girl in the group. I really have my hopes set on having a girl band with a full multicultural mix."

Sacha introduces me to a few women of color she met through modeling in Milan. It's generous of her to help us out, but none of them seem like the right fit for the group. I also get a few responses to the ads I posted in London and Paris, but no one really stands out.

Meanwhile, we have the show booked at Le Trottoir, which is like the CBGB of Milan, and rather than miss this opportunity, we decide to go ahead with the three of us.

Jia comes to stay for an intense week of training with Antonella. The show will be on the Sunday night, the last night of Jia's stay.

"We need to perform eight songs at the gig," I say to the girls when we are all in my lounge room to start the first day of rehearsals. "We have our original numbers, 'Get Naked' and 'Elements,' the two Italian songs, 'Primavera' and 'Tropicana,' and then 'Gimme Gimme' and 'Groovejet.' Then a new Italian song 'Nessun Dolore' that Antonella will be mainly singing, and, great news, we've been sent a new original dance song from Harrison called 'Shine.'"

We rehearse for twelve hours, starting at ten a.m., barely breaking for food. It's grueling, but we have a lot to do. Antonella only knows the two Italian songs, and we have to teach her all the other numbers, plus prepare the two new songs.

The owner of the venue where we have the gig has been calling me asking to see us rehearse. I keep putting him off, and he's obviously getting nervous. The photos he based his booking on were of a four-member group, and now there are only three of us. I hesitate to tell him, as I don't want him to think BBB has fallen apart.

I feel really responsible as he is paying us for this gig, and also the reputation of his venue is on the line. All I can think is thank goodness it's on a Sunday night when it will presumably be relatively quiet. I am confident though that all our hard work will pay off and the show will go fine.

"You have to trust me it will be okay," I assure him.

A couple of days before the show, we finally feel slightly more prepared.

Wow, everything feels so last minute lately. Am I turning a little Italian? A few months ago, this kind of chaos would've made me spiral, but now, somehow, I'm rolling with it. Not exactly relaxed, but ... looser.

Sacha, the good friend of Antonella, has come to many of our rehearsals and enthusiastically helps us with choreography and gives us performance tips. She has a great feeling for the songs. For our newest song, "Shine," Sacha choreographs the whole number for us, and it's set to be our opening act. A great energy hits us when we rehearse it, and it becomes our strongest number.

That day, I receive a text message from an unknown Italian number.

Hi! My name is Nadine and I saw your advertisement. I live in Florence. I am a singer and dancer half African American, half French. Can I audition for the group?

A singer *and* dancer. Fabulous! I reply, asking her to send me some photos by email. She looks great, so I show Jia and Antonella.

"I like her look," says Antonella.

"Me too," I say, admiring her thick, long black hair and full lips.

"I agree, she's really pretty, and lives in Italy," says Jia. "Give her a call. She might be what we need."

I slip into my bedroom for some quiet and sit on the bed, propping up a few pillows behind me as I lean against the headboard. I take a breath, then dial her number, feeling a twitch of nerves. I hope she will be answer for BBB.

"*Pronto.*"

"Hi Nadine? It's Luna here from BBB."

"Hey! So great to hear from you," she says with a North American accent that I can't exactly place.

"We really like your photos. Thanks for sending them through."

"Oh, I'm so glad you like them."

"Can you tell me a little about yourself and your experience?"

"I sing a lot. That's my main thing, but I am also a dancer. I do dance class most days."

"Have you performed much?" I ask.

"I was in a girl band for four years in Spain, and we did a lot of shows."

Oh my goodness. I am struck. I can't believe she's actually had girl band experience. I'm really excited about the prospect of meeting her, but I'm also wondering if she might be too professional for BBB. I'm ready and willing to go professional, but what if *she* rejects *us*?

"I really want to meet you," I say. "What I suggest is, if you can, come to Milan for our gig on Sunday night. You'll see us perform and then know exactly what BBB is all about. If you're interested, we can audition you on Monday."

If I take on Nadine, I really want to make sure this is the last change. It's too much work to teach a new person all the songs and dance steps, and it's not fair to the other band members.

It's Saturday afternoon, and we have eight songs ready. We are finally prepared for the show.

The following night, despite it being a Sunday, we have the venue filled with our friends, acquaintances, and fans, and it is jammed. There must be about one hundred and fifty people there, and the atmosphere is amazing. We're high on adrenaline.

Jia has been working a lot in front of the mirror to practice facial expressions. She's a hit! She has a group of admirers in the audience who during the break ask me if they can meet her.

"She was born to be on the stage," one of the guys says.

This is certainly not the Jia I met nine months ago. She's been transformed into an extremely confident performer.

Antonella is great. She's a natural pop star and is spurred on to give her all by a big group of friends from her university.

While we are performing, Sacha dances along to all our routines on the dance floor in front of the stage. She riles up the crowd and gets them dancing.

Jia's boyfriend says, "Sacha is more BBB than all of you put together!"

Nadine, who arrived that afternoon from Florence, is at the foot of the stage, watching the show and smiling the whole time. I can make out faces in the audience, and it seems clear that everyone loves it.

The show is a huge success. All the hard work pays off and we do all the songs flawlessly.

The owner is thrilled. "You girls are so great," he repeats to me over and over.

Afterward, all of us, including Sacha and Nadine, dance and laugh together for hours. It's so much fun.

The next day, we all meet Nadine for lunch. She suddenly seems very shy, which is a surprise because the night before she had rocked up a storm on the dance floor. Also, her hair is different from her photos and how it was last night.

"Oh, that ponytail is a hairpiece," she explains. "My hair is a 'fro."

Even better. I love her natural look – bold and beautiful, and she would add another strong presence to our diverse crew.

Sacha joins us for lunch as well since she's in the area. As an unofficial member of BBB, she already feels like part of the family.

After lunch, we all go back to my apartment to audition Nadine.

"I'm going to sing The Fugees, 'Killing Me Softly,'" she says. With her short hair, she even looks the part.

She sings. "*I heard he sang a good song, I heard he had a style.*"

We all look at each other in awe. She has the most incredible voice. I can't believe it. Nadine had told me she'd done professional singing training for five years, but I'm also convinced she's just a natural. She confirmed earlier that she loved the show and wanted to be a part of the group. There's no question in my mind that she has to join BBB.

When she's finished, we ask her to sing another song, just so we can keep listening to her amazing voice. *Gosh she is good!* But I feel bad for Sacha who has been so enthusiastic from day one and we all like her so much. I make a rash decision that both girls should join.

"What if we have a five-member group?" I say. "I really want both you girls to be a part of BBB."

All the girls scream out, "Yay!" in a burst of excitement.

"We are really going to be the Spice Girls now," I say.

I put on the "Shine" song and the five of us are jumping around all hugging, dancing, and shouting, "BBB!" The people on the terrace in the building across the road stop what they are doing to watch us. Within seconds of conception, the new five-member BBB group has its very first audience.

A great era for BBB is about to begin.

CHAPTER 29

Do not dwell on the past, do not dream of the future, concentrate the mind on the present moment.

- Buddha

With a five-member group, I feel like I'm managing a small company. I set up my first spreadsheet that shows "BBB Earnings." Before, I had only kept track of "BBB Expenses." Seeing the word earnings in a column feels like a revolution in the right direction.

Just as things are finally coming together with the girl band, the man front begins to unravel. Marek, who once seemed so eager for me to visit, has grown distant. His messages have faded into silence, and though he hasn't said it outright, I sense the shift. I suspect he's met someone else. It stings more than I want to admit but I don't have the space to dwell. The band demands all of me now, and maybe that's a gift in disguise.

There are still a few local flings – moments of warmth, distraction, connection – but nothing that asks for more than I'm willing to give. Salvatore lingers on the edges, charming as ever, but it's very on and off. I try not to give it too much weight. No matter how charming Salvatore is, or how perfect he might seem on paper, I'm not in love. He's more interested in entertaining his friends than offering the kind of depth

I'd need in something real. Right now, the only relationship I'm really investing in is the one I have with BBB.

Corporate Luna: You have a band to manage! Now is your time to keep focused if you want this to work.

Corporate Luna is right. I write my goals:

1. *Sponsors*
2. *More paid gigs*
3. *Increased repertoire and more challenging choreography.*

With both Sacha and Nadine having strong dance backgrounds, and with Antonella and Nadine having such great voices, I see all these goals as imminent.

It's fun with five. Everyone's so different and Jia says, "Now there is really something in there for everyone."

Antonella is the effortlessly cool one – always zipping around on her *motorino* in jeans, trainers, and her signature black leather jacket. Her voice is gutsy and raw, laced with a strong Sicilian edge that gives our sound a fiery kick.

Jia is the elegant intellectual of the group. Her voice is the softest, but there's a quiet confidence in it that draws people in. Her gentle mannerisms and subtle Chinese accent give her a kind of understated grace that balances us out.

Sacha is the wild beauty and party girl who somehow manages to function on minimal sleep and often has a raspy voice that's recovering from the night before. She brings a sparkle to the group and, without fail, she always has a slew of hot guys at her feet.

Then there's Nadine. Despite having the most experience – she's done the girl band thing before, and she's the strongest singer and dancer – there's a surprising shyness to her. At twenty-seven, she's not the youngest, but she sometimes floats through rehearsals with a kind of innocent detachment. Sacha's always teasing her: "Nadine, get with the program!" Jia's actually the youngest at twenty-six, but Nadine somehow feels the most wide-eyed of us all.

Our rehearsals go smoothly and are not too intense. Sacha is already familiar with all the songs and routines, and Nadine picks up everything relatively quickly.

I ask Nadine, "Can you prepare a song that you can sing solo with us doing background vocals? I think it would be great for our shows."

"I could sing Alicia Keyes's 'Falling,'" she suggests.

"Falling" is much slower than the rest of our songs, but Nadine's voice sounds so beautiful when she sings it. It's a wonderful addition to our growing repertoire.

Now that there's a new lineup, we need photos again.

Sacha's ex-boyfriend, a professional photographer who happens to be gorgeous and with just the right amount of charismatic charm, offers to do the shoot. We meet in the Porta di Ticinese area again, with its graffiti walls, crumbling archways, and unmistakable Milan grit. As always, it's the perfect setting to recreate the original urban-look shots that have been my favorite.

We do a mix of poses – some seated, some standing – rotating through setups with jeans, multicolored T-shirts, and our signature street-style vibe. The look is the same as before, but the energy is new. There's something about having five of us now that feels more alive.

I laugh to myself as I watch the group between takes. The first time we did this, there were three of us ... then four ... and now five. Somehow, despite the chaos and the changes, we've made it here.

The shoot is fun – light, spontaneous, and full of movement. Choosing a single shot where we all look flawless? Nearly impossible. But it's the imperfect ones I love the most – the mid-laugh, hair-flying, caught-in-the-moment kind. They feel real.

Then we are off to France to perform at my uncle's sixtieth birthday party. This one is not a paid gig, but it's like a BBB retreat for us to get to know each other better. It's also the first show with us performing with Nadine and Sacha, so a good warm-up.

Sacha, Antonella, Nadine, and I squash into my little Peugeot like sardines in a can. If we can survive a six-hour drive to France in that tiny car, we can survive anything.

There's only one minor drama: Nadine insists on the front seat because of her "claustrophobia," which prompts Sacha and Antonella to mutter that she's being a prima donna.

The road trip itself is surprisingly smooth. We blast music, practice our harmonies between service stations, and laugh way too hard over some terrible French radio. It's cramped, chaotic, and completely ridiculous – but somehow, it works. Kind of like us.

When we arrive in Provence, my family greets us and we relax by the pool. The party isn't until the following night, so we have plenty of time to rehearse.

The weekend unfolds without much drama, though there are a few gripes and problems with the sound equipment. Also, when Sacha's boyfriend, Dante, arrives, she stresses about juggling BBB and looking after him.

Sacha is quite a character. During the day, she's constantly changing into different gorgeous bikinis, dancing around, swooping her long black hair. She is such a larger-than-life personality and arguably the most outgoing of the group, but she says just before the show, "I have to warn you, Luna, I get stage fright."

"Really?" I'm completely surprised by this, and try to soothe her. "You know your part. Don't worry. It's just family and friends tonight – there will only be about fifty people."

"Someone will have to sing all my solo parts for me," she says. "I can't do them."

She seems so worked up about it so I agree, and we ask Antonella to sing Sacha's solo parts in Italian. I don't mind because it's our first show and not a public performance. I'm confident she'll get better with time.

I just find it so ironic that arguably our most extroverted band member is the one with stage fright.

The show goes well and everyone is very complimentary. My cousin Lachlan says, "I think this is by far the strongest lineup BBB have had. Antonella and Sacha are naturals. Nadine has a wonderful voice."

After the slower rhythm of Provence, Milan feels like it's moving at double speed again. A few days later, we have our first public gig with five of us at Le Trottoire, the same venue where we performed just a few weeks before with three BBB members. The owner is rather surprised when I tell him we now have two new members, but he said he trusts it will be okay.

We have the mic stands set up and ready, and our set feels like a full show. Our repertoire has grown to nine songs, thanks to Nadine's recent addition, "Falling," which she sings so well it gives me chills every time. We've saved "Shine" – our unofficial anthem – for the encore.

The energy in the room is electric. People are animated, clapping, moving along with us, and transfixed. It feels right – loud and alive.

The only problem? The stage. It's small. What once felt perfect for three now feels like a crowded kitchen at a house party. With five of us dodging mic stands, and stepping in and out of formations, I swear we're one sharp elbow away from disaster.

But somehow, we make it work. Our singing is tight, the energy is high, and we've never looked more unified. As soon as the opening chords of "Shine" ring out for our encore, the crowd erupts.

The audience doesn't see the squeeze – they see the spark. And the reviews are in: the new lineup is a hit.

"Five women together has an even greater impact," says one friend after the show. "The ethnic mix is even more striking."

From my standpoint, managing the group, I am – for the first time – feeling at ease. I have three girls with substantial performance experience. I'm also very aware that anything could happen over the summer. Maybe Nadine will get another offer and leave, maybe Jia will be busy with her thesis, maybe Sacha will elope with her boyfriend, and maybe Antonella will find a full-time job since she has just graduated from design school at university. With all possible contingencies in mind, I appreciate the comfort of having a larger group because then if someone is missing, it's not detrimental.

The next performance is Massimo's birthday party and it's by far the most exciting gig we've done. Not only is he paying us well, but he has organized everything to perfection, and we feel like real pop stars.

He arranges for a sleek minivan to pick us up from my apartment and take us to Villa Erba on Lake Como. The moment we arrive, it feels like a dream. The villa is a grand nineteenth-century mansion, its stately columns and manicured gardens sloping right down to the water's edge. It's the kind of place that whispers stories of old-world glamour and secrets that were told behind lace fans.

The stage and dance floor are set up on the lakefront, with the golden light of late afternoon spilling across the surface of the water. About a hundred guests are gathered – women in stiletto heels, men in dashing suits, all looking like they've stepped out of a Milan fashion shoot.

The sound check goes smoothly thanks to the team of engineers brought in just for this performance. Everything feels tight and professional. The music swells, the mics are crystal clear, and as the sun begins its descent behind the distant villas, we take the stage.

We're dressed in all black with a touch of gold – elegant, streamlined, and completely in sync. Our show is flawless. The singing is crisp, our steps tight, and energy aligned. Even Sacha, who used to dread her solos, sings her parts without a trace of hesitation. I can finally relax into the performance.

To the right of the stage, Massimo is all smiles, his pride is unmistakable. Singing to him tonight feels like a full-circle moment. He supported us before we had even performed one song, and now here we are, poised and polished, giving it our all under the fading light of Lake Como.

The lake glistens like something out of a painting. I feel a rush of gratitude. I almost have to pinch myself.

Valentina is at the party. She was a founding member of BBB! She looks beautiful as ever, dressed in radiant-blue, glass of prosecco in hand, and eyes glowing as she makes her way through the crowd after our show. It's been only nine months since she left the group, but seeing her again stirs something in me: nostalgia.

"I can't believe you did it!" she says, her voice full of genuine excitement. "You girls were awesome."

I give her a huge hug. Hearing that from her fills me with such warmth I don't know what to say at first. For a second, I imagine what it might have been like if she'd stayed – if she had been on stage with us tonight. Then I look over at Jia, Antonella, Sacha, and Nadine – the lineup we have now is solid. It's taken time, and many hiccups ... but somehow, seeing Valentina here, smiling and proud, makes it feel like we've landed in exactly the right place.

A friend in Milan offers to do a BBB website for free. He is a really talented web designer working for a reputable company. Fabulous! He's attentive to our needs and we seem to work well together. The website is coming together quite quickly.

We have a photo shoot lined up with Angelo Ferrari, one of the most rapidly up-and-coming Italian photographers. Shannon introduces us. He's got extraordinary energy and electric-blue eyes, and agrees to take our photos at no cost because he likes our group's ethnic mix and thinks we will make interesting subjects.

Jia is writing her MBA thesis on fashion production and through her research she has met a talented Italian jeans designer. The label is called "Worldly Women" and they are very trendy, low-hipped jeans. I find the name so perfectly fitting for our group. Jia arranges for me to meet the company CEO and he agrees to give all the BBB girls plenty of jeans. Our first clothing sponsor! Yay! And a great clothing sponsor at that.

My hairdresser, who is the owner of a sleek salon, has been following BBB's progress. As we have some classy gigs in Milan coming up, I ask for some free hairstyling in return for putting his logo on our flyers. He jumps at the chance, and his reaction is, "Why didn't you ask sooner?" He books us to come in one afternoon before a show, and we are each allocated a hairstylist so we can all get it done at the same time. So there we are sitting there having our hair cut, colored, treated, curled, straightened, whatever we want, all for free.

A few days later, our website goes live. We use one of Angelo's photos on our home page. It looks impressive and we have a great photo gallery with a selection of photos from our shows. The site also has a list of our performances, past and upcoming.

I just want to enjoy every wonderful moment.

I manage to carve out a rare moment of stillness between rehearsals and frantic last-minute planning for our next show. I sit in the deep windowsill of my Milanese apartment, notebook on my lap. Outside, scooters buzz down Via Carducci.

These rare writing moments are my secret refuge. When the world of stage lights and nightlife gets too loud, I return to the page and to myself.

Sometimes I think about my friends back in Australia. Most are settled down now – married, building houses, sending me ultrasound photos with pastel captions. Their lives look clean and linear, like neat little rows of tulips.

Mine? It's more like a tangle of wildflowers. Colorful, unpredictable. A little messy.

I have learned Italian, albeit still stumbling through grammar with laughter. I'm living in a country so rich in culture and where beauty is practically falling off the buildings. And somehow, I am singing. In a girl band. In Milan. It still sounds absurd even in my own head. But it's exhilarating. Magical, even. A wild, unlikely chapter of life.

Before I know it, we are off to Sicily for our summer tour.

CHAPTER 30

Twenty years from now you will be more disappointed by the things that you didn't do than by the ones you did do.

- Mark Twain

"Hi babes," Sacha greets us at the EasyJet check-in queue at the airport. "I was wondering when you'd get here."

"Wow, you girls look the part," I say to her and Antonella, mustering up some early-morning vitality. I kiss them both hello on the cheeks. I'm genuinely surprised that they're looking like pop stars at six a.m. They have sunglasses on and are both in tight jeans and sexy black tops, with glossy lips and lustrous hair.

I feel a mess, with my pale face, no makeup on, and my hair tied back. Nadine is not looking so hot either, with her hair wrapped in a cleaning-lady kerchief. Oh well, at least half the group is going to arrive in Sicily in style.

"Look at how much crap we have!" says Sacha, giggling. I look around us and it's true. We're completely surrounded by mounds of luggage and equipment, including microphones, mic stands, and cables.

"Where's Jia?" Nadine asks.

"She had to finish a university assignment," I say. "She'll meet us there in a few days."

I sit next to Antonella on the plane and she tells me about Sicily and its food. I've often heard that Italy gets more and more Italian the further south you go, and well, there is nothing further south than Sicily.

"So when is our first show?" she asks me in Italian.

"It was impossible to set up any gigs from Milan," I tell her. "I tried to talk to the venues and sent BBB packages with photos and our CD, but they want to make arrangements when we get there."

"It's normal for Sicily. It will be fine," she reassures me.

"I spent hours on the phone with your cousin, Beppe," I say. "He's been a wonderful help with everything and organizing the villa rental."

Beppe doesn't speak English, and I find that, thanks to all these Sicilians I have been communicating with (Antonella, Beppe, and Salvatore), I am pretty much fluent in Italian now.

"Beppe has also been going to places in Palermo doing PR for us," she says. "He is so enthusiastic about BBB and loves that we'll all be there over the summer."

When we arrive at Palermo airport, Beppe is there to greet us. It's great to see him in person: he's exactly how I imagined. He's been one of Jia's best friends for years, and she's told me so much about him. He was the person who suggested Antonella should audition for BBB.

He's tall with a slim build and black curly hair. There is something aristocratic and old-world about his looks, like he should have a big black mole painted on his face and wear a massive white wig, like in the *Amadeus* movie.

We rent a car and follow Beppe's miniature brown Fiat into town. Antonella goes in Beppe's car so she can catch up with her cousin. Beppe's car is a typical Sicilian mobile – lucky to fit three people, no space for luggage, and looks like it would break down any minute. Apparently, the Sicilians don't want nice vehicles, since they will likely be hit within the first hour on the road, and with parking being such a problem, they all want really small cars anyway. Such a different world to Milan where the majority of people drive powerful German cars and one of the most common cars I see there is a large five-seater Audi.

Behind the wheel, I am surrounded by thousands of small, beaten-up cars that roam the streets wildly, seeming to ignore all signs, traffic lights, and markings on the road.

I have chosen the smallest, least expensive rental car, but it's shiny and new, so I feel like I'm driving a Rolls Royce. I am super tired, and the driving is stressful. I really don't want to have to pay for some dents on our overpriced rental car – the insurance doesn't cover that. I have to swerve as I drive, trying to keep the car scratch-less at least for the first day.

"Driving here is just awful," I say.

"Let me know when you want help with driving," says Sacha. I'm appreciative of the offer but feel I should take responsibility for the car, at least for now.

We drive into Palermo and I'm relieved when we stop at a café (called a bar). We are fortunate to find parking nearby.

Beppe comes over to us. "Do not open the trunk," he says, almost in alarm as I go toward the back of the car.

"Why not?" I ask.

"If someone sees you have luggage, you will be broken into. Leave it closed for now. Trust me."

"Come on, everyone," Antonella calls over to us. "You have to try real Sicilian food!"

Beppe says the bar we are at is one of the most famous in Palermo. It has an amazing selection of gelato, some savory food that seems to be mostly fried, and then the rest of the store displays a variety of amazingly prepared marzipan treats. The marzipan is made into little perfectly shaped fruit – strawberries, pieces of watermelon, and apples, even with bruises painted on them. The detail is just incredible: they are each a perfect piece of art.

It is still very early, about ten a.m., and she says we should try an *Arancina*. It's a deep-fried ball of rice with a meat stew center. It is delicious, but very heavy and greasy. That is my first Sicilian breakfast. I'm not going to be losing any weight on this summer adventure, that's for sure!

Nadine had been at the gelato counter waiting in line, and comes back with what looks like a bread roll.

"What's that?" I ask.

"It's a gelato sandwich," she says. "I heard about them and have been wanting to try one." She takes a bite into what looks like three scoops of chocolate ice cream in a white bread roll pocket. "Oh, it's delicious," she says.

We eventually head to the house we are renting near the coastal town of Cefalù. The agent had told me the house was out of town. As we drive there, we can see the very picturesque town center in the distance – a mass of whitewashed and golden buildings, with a dramatic backdrop of a large, plateaued mountain that Beppe says is called La Rocca. We turn inland off the coastal highway. The road continues winding up.

We go on and on until finally Beppe turns left into a long driveway and parks his car. I follow. The two-story house is welcoming, with a huge terrace boasting sun beds and an impressive view of the sea. This is to be our home for two weeks before we move on to the Aeolian Islands.

After a few gripes about who gets what room, we launch into setting up gigs. Beppe drives us in our rental car into Palermo so we can talk to some people at a venue called La Cuba, about performing there.

"It's one of the most famous venues in Palermo," he says.

We are on the autostrada to Palermo. With Beppe driving our rental car it seems a rather effortless trip although it is almost an hour from our villa in Cefalù.

We arrive at Palermo's old town center, where the streets are lined with majestic buildings that ooze tales of the city's opulent past. The grandeur of the architecture reflects the layers of history that have shaped the city over centuries.

We pass by lush parks filled with towering palm trees and ancient fig trees, their sprawling roots creating natural sculptures that add to the city's charm.

"It's so beautiful here," says Nadine. "What's that building? It looks like a castle."

"That's the Palermo Cathedral," Beppe replies, pointing to the imposing structure with its mix of architectural styles.

"And those buildings there? They remind me of Paris," I say, gesturing towards the elegant facades lining a square.

"That's the theater," he explains, as we take in the vibrant atmosphere.

Our meeting at the venue isn't until later, so we head to dinner first at a place called La Focacceria. Tucked into a charming piazza, the setting feels like something out of a film. We sit alfresco, soaking in the old-world architecture and golden light. The street is closed to traffic, so there's a rare kind of calm – just clinking glasses and the constant hum of conversation.

The food is exceptional, and the local Sicilian wine, Corvo, is both delicious and surprisingly affordable. There's a relaxed joy in the air, the kind that comes when time slows down just enough to let you savor it. We're here. In Sicily. I can't believe our tour is about to kick off. My heart is full of anticipation.

After dinner, we head to La Cuba, which seems to be in the ritzy part of town – grand villas, tree-lined streets, and a quiet kind of elegance that's hard to miss.

La Cuba is an outdoor lounge with a tropical feel, and a lot of palm trees adorning it. I speak with the DJ who's in charge of the shows, and she seems enthusiastic, penciling in a gig in ten days' time. I leave her with our CD, and she says she will get back to me to confirm.

The next day, we head to the beach to settle into our surroundings in Cefalù. The golden sand stretches along the Tyrrhenian Sea, framed by the dramatic cliffs of La Rocca and the charm of the old town just a short walk away. The beach is packed with sunseekers; families with colorful umbrellas, and kids squealing in the shallows. The sea is clear, glittering in the sunlight.

In the evening, we make our way to Casa Cuba, a venue situated along the coast near Palermo. La Cuba yesterday, Casa Cuba today ... we chuckle at all the Cuban references.

"We must have got off on the wrong island," I say.

"With all these Cuban connections, our signature drink will have to be a mojito," Sacha replies.

"You're on!" I laugh.

At Casa Cuba, we have another meeting set up by Beppe. It's a sprawling outdoor nightclub set right on the beach with wonderful sea air. We're all invited to sit at a long wooden table under string lights swaying gently in the breeze.

The owner is a well-tanned man in his late fifties and has the air of someone who's seen every kind of party. The DJ – broad and bald – is wearing a black and white tank top exposing his tattoo-covered arms.

In true Italian fashion, the conversation meanders. There's a lot of shrugging and gestures exchanged. Finally, the owner nods slowly and says, "Maybe in a few weeks."

"We are leaving the Palermo area for the islands really soon," I say in Italian. "If we don't do it now, we won't be able to do it at all."

There is a pause, and the owner says nothing.

"What about on Thursday?" the DJ asks the owner. "We have the *pareo* party."

The owner looks at us, and finally nods to the DJ, and then it's a deal. We have a confirmed gig. Yay!

Then the realization hits me, oh dear, a *pareo* party ... We'll have to wear bikinis and sarongs on stage. I don't like the idea of performing with so few clothes on. I'm really not sure I'm ready for that much Sicilian exposure!

Before we know it, it's time for our first big Sicilian gig, the *pareo* party. Antonella takes me to Palermo for shopping so I can buy a new bikini. We have worked out a bikini and sarong color scheme that matches the T-shirts on our flyers. It will be Antonella in black, Sacha in cream, Jia in yellow, Nadine in white, and I need to be in red. Eventually, we find a suitable red bikini for me, beaded with sequins and quite glam.

The large, raised stage at Casa Cuba is beautifully set, facing the beach, and rehearsals are breathtaking, looking over the sea.

"Where's Jia?" Antonella asks. "Shouldn't she be here by now?"

"She missed her flight, but she'll be here soon," I say.

Jia eventually arrives, we do a sound check very late in the afternoon, and we're all set for the show. Arriving back at the club that night dressed in our color-coordinated bikinis and *pareos*, we park our car in the club's huge sand-covered lot, and I am dismayed when we look around to see mobs of people in regular clothes – short dresses, jeans, and T-shirts.

"Nobody else at the party is dressed in bikinis!" I say, glad that I have a blouse on to cover my body. But none of the other BBB girls seem to mind. They are bronzed and slim, and for them it doesn't seem to be a big deal to do our show in a swimsuit.

"That's fine, we're the performers!" says Sacha in her optimistic way.

We go to the stage above a large dance floor that's already filled with people, and the DJ is in his booth to our right. The club arranges for us to have free drinks all night and we even have our own private VIP section with lounges protected by a bouncer.

"The bouncer won't let Beppe and his friends into our VIP section," complains Antonella.

"We can go join them in the club for a while," I say. "We still have a little time before the show."

Moving through the crowd makes me realize how tightly packed the place is. It makes me have jitters. Soon we will be performing in front of all these people! There must be more than a thousand of them.

"This is our biggest audience so far," says Jia, seeming quite excited.

As soon as we get back, we are up.

It's a full moon, which creates a magical effect. The dance floor below us is a flood of faces and camera flashes, and the sea lapping against rocks provides a perfect backdrop. The bikinis turned out to be a great idea: I can appreciate how we complement the setting.

I never thought I'd dance confidently in a swimsuit – *never*. But here I am, moving freely, owning every step, not hiding or apologizing. Back in New York, I used to feel disconnected from my body – like it was something I was supposed to fix, not live in. I wasn't exercising, I wasn't taking care of myself, and I felt it in every mirror. But Milan has changed me. Dancing, moving, sweating it out with the girls – something shifted. I'm not the thinnest girl on stage, but I've stopped comparing. This is my body and I'm wearing it with pride.

It's a unique evening, and none of us are nervous. I'm on automatic pilot, mesmerized by the moment. We only have to perform six songs, and we sail through them without any glitches. Our singing and dancing flows smoothly – I feel it's one of our best gigs.

"Great show, guys!" I say, buzzing on a high. "I just can't believe we were actually up there in bikinis and *pareos* doing our BBB thing."

I give Jia a hug, so pleased she's here to share this special night.

"I would have never thought we would do that," she says. "But it does seem fitting for the debut performance of our Sicilian summer tour."

"Yay BBB!" we shout in unison.

We are pretty much mobbed by guys after the show, but in a complimentary way that makes us feel good. We stay at the club for a while, and from time to time seek refuge in our VIP section.

During our remaining time in Cefalù, we go out relentlessly. Every night involves PR mixed with drinking and dancing. We are constantly working on promoting BBB, except for a few hours in the afternoon when we relax on the beach. I think we're doing way too much partying, but the nature of our work revolves around bars and clubs. We're constantly meeting people to get gigs and seeking out new venues to perform at. The proprietors want to chat and offer us drinks. Having a night staying home at our villa feels like a missed opportunity.

We quickly become very well known in Cefalù and during the daytime we are asked to perform our original songs a few times on the crowded beaches. We do these free performances in our bikinis and sarongs. They are aired on Sicilian radio, and we just lip-sync and dance to our recorded tracks.

After not much time at all, we have people on the streets calling out to us, "BBB!" Young and old seem to remember us, likely because we look so different.

One little girl, about eight years old, comes up to us and says, "I like the cream one best." I presume she means Sacha who is wearing a cream bikini and sarong. Another girl points to Nadine and says, "I like her best because of her hair."

Soon it's time for us to do the show in Palermo at the rather elegant La Cuba. We decide to wear fitted designer jeans with a variety of gold, silver, and black tops. This is a serious gig at a quality venue, and we have to perform ten songs. I really treasure having Nadine there with her polished voice. We do quite a few slower songs that we wouldn't have been able to do had it not been for her. I was surprised though that I had to coax her to sing extra songs. I thought she'd jump at the chance to be in the limelight, but maybe she's still finding her feet among us.

Our remaining time in Cefalù passes quickly. We do a gig at a nearby beach called Salinelle, which has a popular club. They don't pay us as well as the other venues, but at this stage we are running out of places in the area to perform at, so we can't be too fussy. They make us feel like superstars, however, as they arrange bodyguards. The tall, heavy-set bodyguards insist on walking us to the bathroom and being by our sides at all times, which seems rather unnecessary but I must admit it's fun. I never imagined my girl band career would involve sequins, sand, and VIP bouncers guarding my bikini-clad self. Sacha particularly loves all the attention, but I would have preferred more cash from the club.

We have another great venue lined up by the water near Cefalù. The day before the show, we turn up for a sound check with our equipment and find that the owner who's meant to meet us is away in Palermo. A guy who works there soon tells us our show is canceled.

"Why didn't the owner call me to let me know?" I ask. "We came all this way for the sound check."

"This is Sicily," he explains.

Another guy who promises to set up some gigs for us suddenly falls off the face of the earth as well. *Why won't he return my call?* Creative Luna wants to shake it off and dance. Corporate Luna wants to fire every unreliable Sicilian club owner on the island.

"I think some of the men here look at us as foreign women and don't have enough respect to bother keeping their word," I confide in Jia.

"You've been doing a great job so far, don't let them get you down," she says.

I find myself getting more and more frustrated with Sicilians and their way of doing business, but we still have the rest of our tour left on the Aeolian Islands, so I plan to make the most of it.

CHAPTER 31

Life isn't a matter of milestones, but of moments.

- Rose Kennedy

Salvatore's friend who I know from Milan, Vincenzo, is also in Sicily. He's offered to host us on the Aeolian Island of Vulcano. After everything Salvatore told me about Vulcano, I'm so eager to see it, and hope it has good things to offer performance-wise.

We catch the ferry from Milazzo. Vincenzo greets us at the Vulcano port. "Luna! *Ciao bellas! Benvenute a Vulcano!!*"

He gives us all embraces and kisses. He has a tall, slim friend next to him who also welcomes us warmly.

Vincenzo introduces him. "This is my friend, Luca, whose place we stay at," he says.

We walk into the town center that is laced with streets so small they are like walking paths, not roads. There are stalls on either side of us, colorfully adorned with T-shirts, sarongs, jewelry, and chintzy tourist items. Before long, we arrive at a white, low-rise apartment complex surrounding a pool. There are outdoor showers, lots of trees, and a lawn sprawling with families.

Luca's place is on the ground floor. We enter to see an open plan kitchen, a small bathroom, and one large room filled with single beds. There's a garden-style patio at both the front and back, but the grass is brown and dry, obviously uncared for. He explains that his family usually rents it to tourists, but this August they have kept it free for him to use.

"Where's the beach?" I ask.

"See that road there?" Luca says in Italian, pointing to a small but busy street along the side of the apartment. "Just at the other side. It's a two-minute walk."

Now he's talking – anywhere near the beach is synonymous with heaven for me.

We leave our bags, put on our swimsuits, and head to the beach. The two-minute walk is really a five-minute trek over gray sand that burns my feet. I promptly decide to leave my shoes on, and become overwhelmed by a smell that becomes more and more prominent.

"What is that rotten-egg stench?" asks Sacha in her usual straightforward manner.

"This is a volcanic island and there are sulfur baths, see?" Luca says in Italian, pointing to what looks like a small, khaki-colored lagoon at the end of the beach.

When we get closer to the beautiful, clear sea, we set out our towels and see a couple of girls about our age walking along the shore, talking. They are covered head to toe in green mud.

"The mud is extremely healthy," Luca explains. "Many people believe in its healing properties. It's unique to our island and is why so many people like to come here."

"Yes, Salvatore had told me about the magical, bubbling mud," I say.

We're on the beach, relaxing, with the sulfur smell in our nostrils. Antonella and Luca are engrossed in conversation, about four meters from us, with the water lapping at their legs, chatting nonstop.

"Look at those two. You'd think they've known each other for ages!" says Sacha.

"I thought they knew each other before?" says Nadine.

I shrug. "No, they just met today."

Nadine gives me a look framed by a raised eyebrow. I feel like we're teenagers, and I wait for her to say, "Woo-hoo, lovers ..." but she doesn't.

I soon understand why the beach is called "*Aqua Calienti*" (hot water). As I swim, bubbles of air come up through the water. When I put my feet down on the seabed, all I can feel is hot sand, but when I move my foot near to where the air comes out, it almost burns me. I quickly move my foot away in fright. There seems to be some serious volcanic activity going on under there.

"So how do you like Vulcano so far?" asks Vincenzo.

"I love it, thanks so much for the invitation," I reply.

"I have to go do some things," he says. "But be ready tonight at seven. We'll have a nice night."

That evening we have *aperitivo* at another small beach called Sabbie Nere. The beach is spectacular, with black sand that looks like a crystallized bed of tar. It's still hot from the sun, so once again I have to leave my shoes on to cross the sand.

Bottle of prosecco after prosecco, jokes after jokes ... we have a blast with Vincenzo, Luca, and their friends. The sun is setting and it feels like our own private Café del Mar in Ibiza. We have a superb view of the bay, the sun sets over a rocky point jutting out of the sea, and we are surrounded by rich black sand that creates an other-worldly effect.

After dinner at the most famous seafood restaurant on the island, we go to Il Castello, which is the only late-night spot. It's a great outdoor bar-nightclub with two different DJ booths: one under a straw hut with dance music, the other close to a castle-type building playing chart and retro music. Soon we are having a blast dancing. The place is packed.

Vincenzo introduces me to the owner, who comes across as both professional and approachable. I'm thrilled – she's keen to have us perform. She shows me a raised section and say they have a music mixer that covers our equipment needs. Great! We exchange numbers and agree to be in touch to fix not just one, but two shows. If we can arrange two more gigs on the other islands, I'll have most of our tour costs covered. No profit, but a great all-expenses paid summer holiday.

Antonella and Luca seem to be stitched at the hip and very much in their own world. Luca is very sweet, and I feel bad that his love nest is crammed with all of us. Luca's little apartment is full of beds and luggage, and full of action with everyone coming and going throughout the day and night. We not only have five BBB girls, but a growing entourage – including Beppe, and Sacha's boyfriend, Dante. Sacha is rather preoccupied. She loves Dante so much that she's always super-attentive to make sure she is pleasing him one hundred percent.

Beppe and Jia seem to be partying all the time. One night they go skinny dipping in the sulfur mud, which is called *fango* in Italian. Jia screams out at the club as they are leaving, "*Fango nudi!!*"

Nadine's Grace Jones-class muscular physique, with idyllic pert butt, means that the men go crazy when she wears her short little tops exposing her perfectly taut stomach. She attracts a following of guys, but she keeps them at a distance. They start to call her Lolita, because she seems so young and innocent. Some nights when we're all out, she'll have a few sips of our mojitos and we laugh with her that she's going to start drinking. She never would, however. She is very disciplined.

During our time on Vulcano we attract a great following. We hang out with Italian vacationers at *aperitivo*, and they take photos with us and tell us they are BBB supporters.

Salvatore couldn't join us in Vulcano, but his presence lingers in sweet messages. He has a way with words – especially over text. His notes feel like sun-drenched poems, full of warmth and old-world Sicilian charm, as if he were raised on Quasimodo verses beneath the shade of a fig tree in Palermo.

```
Your eyes are like the sea off Taormina … dangerous,
deep, and impossible to leave once you're in.
```

He also continues to be wonderfully supportive, always introducing me to anyone he thinks might help with BBB. He puts me in touch with a guy named Cico – pronounced Chicko, short for Francesco – who's just arrived on the island. He is a classic Sicilian; dark eyes, olive-skinned, and a tangle of chest hair that peeks out like it has a personality of its own. Naturally, he turns out to be Salvatore's cousin. The island is so small that all the locals know each other, and it also seems most of them are related. For them, "*cugino*" (cousin) is a very loose term.

Cico's business is in Lipari, the largest Aeolian Island, but he's holidaying on Vulcano. He drives me around, shows me the sites, and is a real gentleman.

"I know a lot of people on Lipari," he says. "I'll set up a gig for you."

But in the usual Sicilian way, this is the last I hear of the offer.

It's time to visit the other islands to check them out in the hope that we can get more gigs. Nadine and I go on an organized boat tour to "see the Aeolian Islands in a day."

First, we stop at Lipari. The island is so big compared to Vulcano. There are loads of stores, restaurants, and bars. There's a huge main street that allows only pedestrian traffic, and it's teeming with people. There's a nice beach with a huge port.

"Wow, this is the place with all the action," I say.

It's still very early in the day, so all the venues are shut, but Cico will know which places to approach for gigs. I have to talk to him as soon as I get back to Vulcano.

"I have an idea," I say to Nadine. I call Antonella.

"*Ciao* Antonella! I am thinking we should have a get-together tonight at our place. Can you check with Luca if it's okay? I was thinking it could be in his courtyard."

"I know he'll say yes," she says. "Just come back. We miss you already."

"We won't be back too late, and I'll be there to help buy what we need for the party. Make sure Sacha, Jia, and everyone know!"

I send Cico a text to make sure he can come.

Next we go to the island of Panarea. We have time for a walk around the town. It is beautiful, but seems so sterile compared to Vulcano. It is pristine and white, and feels more like Mykonos in Greece than an Italian town. There's one famous club there, but I can see it's a venue that would have to be arranged well in advance.

We then visit Stromboli. It is so lush and quaint. The small town is picture-perfect, set on a steep face of the volcano that rises out of the ocean. There are huge puffs of black smoke ejecting out of the top of the crater. Wow! The tour guide tells us it's always like that. I can't fathom how anyone would ever want to live at the base of a live volcano, but it's so incredibly beautiful that I can understand how someone could fall in love with the place.

We walk up the hill in the main town and have gelato looking out over the sea. The sun is starting to set, and our boat soon leaves to take us around to the other side of the island. There, the guide explains how the whole side of the volcano plummeted into the ocean during the last eruption. A sheer face is covered with smooth, gray dried lava. As the darkness draws in, the volcano lets out a couple of bursts of molten lava. I find it magical against the dark sky. It's such a bright orange spurt with sparks that look like fireworks. Enormous blobs of lava are thrown into the air and then ooze onto the sheer face of the volcano before gradually melting into the gray.

Back on Vulcano, we all put in a team effort to brighten up our dry and bare courtyard with candles and lights. We cover small tables with bright sarongs and put out colorful cups and napkins. Soon people start coming over, and our gathering grows by the minute. By the time you get a Sicilian and his *cuginos* involved, word gets around fast.

We have a barbecue, and Beppe and Sacha make sure that everyone is sufficiently intoxicated with an extremely strong watermelon concoction. They cut a watermelon in half and mash up the flesh, mixing it with copious amounts of vodka and I dare not ask what else. They hand out multicolored plastic straws and coax everyone in groups to simultaneously down the contents directly from the watermelon, as if in a race.

By midnight, a lot of people leave to go to the club. There are about twenty of us sitting around and Cico starts singing in Italian. Before we know it, Vincenzo joins in. It sounds great.

Hang on. Aren't we the girl band? At this late stage in our tour, I'm rather fed up with pushing us to be in the spotlight, but I do like the idea of impressing Cico with our talents. After all, that was the main reason I thought of arranging this party. I really hope he might help us set up one last gig on the islands, this time on Lipari.

"Why don't you sing for us, Nadine?" I ask.

"Yeah, come on Nadi, that would be great," says Sacha, slightly slurring. She's propping herself up against Dante.

"You don't want to hear me," says Nadine. "You know I'm shy."

"Nadine, we really do want to hear you," I urge her. "You know loads of songs. C'mon."

"I don't know. What d'you want to hear?"

"Why don't you do 'Killing Me Softly'?"

"I find that hard without a backing track," she says.

"Well, sing anything then. You know better than me. We'd love to hear any song you know."

"I know some Whitney Houston."

"Perfect!"

There's complete silence from the group as we wait for her to start. I watch her eyes move across the group, uncertain. It hits me how even the boldest voices can retreat when they are the center of attention. She looks around and smiles at us, but still won't sing.

"C'mon," I say.

"Well I just hope you like it," she replies with a shrug.

She then starts:

"If I should stay, I would only be in your way."

We're all spellbound. I've never heard her sing with so much emotion. I wonder which guy in the group she is singing to. Then she finishes:

"Ooh, I'll always, I'll always love you."

We break out in loud applause. Antonella is sitting near Nadine and gives her a big hug. Beppe does a woo-woo noise in full appreciation and Cico gives me a look, saying, "That was fucking great."

I'm actually surprised at how fabulously she sang. She is always great, but never *this* great. Why hadn't she done this before? I personally find intimate settings much more difficult than performing on stage. I'm in awe of her talent.

"Nadine, that was amazing," I say. "The best ever."

"Really? You really liked it?"

"Completely."

Cico says, "I want to hear more. What other songs do you know?"

"Why doesn't somebody else sing?" says Nadine. "You don't want to hear me again."

"We do, Nadine," I say. "You have a fantastic voice."

I always thought she had a slight princess attitude because she knew she was so talented, but I can now see she's genuinely shy. No matter how clear it is to us that she has the voice of the group, she has no idea what a pleasure it is for us to hear her.

I'm sure her singing for us in a private setting, all enthusiastically cheering for her as a solo artist, does wonders for her confidence. We urge her to sing another, and then another, and another.

As the night stretches on, so does the playlist – and the cocktail list. We sample everything, but keep returning to the watermelon vodka mix Beppe and Sacha served earlier. It's dangerously good.

In the early hours of the morning, someone suggests dancing. Sacha, naturally, takes the lead, yelling, "Mojito!" as she skips ahead with her arms raised like a wild parade leader. We follow her down the winding garden path toward the main road into town, laughing and stumbling.

I hang back a little, near the end of the group, and suddenly see Dante heading the opposite way, back toward the apartment, carrying Sacha in his arms like she's made of feathers.

"She okay?" I ask, catching up.

"She's fine," he says, smiling. "Just needs to sleep it off."

Sacha mumbles softly, almost dreamlike: "Mojito..."

I can also feel the fatigue settle into my bones. We're all running on fumes, high on music, sun, and each other. It's like no one wants these magical nights – and our Sicilian tour – to end.

Cico is true to his word and sets up a gig for us in Lipari. He has some friends who are all called Francesco, and between them he says they have a plush hotel to accommodate and feed us, a venue for us to perform at, and the equipment we need for the show. Yay!

When we are walking down the street in Lipari toward the hotel, a group of young guys yells out to us, "BBB!" They must have seen us performing at another venue. A few of them pull out their phones and snap photos, like we're celebrities. We instinctively strike poses – half serious, half playing up as over-accentuated divas. At moments like this I am loving that Sicily is such a small-world. We are pop-up popstars! We soak it up.

Having rehearsed already in Vulcano, we can enjoy hours lazing around the pool at the hotel in Lipari. We're given a big room with a large terrace. The hotel is a fabulous luxury for us after our cramped quarters at Luca's place. The owner is really friendly and lets us eat and drink whatever we want, so we treat ourselves to a wonderful dinner before the show.

We are set up outside the venue on the main street. We are all dressed up in short dresses with scoop necks, belts, and high heels. We look like a colorful selection of James Bond girls. Nadine is in white, Antonella in orange, Sacha in black, Jia in yellow, and I am in aqua blue.

Every person who walks past during the forty minutes of our show becomes a part of the audience. There are hundreds of people there and everyone has flashing cameras.

Some people in the music industry stay after the show to tell us how impressed they are, taking my phone number and email, and promising contacts in Milan. It's the perfect finale to our tour.

I reflect over the last month. During this time in Sicily, I've learned a lot about Italians, and I swear I will never, ever, try to do business in Sicily again. The number of promises, the amount of time running around, and the quantity of promotional DVDs and CDs given out for nothing ... It's like they don't know how to just say no. It's always, "Yes, everything is okay. No worries, *la la la, cara*." But so many times it was all fluff.

On the girl band front, despite some disappointments, our summer tour was a truly irreplaceable experience together. We developed into a real group and became like family. Now back to the real world in Milan.

CHAPTER 32

Build your own dreams, or someone else will hire you to build theirs.

- Farrah Gray

I arrive back from Sicily to a very tranquil Milan. There are a few days of August left and the city is still quite empty. I love it.

The tour in Sicily was a lot of fun, but I pushed myself to the limit. I look at my face in the mirror and it's as though I have aged ten years. I haven't looked this haggard since I left the stress of New York.

I know it's a combination of things. The sun might be a factor, but I'm always careful to wear a hat. The drinking was probably the worst of all. That's the lifestyle associated with working in clubs and nightspots, and we even drank on nights off when we were socializing. It seems we didn't know how to stop.

Now back in Milan, I'm so sick of partying that I can't even fathom going out. I'm invited to go away with friends for the weekend, and have other lovely invitations, but I just want some time to chill and be alone. I need quiet time, and I know I'll soon be busy again with BBB.

"Go placidly amid the noise and haste." The words of *Desiderata* echo in my mind. I left New York chasing a slower, more balanced life – something sustainable. But this girl band pace? The late nights, constant movement, endless social energy – it's starting to feel like another version of burnout. Maybe Corporate Luna didn't stay behind in Manhattan after all. Maybe she just changed outfits.

Still, there's so much I don't want to lose: the music, the magic, the spark. I just need to find a rhythm that works for me. Less alcohol. More time to write. A little more me-time between the mayhem.

Balance won't come gift-wrapped. I'll have to carve it out for myself.

I focus on the next steps. We have more gigs lined up, but in a way I've already achieved so much with the group. *How much more performing and partying can we do?*

I start to embrace a healthier lifestyle. I get into the routine of going to my local outdoor pool, doing laps, and lying in the sun reading. I then go home, cook, and write pages on my computer, like a diary. I don't want to forget any of the details of my wonderful Sicilian experiences and beyond.

Before I know it, it's September again and everyone comes back from vacation. The city is back to its usual busy buzz and the weather starts getting considerably cooler. I replace laps at the pool with kickboxing workouts in my apartment.

Shannon is back from holidays too so it's fun to exercise with her and have good chats.

"What's the latest with BBB?" she asks.

"It's getting pretty hectic again, but all good."

"Your voice sounds raspy," she says.

"You can still hear it?" My throat has been suffering since the summer. "I'm back doing regular singing lessons which has put a bit of strain on it. I'm being super healthy and avoiding too much nightlife, so hopefully I'll be sounding like myself again soon."

"It sounded like your summer was tour amazing."

"It was wonderful, but also came with many frustrations. We almost broke even, but not quite."

"It's been a long time for you without a real income. How is that side of things?"

"I still have savings, but it's time to renew the lease of this apartment. Financially, I can't do it. I'd need to commit to a whole year ..."

"Wow." She looks genuinely surprised. "So what's your plan?"

"Not sure, but somehow I need to change things to make my life more sustainable. Right now, this lifestyle is too expensive and too unhealthy! It can't go on ..."

That evening, I sit quietly, the soft beat of the city outside my window. I can feel the weight of the whirlwind months behind me – late nights, endless rehearsals, the constant push and pull of the band. I know I've come a long way and there's still more to do, but something inside me whispers the need for a pause.

I start to write in my journal, feeling the need to set some new intentions. Balance – that's the next goal. Maintain a healthy outlook, and take a few days off.

My Italian is finally flowing, which makes me think about my French. It's getting rusty, and for a second, my mind drifts to possibly visit Paris. But no ... it isn't calling me right now. The pace is not what I need.

And then I remember – Elena, my Dutch friend whom I met in Paris, is doing a three-month internship in Barcelona, a city I've been intrigued to visit for ages. That stirs something. Barcelona. A bohemian energy, warmth, and the beach. A place to breathe. That's it. I'm going to take a mini break in Barcelona.

CHAPTER 33

We must be willing to let go of the life we planned so as to have the life that is waiting for us.

- Joseph Campbell

"*Hola Guapa!*" says Elena, putting on her best Spanish accent as she greets me at the Ryan Air bus station in Barcelona. She looks as stylish as ever with knee-length brown boots, tight jeans, and a cream wrap casually slung around her tall frame.

"It's so good to be here!" I say, hugging her. "I can't believe I haven't seen you since Paris."

We head to Elena's apartment in the Gothic Quarter. I pull my small black Samsonite suitcase through a maze of pedestrian streets, then carry it up four flights of stairs to her flat. "Thank goodness I packed so light!"

"I'm sorry for my place, it's so tiny," she says as we enter.

"Not at all, it's gorgeous and bright. You seem to be right in the center." I admire the view from her small balcony. As I gaze out, a tapestry of rooftops unfolds before me. The city looks like it's made of sun-bleached gold. "The view is amazing."

"Barcelona is very beautiful. Much more than Milan, but that's only my opinion. You have to see for yourself. What would you like to do today?" she asks.

"Only one request – the beach."

To get to the beach, Elena and I go for a long walk around the center of town. The architecture is breathtaking. I never know what's going to be around the next corner. There are small, crowded streets lined with specialty stores, and countless cafés where people take their time drinking coffee or beer, engaged in animated conversation. Everywhere smells of garlic and freshly cooked food. We walk past the old port through Barceloneta, which used to be the fisherman's village, with its rows of almost crumbling buildings and washing hanging on small balconies. I love it as it looks so South European.

We then reach the beach. The sand is soft, the water clear and a brilliant blue. There are locals, foreigners, children, and musicians who are playing and singing. Everyone is in a good mood and having a great time in the sun. I can't stop smiling. Even the water seems happy as it laps against the golden sand. The distant yachts look like small origami swans stuck against a blue watercolor. I'm tempted to dive deep into the cool sea. What bliss!

"There's a kind of bohemian feel that reminds me of Amsterdam," Elena says. "But it's better because it's warm with blue sky and the sea."

"Seems ideal."

"Tell me, how do you enjoy Milan?" she asks, her blue eyes bright and full of interest. She looks at me intently, twisting a strand of her thick blonde hair absentmindedly.

"As you know, it's a really fun city," I say. "I brought some photos of the girl band to show you."

"That's so great," she says in her deep Dutch accent. "So you found your home there."

"Not exactly. It's a very expensive city to live in and I don't see myself there forever."

"But the girl band is a success?"

"Yes, it's going great," I say. "Partying nonstop, but it's been amazing."

I show her photos of BBB and of my apartment. "Wow, your place looks beautiful," she says.

"The reality is though, while my apartment is fabulous, and ideal for BBB, I just can't afford to keep paying such high rent indefinitely. I've been thinking of making a change so that's why I'm super keen to check out this latest town of yours."

"Barcelona? Yes! It might be better for music too. They have so many concerts and festivals going on all the time."

"I heard that. I also love the idea of living near the beach."

We take a seat at the outdoor bar-restaurant, which is on a square wooden platform on the sand. There are no obstructions between the vibrant sky, the sea, and us. The locals call these open bars that line the beaches *chiringuitos*. Our *chiringuito* has a great atmosphere with Latino music playing and a small colorfully painted hut at one end where the food and drink is prepared.

We watch families walk along the esplanade by the beach. Small children enthusiastically run at the feet of their parents with the palm trees gently rocking in the distance. As I look around, I wonder why it's taken me so long to consider this city as a place to live. I know I could settle here.

"It's a fun, international city," says Elena. "You would be happy here."

"It's kind of like a European Sydney," I say. "Now I know why people say Barcelona is the best city in Europe."

"The cost of living is much lower than Milan."

My eyes engulf every image in front of me. The sun is penetrating so strongly that I have to take off my sweater. I want to dig my heels into the sand. I want to rip off all my clothes and feel the heat of the sun on my bare skin.

"Decision made. I'm moving here." While I make out I'm joking, I am completely serious. Elena gives me a knowing look. She no doubt remembers how decisive I was when we were in Milan and I said I would move there.

Part of me would love to move to Barcelona immediately, but I know I can't. I have to see the BBB venture through. We've all made sacrifices to make it happen and there's no way I want to walk out on my dream just yet. However, at least I know that Barcelona is waiting for me.

I look at the horizon. The world is suddenly so open and immense. Because I grew up in Sydney, it seems so natural to live by the sea again. Milan is an inland city, and I realize now I've felt the confines of its heavy architecture and car-filled streets.

I arrive back in Milan in high spirits. I'm so excited about the idea of moving to Barcelona and motivated to ensure BBB truly leaves its mark in Milan before I leave.

Everything with the group is running smoothly. We are regulars at Le Trottoir, with gigs lined up there every few weeks. We perform at Executive Lounge, an upmarket venue with a good crowd in a fabulous location at Corso Como, a district known for its elegant clubs and restaurants. Ironically, Corso Como is where Massimo, Valentina, Ilaria and I had dinner a year and a half ago – when the very first seeds of the girl band idea were sown.

At Executive Lounge, we wear all black and add some numbers to our repertoire that suit the venue. Our gigs are sponsored by a luxury car brand, so they pay us about three times as much as we usually get, and we only have to perform six songs.

We do "Leave Your Hat On," using bowler hats and chairs as props with some highly choreographed moves. We start by slowly taking off black trench coats, to reveal slinky black dresses. We wear long black gloves that we also take off and fling into the audience. We also do a BBB adaptation of The Rolling Stones' "Satisfaction." It brings back memories from the early days of singing training with Harrison when he asked Jia, Ilaria, and me to "go wild" to that song.

Our performance at Executive Lounge is a great success so they also book us to do a special Christmas show in December.

A reporter contacts me, saying he wants to write an article about us for the largest newspaper in Italy, *Corriera della Sera*, which is a great chance for some wide publicity.

I give notice to my landlady that I'll leave my apartment toward the end of December. It seems so strange to be making plans for my move out of Milan while at the same time I feel that things with the girl group are still taking off.

I have grown to love my Milanese life, and start to feel nostalgic. *"I can take BBB with me,"* I convince myself.

Corporate Luna: You're finally making money with BBB and doing what you wanted – performing! I am now baffled as to what more you want. Barcelona??

Creative Luna: You've achieved what you wanted with BBB and it's time to move on. You're not going to party and hang out at nightclubs indefinitely. Give the beach life a whirl. Let's see where a new phase takes you.

Corporate and Creative Luna are now fuzzy to me. Corporate Luna wants me to stay? I thought Creative Luna would want to stay. Maybe Corporate Luna is the voice that always wants to hold me back? Is she the voice of fear?

In November, we perform at The Rocket, a really popular club with what seems like over a thousand people rammed inside. It is so different to everywhere we have previously performed. It's a retro-style space with street art murals all over the walls and a trendy but almost grungy crowd. Most of our friends can't even get through the door because the place is so packed.

We perform a few new numbers that suit the venue, like Donna Summer's "I Will Survive." The Italians go crazy over that song, and I love it too. We also do a disco version of ABBA's "Mama Mia." The crowd sings along and dances with us.

Ilaria, who has started her own Milanese fashion-tour business, has turned into a wonderful supporter at our shows. She has fun socializing and sharing a glass of wine while we prep for the shows and perform. She knows the lyrics, remembers some of the routines, and now gets to enjoy it all from the sidelines.

I love that we're still friends – and that she's meeting the new BBB members with such warmth and enthusiasm. Without Ilaria, BBB would never have been possible. She was there at the beginning, and seeing her still cheering us on means everything.

One morning, I sit down to write, but my computer keeps crashing, refusing to cooperate. I give up and decide to take a long bike ride through the city, no destination in mind, just a quiet urge to absorb everything around me.

I recently bought a new camera, loaded with megapixels and a zoom, and today feels like the right time to try it out. I ride my bicycle and stop often, capturing shots of my favorite corners of Milan: cobblestone streets, majestic architecture, and little cafés where patrons lose hours to cappuccinos and daydreams.

The sky is a brilliant blue, the kind that makes everything feel more vivid. As I ride, the thought of moving to Barcelona drifts in again – it's exciting, and full of promise. But suddenly, I feel a wave of nostalgia. Milan has become part of me. Letting go, even for something new, won't be easy.

When I get home, my computer decides to work perfectly. I take it as a sign that I was meant to have that Milanese outing today. I download the photos, and when I look at them it makes my eyes water. I feel such a connection with Milan.

I'm so happy I have these photos that will forever serve as a great memory. For me, it is a phenomenal city – and where I experienced such a turning point in my life to release my corporate self and go creative. I can't believe I'll actually be leaving Milan in a month. *Will I go through with it?*

CHAPTER 34

Accept what is, let go of what was, and have faith in what will be.

- Sonia Ricotti

Free hair, free jeans, free drinks, and free press! After working so hard to push BBB out into the world, it seems the world is finally coming to us. I answer questions from the *Corriera della Sera* reporter: "How did the band start? Why did you come to live in Milan? Do you like it here? What are your favorite places in the city? How did you all meet?"

The following Sunday, the article is published on the front page of the Milano section of the *Corriera della Sera* with a photograph of all of us. He says we are the Milanese Spice Girls. The photo is attractive. It was taken by one of his photographers before a gig at Le Trottoir. The article is written with a big push toward how Milan is such an international city and how we all chose to live there because it's the lifeblood of Italy. He talks about our education, also about how I founded the group.

A few days after the newspaper article runs, things start to snowball. We get calls from a handful of TV producers who've seen the piece. One, in particular, stands out: Markette – a late-night talk show on LA7 known for its quirky satirical edge, and its eccentric host, Piero Chiambretti. It's often described as Italy's answer to Letterman.

Before we know it, we've been booked.

We arrive at the studio wide-eyed, ushered into a swirl of activity. The set is bigger than I expected, with cameras swinging, lights blazing, and staff buzzing in every direction. We arrive in black dresses, fitted and flattering, and are pointed toward the makeup chairs, where professional artists layer foundation, blush, and enough eyeliner to make us visible from space. It's over the top – and kind of fabulous.

An assistant producer hurries over and runs us through what little plan there is. "You'll walk in dancing," he says, clipboard in hand, "then there'll be a short sketch, a quick interview. Luna, you're miked." He points at the tiny microphone now clipped to my neckline. "Just follow Chiambretti's lead. And smile!"

My heart skips. No rehearsal. No retakes. And a live studio audience. I nod, trying not to show how nervous I am. It's all going to be in Italian. What if I don't understand what he's saying? What if I say something stupid on national television?

The music starts – it's bold, with a heavy beat – and we step onto the stage. Lights hit us instantly. We dance as we've been told, walking in rhythm toward our marks. The crowd cheers. Piero is in a tailored black suit. He's shorter than I imagined and, especially in heels, I'm towering over him. He radiates confidence and is a born showman.

He starts dancing too, and the audience eats it up.

Just as we settle into place, a Jack Russell terrier – belonging to a guest waiting backstage – slips free and bolts across the stage. The crowd erupts. We freeze, half laughing, half unsure what to do, as the little dog zips between our legs and circles Chiambretti, tail wagging furiously. One of the crew finally scoops it up and carries it off, still wiggling.

Chiambretti doesn't miss a beat. Once the laughter dies down, he launches into his introduction at lightning speed. His Italian is fast, playful, full of puns I only half understand. But I catch the essentials: "BBB ... ragazze internazionali ... tutte laureate." International girls. All with university degrees. I breathe a little easier. At least he's being kind.

As he talks, I nod and smile, glancing occasionally into the camera, trying to appear relaxed. This is surreal. Just a few months ago we were rehearsing in living rooms, and now we're on national TV with Chiambretti dancing beside us.

As he speaks, I look at him but also turn from time to time to look into the camera.

Then he asks me, "*E come si chiama il gruppo?*"

"BBB," I answer.

"BBBB?" he asks.

"No, BBB." I laugh. "*Solo tre B.*"

"*Ah! Bella Bella Buona Buona!*" And then he says, "*Minchia,*" which is a rather inappropriate slang term to use on national television. The whole audience burst out laughing.

He's a really entertaining show host. The interview and whole segment is lighthearted and fun.

Then we perform "Come Get Naked With Me" to close the show. The show producer is really happy with it. He calls me a few days later to say their ratings were high that night, and 98 percent of the television audience kept watching to the end of the program. He said usually half the viewers have switched channels by the time the credits start coming up, but because we were performing they stayed watching.

Salvatore and I naturally drift apart with a quiet understanding. We still wave at each other across crowded bars, and he's always at our shows, cheering us on. Some people aren't meant to stay, but they make the city feel more like home while they're there.

As my pending departure approaches, I start to freak out about whether I really should move to Barcelona. In general, I feel so happy and settled in Milan. I could easily stay another year and love it. Our gigs are packed and everything is going smoothly. BBB is invited to loads of fun social events, including hotel openings, parties, and dinners – and everywhere we go it seems people know who we are. We are pop stars. *Why am I going to leave all this behind?*

I suggest to Shannon we go for *aperitivo*, and we meet at Bar Magenta. I can't believe it's been almost two years since we had our first drink here together – back when we were just getting to know each other.

"You've said for a long time that you want a change of lifestyle," she reminds me. "Barcelona has the beach, a new culture, and it's a cheaper place to live. You said you can't afford to keep renting your apartment in Milan."

"I know," I reply. Her response is a perfect reminder of my reasons to leave, but I remember all the challenges of starting over again in a new city. "New friends and new language? Elena was living there, but she's back in the Netherlands now. I don't know anyone in Barcelona."

"I don't think you need to worry about that," she says. "You've done it before, and you'll do it again. My biggest fear is that leaving Milan might mean the end of BBB."

I shake my head. "No way. I don't want that to happen. It would be amazing to keep doing gigs here in Milan – and I'm already thinking about how we can start performing in Barcelona too. BBB was never meant to be just a Milan thing. Why not go international?"

She smiles, but I can see she's still unsure. "Still, you've done so much already. Aren't you ... satisfied?"

"Honestly?" I pause, thinking about the wild ride we've had. "I'm incredibly proud of what we've built. We started from nothing – just a few contacts and enough promo to sink an ocean liner. But we made it happen. We were raw, unpolished ... and somehow, we pulled it off."

She raises her glass. "When I think about how it all started with Ilaria and Valentina, and all that chaos – it's kind of unbelievable that BBB actually made it."

"To BBB," I say, clinking my glass with hers.

"So ... what are the next steps for you in Barcelona?"

"I want to carve out some time to write. Really write. But BBB isn't over. It's just ... evolving."

"That sounds wonderful," she says softly. "You know I'm going to miss you."

"I'll miss you too." My voice wobbles, and I blink fast. "But I'll be back in Milan all the time. This city – and this band – are still part of me."

We have the Executive Lounge Christmas gig coming up and I want us to have some festive attire for the occasion. My hairdresser recommends a lady who's a talented stylist. She has contacts in boutiques and can get us clothes that we can borrow for our shows. She kindly offers her services for free. She takes us to a store run by a really tall lady with thick makeup and a flamboyant personality.

"*Cara mia, sono Dora,*" she says to me in a husky tone and kisses both my cheeks. Dora stands back to look us all up and down. "*Siete belli.*"

I am pretty sure this is no ordinary woman I am talking to ... maybe *she* was once a *he?* How fun. I love her camp demeanor and the fact I'm experiencing a completely different side to Milan.

The store is also a showroom and has racks and racks jammed with twinkling gowns. Dora chooses a selection of red and black dresses. They're a mix of lace and sequins, all different styles yet similar enough that we'll look like a group. We try on the black first and stand in front of a large mirror together. We look so glamorous and elegant. It's a good look for BBB. Then we put on the red dresses, which are particularly striking. So we have two amazing outfits for our Christmas show – we'll do three songs in black, and three songs in red.

I now feel like I'm living an incredible dream. BBB was born out of a random idea; an idea that I thought was so off the charts that I didn't even think I could go through with asking Ilaria and Valentina. But then BBB went on to become my Milanese life.

Executive Lounge let me have my farewell party there and offer to put on free food and wine. A-M-A-Z-I-N-G. I particularly like the idea of not having to face any cleaning up in the morning!

Sacha designs a cute invitation with a blonde female cartoon character looking very chic lounging in a margarita glass. It is a BBB party and has a glamour theme, but we don't perform, we just want to have fun. All of our friends are there, of course, but other than that it is teeming with men, men, and more men. It's a really great group. We all have a fabulous time, and I can't remember feeling quite so sad to leave a place.

My departure is approaching. I'm still in denial that I am leaving, and I haven't even started packing. I have a flight booked to Sydney for Christmas. Then I plan to visit New York. I haven't been there in ages, and it'll be a good chance to catch up with friends and see Bob before I move to Barcelona.

With many, many hugs and tears saying goodbye to friends, I make it through my last week in Milan. Packing is quite emotional, but the more I plow through it, the more excited I am about my journey ahead.

I've packed my life into three bags: one for summer in Australia, one for winter in New York, and one for the next chapter – Barcelona. It feels like I'm finally shedding the cold, grey winters that have followed me through every city since I left Australia nearly twelve years ago.

Now, I crave warmth. I want to run along the beach, dive into the sea, and feel the sun on my skin and the salty breeze in my hair.

As I fold a pair of jeans into my suitcase, the thought creeps in like a shy old friend: "Remember that language course you wanted to enrol in when you lived in London?"

I hadn't thought about it in years. Or maybe I had, somewhere deep in the recesses of my mind, behind the law studies, the banking, the singing, the shows, and all the new beginnings. Maybe my conscious brain had let it go, but the rest of me hadn't.

Because here I was — fluent in French, conversational in Italian, and now, on the cusp of moving to Barcelona, Spanish was next. Not in a classroom, not through textbooks, but in life.

I almost laughed. I hadn't studied that language course, but I'd lived it. I was about to become fluent in all three Romance languages, without a diploma to show for it. Just songs, mistakes, moments. Life itself.

Sometimes, it's like the universe files away the dreams we're too afraid to chase and brings them back to us when we're finally ready.

And if it could do that with languages ... maybe, just maybe, it could do the same with the stories I used to write as a child. The ones I'd tucked away long ago.

I hope leaving Milan isn't the end of BBB, or the end of my singing days. But I also know this: I did what I came to do. I have said "yes" to life again.

Barcelona isn't just another stop — it's another new beginning. I can't wait to see what it has waiting for me.

CHAPTER 35

The only person you are destined to become is the person you decide to be.

- Ralph Waldo Emerson

Four months later

It's four a.m. and the remnants of the crowd that's been watching a flamenco-rock performance in Barcelona's Raval are now dancing to eighties music. I grew up with eighties music as a teenager, and I love the fact I'm in Barcelona, listening to all my favorite songs in English. The flamenco-rock concert was certainly unusual, and where else but in Spain would you get such a musical fusion? But the eighties music is certainly more my cup of tea.

Gin and tonic in hand, I sway with the music, surrounded by Italian and Irish acquaintances. I still find it hard to believe I'm now living in Barcelona. I'd anticipated this move for months, and here I am finally. I arrived less than a week ago and have already started my Spanish course. The world I left behind in Milan seems an eternity ago. If I was still in Milan, instead of hanging back and listening to the concert and dancing, I likely would have been hustling for a gig for my girl band. But here I am, feeling free as a bird, and glad to have met some nice people here already. I'm very eager to get my Spanish up to speed and delve into my next venture as a writer.

As I sing along to the words, a blond hunk passes me a beer. I'm already full of gin and tonics, but can't resist this friendly advance. I smile at him in appreciation, my vision slightly blurred. It's incredible, like *déjà vu*. Is it Marek? There he is, tall with long blond hair, bronzed skin ... but as I make out the detail, he's not as lanky as Marek, and this guy has steel-blue eyes instead of brown. Actually, he looks like an Australian surfer dude. *What is such an Australian-looking guy doing in Barcelona?* Australian men are known to be blond with a golden tan, but Spanish men are more like Italian men – shorter, dark-haired, and olive-skinned. Where is this guy from?

I watch him for a while from the corner of my eye. He's with some friends, and seems to laugh and joke a lot. He looks like fun. His friends look more like the locals, and I realize they are all speaking what sounds like Spanish. Maybe he's from here? I'm keen to find out.

I try my best to draw on my rudimentary Spanish. I ask him, "*De donde estas?*" (Where are you from?)

"I am Catalan," he says in English, and I sense an air of pride.

"De Barcelona?"

"*Si*," he said. "What your name?" He has a husky voice. I find him very masculine. He has large hands, and a strong physique.

"*Soy Luna, y tu?*" Our conversation is limited, with my minimal Spanish and his seemingly basic English, and I'm not even sure if I'm speaking Spanish, Italian, or French at this stage, but at least we keep the conversation simple.

"My name is Oscar."

That's my father's name. I didn't know Oscar was a name used here.

We continue to enjoy the fun tunes – ABBA hits, "Tainted Love," "Come on Eileen," – and he knows all the same songs as me. It brings back so many great memories from growing up, and it's so much fun to

232

have a dedicated dancing partner. He has great rhythm and we smile and laugh. He spins me around and around.

At this late stage in the night, the new friends from language school that I had come to the concert with have all dispersed, so I'm on my own with Oscar. He now seems on his own as well. From time to time, he takes both my hands as we move – his grip is strong, his touch is warm. We dance together until five a.m., when the venue finally closes.

"Where you stay?" he asks me as we get herded out the doors onto a narrow street.

"Near Via Laietana." It's a very central location in the Gothic Quarter.

"Raval not a safe part of the city," Oscar says. "I walk with you." His English is broken but his deep voice and ruggedness give him an air of confidence with his words. I like that he takes this protective role. It's true, where we are in the Ravel is slowly up-and-coming, but I've heard it's known for theft, and with Oscar, I am completely at ease.

He accompanies me home, which is about a fifteen-minute walk through the winding back roads of the old town. Narrow pedestrian streets weave into one another, and we pass what look like prostitutes and drug dealers, but I feel safe. He knows every turn by heart.

We cross Las Ramblas, and the magic Plaça Reial, which is still quite vibrant despite the late hour. It's an open square with an ornate fountain in the middle and tall palm trees, surrounded by majestic buildings with bars and restaurants on the ground floor, all of which are now closed. To me, this spot is quintessential Barcelona. The Plaça has people selling beers and letting off glowing spinning tops that fly into the air. We are being hassled to buy beer or trinkets – we both look like such foreigners. "*Cerveza, cerveza,*" (beer) they insist, and Oscar answers them with an abrupt, "No."

At the spectacular Plaça Sant Jaume, where the city town hall is in all its grandeur, we turn left up toward my apartment. As we cross the square, a man with dark skin and eyes approaches us and wants to sell us red roses. I'm surprised when Oscar agrees to buy one. "For Sant Jordi," he says and hands it to me. "It a special day here in Catalunya." I am chuffed to have a rose! I make a mental note to look up Sant Jordi.

When we get to the front door of my building, Oscar gives me a kiss on both cheeks. "I call you tomorrow," he says.

"*Hasta mañana*," I say. It's lovely that he says he'll call the next day, and I do hope he will, but my experience in Italy was that the men would say that, but then call, or usually text message, days later. I keep in mind that Spain is still Southern Europe, and I'm not confident my experience here will be any different to that in Italy.

I'm renting a single bed in a small room in the house of a lady I've never met. It's a cheap option I found through my Spanish school, and it's a good starting point while I look for my own apartment to rent. It's super basic with a thin mattress, slightly musty smell, and has a rather dismal shared bathroom, but the location is fabulous. I still have to work out which neighborhood ("*barrio*") of the city I want to live in, so that's my current focus, to find my next home in the right part of Barcelona.

Before nestling into bed, I look up Sant Jordi. It's Catalunya's equivalent of Valentine's Day. Sant Jordi saved the beautiful princess from the dragon, and now it's a huge tradition in the whole of Catalunya on April 23 where men give the women roses, and women give the men books.

The Sant Jordi book tie-in is very fitting. I'm getting more and more ready to delve into writing to follow a dream that I've had since I was twelve years old. The girl band venture filled my yearning to be on stage, and now I'm going to write.

And here I am, the morning after an iconic Catalonian day – a day about love and books. Perhaps this is a message that I'm on the right track. How romantic that Oscar and I met on this day. I do hope he'll call soon.

I get a lovely surprise the next day; Oscar calls at midday. Through our broken conversation, we know we are both keen to meet again. *I've only been in Barcelona for five days and I've met a guy.* I can't believe it! I love that Oscar called the next day, like he said he would. After many disappointments with men in Italy, I'm craving a relationship with a man who's ready to reciprocate my dependable nature.

Oscar knows I'm looking for an apartment and need to get to know different areas of the city. "I show you all Barcelona," he says. As the first date, he invites me to his *barrio* in Barceloneta. I'm thrilled – the beach was always my dream, so now I'll get to see it first hand from a local.

He shows me a few of his favorite spots in Barceloneta by the beach – including his local bar, the Bitacora – and introduces me to his friend Carlos who owns a lovely fruit shop. We have a traditional Catalan dinner – pan con tomato, patatas bravas, fried calamari, and sardines, all dripping with olive oil and absolutely delicious.

While Barceloneta has the magical charm of the beach and rows of palm trees, it's grungier than I expected. I remind myself that this reaction comes from my Milanese conditioning. Milan had been an almost unreal life of wealth and glamour – sleek sports cars driven by impossibly good-looking twenty-somethings in the latest designer clothes and shoes. But behind it all, most were still students living with their parents. I'd been swept up in the allure, yet I also sensed the emptiness behind it. With time, I began to wonder if that life really suited me. Do I really want to wear designer outfits and stilettos every day? After Milan, I'm ready for a more bohemian experience – and here in Barceloneta, I'm certainly getting one.

Oscar tells me he's a sailor, a qualified ship's captain. I have dreamy visions of us sailing to the Balearic Islands and having a wonderful life.

The next day, he calls again, and that night he shows me Calle Verde in Gracia. Oscar says this street is the most famous in the *barrio* of Gracia. It's blocked off to cars, people walk or ride their bikes down its long expanse, and it's scattered with a multitude of restaurants and bars. We go for a delicious shawarma feast. I like Middle-Eastern food, and it's a great choice.

After dinner, as we are walking, Oscar looks over and says, "You look like you could be my sister." And yes, it's true – if he did have a sister, she could well look like me! Our hair is the same color, and his hair is almost as long as mine. Oscar, however, tells me he has two brothers, no sisters.

The next day he takes me to Poble Sec, just at the base of Monjuic, which is another *barrio* filled with small hole-in-the-wall bars and restaurants. We eat at Can Margarit, and we have the most delicious baked rabbit filled with garlic, onion, and spices.

That night we walk back to my apartment hand in hand under a full moon. The streets are so light under its huge gaze. It's a fair walk, over half an hour, but every moment is magical with it shining down on us at every turn. No man in Italy ever gave so much of himself to me, let alone so quickly. Oscar is making such an effort to make me get to know his city, and I get the impression he wants me to fall in love with it. With the moon beaming down on us, it's like the universe is giving its blessing. It feels like this is really meant to be. We have our first real kiss. *I am in Spain! With a wonderful man!* I have to pinch myself.

I came to Barcelona looking for space – to write, to breathe, to be.

I didn't expect to find love. But maybe that's the point.

When you stop chasing the perfect plan, something real has a chance to arrive.

And somewhere along those winding streets, between shawarma and pan con tomate, I realize something: I want to write *a lot*. Really write. I still have the music in me – BBB will live on, in whatever shape it takes – but right now, there's another voice inside me that wants to come out.

I think of that girl in London, choosing law over language. Of the woman in the Manhattan office tower, telling herself this was success, even as something inside her quietly shriveled.

I could have stayed on that path. Safe. Predictable.

But I chose to leap. To risk. To live the kind of life that Corporate Luna didn't think was possible.

Maybe it's time to start writing the story I've just lived. The story of how I got ... UnStuck.

POSTSCRIPT

The biggest adventure you can ever take is to live the life of your dreams.

- Oprah Winfrey

Looking back now, I realize just how crazy that time was. What made me think I could start a girl band? I wasn't a trained singer. I wasn't even sure what key I sang in. All I had was high school dance training, a stubborn streak, and a feeling, deep down, that there was more to me than numbers on a screen or suits in a boardroom.

And ... somehow, I did it.

I went from zero girl band experience to managing a group that performed in Italy, England, and France. We toured Sicily. We sang under the stars. We made it onto Italian television. We wore *pareos*, lost our voices, danced our hearts out, and had to figure everything out along the way.

No, we didn't get the record deal. No, our summer hit didn't break the charts. But we created something from nothing. We made a mark. I carved out space for myself in a country that wasn't mine, in an industry I had no map for. And for a moment in time, we lit up Milan.

That, to me, is success.

Not because we became famous, but because we were brave enough to try. Because we said yes. Because we turned our blank canvas into something unforgettable.

And now, as I sit in a new city with that same open-hearted curiosity, I know this: the artist in me is just getting started. I am no longer chasing a path that's been laid out for me. I'm creating my own.

Whether it's music, love, language, or whatever wild idea comes next, I'm not afraid anymore. I've learned that sometimes the boldest thing you can do is trust yourself enough to begin again.

NATALIA HOOKER

CORRIERE DELLA SERA, MILANO 2004
Five girls of diverse nationalities: BBB

A multi-ethnic girl group was born in the city of Milan.
From the Duomo to *The Last Supper*, the metropolis has inspired them.
Foreigners, models, and pop stars: the Milanese Spice Girls
Blonde, brown, black ... that is, BBB, or the living proof that Milano (in Italian)
has become Milan (in English). That's to say, one of the most international cities
of the world.
BBB are five girls from five different ethnicities, with parents, in turn, from
diverse nationalities. They met in Milan and have created a pop group, a
sub-species of the Spice Girls Milano-style.
Luna, the blonde, Australian with a Polish mother, is the founder of the group.
Having graduated in law, an aspiring novelist, she was in Milan with friends
when one evening at a party "the idea came to me to start a pop group with
two other girls who were there. I had already sung in Australia." That was at the
beginning of 2003, and from there it took off.
Of Milan she knew little – "Gattopardo and Roialto, Prada and D&G" – but
gradually she oriented herself. "We went up onto the roof of the Duomo and
also saw *The Last Supper*. We liked the lake district where George Clooney has
his villa." The girls rehearse in the evenings. The group came together in a few
months with subsequent additions and replacements.
Jia is a twenty-six-year-old from Hong Kong. Studying business and fashion, she
commutes back and forth between Bologna and Milan.
Sacha is a twenty-eight-year-old with oriental features, of Philippine heritage.
She studied design in Milan when she met Luna and became a part of BBB.
The African-heritage member is Nadine, twenty-seven years old, with a French
mother and African American father. She now lives in both Florence and Milan.
The final member, Antonella, twenty-nine years old, is from Palermo (Sicily) and
she goes back and forth between the two cities.

240

They speak English together and they love Milan "because it's the most international city" and because "the Italian way of life is very open and this is where the melting pot is." They sing, they are models, but also aspiring designers and writers. They have performed in London, they have recorded their first album, and tonight, for pop-music lovers, they will jump up onto the tables of Le Trottoir.

This photo shows the real BBB in 2004 – the fearless, fabulous girl band that inspired this story. Names, details, and a few mojito counts may have been changed ... but the spirit remains the same.

Coming Soon: *UnBlock*

Luna is finally writing. Her new life in Barcelona is full of possibility with the sunlight, sea air, and stories pouring onto the page. But as the words begin to flow, she senses that something deeper is missing.

As her relationship with Oscar begins to unravel, Luna is forced to confront the restlessness within her. The old questions return in new forms: *Who am I when I'm not partying? What does peace look like when no one's watching?*

From Ibiza to Sedona, from the Black Rock Desert to La Gomera, *UnBlock* is the story of a woman searching for wholeness. From heartbreak to quiet breakthroughs, from beachside yoga to silent meditation retreats, it's about letting go, slowing down, and daring to face the truth.

www.alayabooks.com

Thank You

To everyone who read *UnStuck*, cheered me on, shared your thoughts, or simply took this journey with me – thank you from the bottom of my heart. Your encouragement means more than you know.

If you would like to keep in touch and follow along with the next adventures, you can find me here:
Instagram: @alayabooks

Here's to saying yes to life – again and again.

Listen to BBB's Music:

Scan the QR codes below to hear the original songs.

"Elements"

"Come Get Naked with Me"

The world needs your story.